THE LETTE

OF A

STRANGER

Cathy J Hopkins

Copyright © Cathy J Hopkins

All rights reserved

ISBN: 9798759202691

No part of this publication may be reproduced, distributed, or transmitted in any form or by any means, including photocopying, recording or other electronic or mechanical methods, without prior permission of the author, except in a case of brief quotations embodied in critical reviews and certain other noncommercial uses permitted by copyright law. For permission requests, write to the author at www.cathyjhopkins.com

The names, characters, places, and incidents are a product of the author's imagination. Locales and public names are sometimes used for atmospheric purposes. Any resemblance to actual people, living or dead, or to businesses, companies, events, institutions, or locales is completely coincidental.

Art by Christopher Gibson at chris@radargraphics.ca

DEDICATION

Thank you to author James Kochanoff for guiding me through the journey of writing and publishing my book.

Thank you to my husband and daughter for their support, encouragement, and love during the development of my story.

Thank you to my wonderful readers. I hope you enjoy the book.

Chapter 1

As the ambulance speeds out of the warehouse driveway, rushing me to the hospital, I am wondering if this time I will die.

They say that when you are facing death, you relive your life. The first memory I have is when I was about four years old.

It was winter, and we were playing outside in the snow on the front lawn while our dad was shoveling the driveway. We decided to make a snowman. Nancy made the bottom part, Billy made the middle, and I would make the top.

After Dad was done, he asked if I wanted a treat at the store. Now, when you ask a four-year-old a question like that, you should know what the answer will be. Of course, the answer was yes, and I got a bag of chips. At that time, it was my favorite snack.

We were just a typical family, or at least that was what I thought. We lived in an ordinary three-bedroom bungalow on a quiet street in Tignish, Prince Edward Island. The outside of the house was white, with purple shutters on the windows. I remember the color of the shutters since that was my favorite. The backyard was all fenced in; that way we could play outside while Mom was cooking supper.

The house had two levels. The top level had three bedrooms and a full bathroom. On the main level there was a kitchen, living room, half a bathroom, and a porch off the kitchen that had the washer and dryer in it.

My mom stayed at home and took care of the house and us kids, which I now realize is a full-time job. I had two siblings, Nancy, who was seven years old in grade two, and Billy, who was two. I, Rebecca, was the middle child.

My dad worked two jobs to provide for us, one in an office on weekdays, and on Saturdays he would cut trees down for extra money. With three growing children, car payments, and a mortgage, the extra money came in handy.

Just before Dad left to go to the store, Mom came outside to play with us kids when a man came up to her and started talking. I could only hear bits of the conversation in between Nancy and Billy laughing, and at that time it didn't make sense to me. I notice that my mom was getting upset, but why. At that time, I didn't know the impact that person would have on my life. I was too young to realized that no matter how terrible things get, you can't do it alone. Sometimes you need the help of your family.

My next memory is of when I was five years old, and my family was getting ready to move to a different province. My dad had accepted a new job in Halifax, Nova Scotia, which meant that he didn't have to work evenings or weekends. My mom was happy that he would have more time to spend with her and us kids.

Nancy, Billy, and I were driving my mom crazy while she was trying to pack, so she took us to the park to burn off some energy. It was a sunny spring day, and I was playing in the sandbox while Nancy and Billy were playing on the slide. I had a feeling that someone was staring at me, and when I looked for my mom, I saw her talking to the same man as before. At first, I couldn't hear what they were talking about, but then their voices got loud. I heard the man say, "If you take her away from me, you will regret it for the rest of your life."

I kept going in and out of consciousness while I was in the ambulance on the way to the hospital. I could hear someone saying, "You have to go faster, we are losing her." I knew that I lost a lot of blood, and time was against me.

*

I remember being rushed into the hospital, where there were a lot of doctors and nurses trying to save my life. There was a lot of commotion, they were saying, "she needs to go to the operating room if we are going to save her life." At that time, I wasn't sure that if they put me to sleep, I would ever wake up or want to. I was also tired of fighting to stay alive.

*

The next thing I remember, we had been living in Halifax, Nova Scotia for two years. I can't remember the exact time of year, but I believe it was in the fall. There was no snow on the ground, but it was a little chilly, and I needed a light sweater. I was five years old and just started primary school.

It was the end of the day when I went outside. Our mom wasn't there with Billy to walk Nancy and I home from school. That was the first time she didn't come, so we walked home from school with one of Nancy's classmates who lived on the same street as us. Nancy went over to her friend's house to play before supper.

I couldn't wait until I got home to show Mom the test that I got A+ on. I was halfway across the street when a car sped in front of me. If it weren't for the crosswalk lady that pulled me back, I would have been hit.

"Slow down before you kill someone!" the crosswalk lady screamed, and then she turned to me. "Are you okay?"

I don't know if I was in shock, but it took me a few seconds to answer, "Yes."

I got a funny feeling in my stomach that I thought it was just the adrenaline rushing through my body from almost getting hit. It was like I knew that something was wrong, but I didn't know what. I ran up the street and into the house to see my mom on the floor, crying.

I ran over to her. "Mommy what is wrong?"

My mom lifted her head, and I could tell by the look in her eyes that she was scared. I saw her face was bruised and swollen. My mom wouldn't answer at first.

"Mommy, what happened to your face?" I screamed.

All she could say was, "I am sorry, I am so sorry, Rebecca."

"What happened? Why are you sorry?"

"I made a mistake, and I can't stop him."

I was trying to make sense of what happened when I heard the front door open. My heart started to beat extremely fast, my breath became shallow, and my hands were sweaty. What if the person who hurt my mom came back? Before I had another thought, I saw it was my father that had come home and rushed over to my mom and me.

In a confused voice, he asked, "What happened?"

"I was coming up the stairs, tripped, and fell down to the bottom of the stairs," my mom replied.

He looked at me for confirmation of what happened. I don't know why, but I answered, "That is what happened."

He looked at my mom. "Are you okay?"

In a faint voice, my mom said, "Yes, I will be. I just need to rest for a little while."

Dad believed her story, but I was confused about what mistake she made and who she couldn't stop.

Chapter 2

Over the next three years, everything was going great. I just started grade two, Nancy was in grade five, and Billy was in primary. My parents were planning a trip for the whole family to Walt Disney World at Christmas break. It was three weeks before our trip, and school was getting out for the weekend. All the way home, Nancy, Billy, and I couldn't stop talking about our trip. We talked about all the characters we were going to see such as Mickey Mouse, Minnie Mouse, Pooh Bear, and Cinderella, and what rides we wanted to go on and the theme parks we wanted to visit.

When we got to our street from school, I saw a lot of cars parked on the street by our house, which was unusual. Nancy and I looked at each other and knew something weren't right. We walked into the house; at first no one noticed us. There were neighbors, close friends of my parents, and some relatives. I remember thinking I had never seen our house with this many people in it before.

Our Aunt Debbie, my mom's sister, saw us looking around and came over to us to give each of us a big hug. I looked in her eyes and could tell that she had been crying for a long time.

She took us downstairs into the TV room to tell us, "I am sorry, your parents have been in a car accident. They were rushed to the hospital, and the doctors and nurses did everything they could, but it was too late. I am so sorry; your parents have died."

I just stood there looking into space. I couldn't believe they were gone. I just saw them six hours ago at breakfast, healthy and alive.

Once the news registered, Nancy and I started to cry and couldn't stop. Billy wasn't accepting our parents' death. He had the hardest time out of the three of us. I thought it was because he was the youngest. Aunt Debbie hugged each of us as tight as she could and told us she loved us.

After I wiped the tears off my face, I asked, "How did the accident happen?"

"A truck lost control and hit your parents' car head on. It happened so fast, there was nothing your dad could do to prevent the accident," responded Aunt Debbie.

"What is going to happen to Nancy, Billy, and I? Where are we going to live?"

"All of you are going to come and live with Uncle Jeff, Monica, and me. Your parents appointed us the guardian of you three children if something happened to them," Aunt Debbie told us.

Over the next few days, all the relatives arrive at the house for the funeral. This was the first funeral I had ever been to, and I didn't know what to expect. Everyone was dressed in black, crying, hugging me, and telling me they were sorry. I never had so many hugs before in my life. I guess I was too young to understand that there was nothing anyone could say or do to ease my pain. Every night, I cried myself to sleep just wanting to be hugged by my parents one last time.

It was decided that Aunt Debbie would take a year leave of absence from her job to be there for us during the transition, since Uncle Jeff made more money.

It had been a month since the funeral, and it was time to pack up the house to put it on the market. Aunt Debbie and Uncle Jeff lived in Enfield, a half hour away from our house, and that meant that we had to change schools and make new friends. I remember that Nancy and I are sad about leaving our friends behind. It just didn't seem fair to us that we lost our parents, our house, and now our friends.

We had been over to Aunt Debbie's house many times for visits and special occasions such as birthdays, holidays, and BBQ, but this time was different. Our lives were forever changed.

Their house was beautiful; there was a big oak in the middle of the front yard and a swing on the front porch. Every time our mom would take us for a visit, I would just sit on the porch, swinging for hours, or it seemed like it. It was a split entry house with a big front entranceway. When you went upstairs, you were in the living room that had the most beautiful brick fireplace, an eat-in kitchen, and full bathroom with three bedrooms. Downstairs, there was a half bathroom, TV room, laundry room, and a small bedroom.

    Since Nancy was the eldest, she took the downstairs bedroom. Monica and I shared her bedroom, while Billy had the spare bedroom upstairs.

Chapter 3

It had been a couple of years since our parents' deaths, and life seemed to be returning to normal. I was adjusted to my new school and even made some friends. I still had some bad days where I would miss my parents a lot, but Aunt Debbie was there for me to talk to, which made it easier.

School just got out a week before, and Monica and I were doing cartwheels on the front lawn when we heard a loud bang. At first, I didn't know what it was. I looked up and down the street but didn't notice anything. When I looked back at Monica, she was on the ground, crying in pain. I went over to her and noticed the blood on her top.

I yelled at the top of my lungs, "Help! Help!"

Aunt Debbie came running out of the house toward Monica and me. At first, she didn't notice the blood on Monica's shirt until she moved her. Immediately, Aunt Debbie looked at the wound and realized that Monica had been shot. She put her hand on the wound to apply pressure and slow down the bleeding.

When Uncle Jeff came outside, he could tell by Aunt Debbie's expression that it was bad. She picked up Monica while Uncle Jeff grabbed me and ran back into the house.

"She was shot! Jeff, call 911 and tell them she was shot," Aunt Debbie yelled.

Uncle Jeff stayed on the line with the dispatcher until the police arrived. Nancy, Billy, and I just stood there and kept staring at Monica. Uncle Jeff was relaying information that 911 was telling him to Aunt Debbie. Monica stopped breathing, so Aunt Debbie had to do CPR while we waited for the ambulance to get there.

Finally, the ambulance and police arrived, which seemed like a long time.

The police and EMS ran into the house. The police looked all around to secure the area while the ambulance attendants worked on Monica. Everything was happening extremely fast. The next thing I knew, Aunt Debbie was getting into the back of the ambulance with Monica and being rushed to the hospital.

The police asked Uncle Jeff, "What happened?"

Uncle Jeff said, "Debbie and I were in the house while Monica and Rebecca were playing in the front yard when we heard Rebecca yelling for help. Once we realized what happened, we brought both girls in the house in case the person came back and called 911."

"It would be helpful if we can speak to Rebecca. She could have saw something that could help us," the policewoman asked.

"Yes, of course. Anything to help figure out what happened," Uncle Jeff replied.

Uncle Jeff sat on the couch next to me and said, "Rebecca, this is Sergeant Neilson. She would like to ask you a few questions, okay?"

I never had to answer questions by a police officer before, so I was nervous. I wasn't sure what to tell them since I didn't see anything.

Sergeant Neilson said, "Hi, Rebecca, my name is Stephanie. Can you tell me what happened?"

I said, "Okay. Monica and I were having fun doing cartwheels on the front lawn when I heard a loud bang. I looked around, but I didn't see anything, and I didn't know where the sound came from. When I turned around, Monica fell to the ground crying. I ran over to her and saw the blood, which made me scream. Then Aunt Debbie and Uncle Jeff came running out of the house."

"Did you see anyone come into the yard or the driveway?" asked Sergeant Neilson.

"No."

"Okay, thank you for talking to me," Sergeant Neilson replied.

While I was talking to the police, Uncle Jeff couldn't stop looking at his phone for a text or call from Aunt Debbie on Monica's condition. As soon as we were done, he asked, "If that is all, I would like to go to the hospital to see how Monica is doing."

Sergeant Neilson said, "Yes, of course. We are going to talk to the neighbors and see if they saw anything and look around the area. We will keep in touch with you."

"Thank you. Nancy, Billy, and Rebecca, let's go," said Uncle Jeff.

When we arrived at the hospital, the emergency nurse took us to a room where Aunt Debbie was waiting while Monica was in surgery.

In a scared voice, Uncle Jeff asked, "How is Monica doing?"

"I am not sure; they took her to the operating room a little while ago, and I haven't heard anything," replied Aunt Debbie

We sat there waiting and waiting to hear anything from the operating room. About an hour later, the doctor entered the room. We were the only family there.

"Monica had lost a lot of blood, and the bullet hit her liver. We had to take a section of liver out, and she will have to stay in the hospital for a couple of days but will make a full recovery."

Uncle Jeff grabbed Aunt Debbie and gave her the biggest hug possible. We all started to cry, but they were happy tears.

"Can she live a normal life with only part of her liver?" asked Aunt Debbie.

"Yes, the liver is a remarkable organ. It will grow back again. She will just have to take it easy for a few weeks."

"When can we see her?"

"In about a half hour, a nurse will come and take you to her in a room, then you can visit with her."

I remember walking into Monica's room, and the first thing I noticed was that she was hooked up to all kinds of tubes and machines. I was scared to touch her because I thought I might hurt her.

"It's okay, Rebecca, you can touch her. You won't hurt her."

"Why does she have tubes in her arm and nose?"

"The tubes in her nose are supplying her with oxygen to help her breathe, and the ones in her arm are giving her fluids and medicine," Aunt Debbie replied.

The police came into Monica's room to check on how she was doing. Aunt Debbie, Uncle Jeff, and Sergeant Neilson went out in the hallway to talk, but they left the door open, so I could hear what they were saying.

"Do you have any leads on who did this?"

"No, we have no eyewitnesses and there is no evidence. The only thing we have is a bullet, which is being sent to the lab for analysis and fingerprinting."

A few days later, we just arrived home after picking Monica up from the hospital when Sergeant Neilson came over to the house to advise Aunt Debbie and Uncle Jeff there was no evidence on the bullet. The sergeant believed it was a random shooting. Over the next few months, Aunt Debbie and Uncle Jeff seemed to relax, and Monica made a complete recovery. Summer was over, and it was time to go back to school.

Chapter 4

The fall went by fast, and the next thing I knew it was November and we had our first snow day of the year.

A couple of weeks later, Aunt Debbie gave me some money to buy everyone in the family a small Christmas gift. I was ten years old and wanted to go shopping with my friends at the mall without her or my uncle. Aunt Debbie wouldn't go for that; she told me I was too young. The deal was she would drop off and pick up my friends and me at the mall. We had two hours to shop, and Nancy, who was thirteen, had to go with us.

We shopped for one and half hours and bought all the Christmas gifts I needed, so we decided to go to the food court for a snack; shopping makes you hungry. When I was eating, I kept getting a feeling that someone was watching me. I look around but couldn't see anyone that I knew.

Just as I was about to take a sip of my pop, I spilled it all over my top and jeans.

"Shit!" I said.

"Rebecca, don't say that word!" Nancy replied.

Of course, being the saucy sister I was, I retorted, "You say it."

"I am older than you."

"I can't believe you missed your big mouth," said one of my friends.

"Very funny, ha-ha, I will be right back. I'm going to the bathroom to clean up."

When I came out of the bathroom, there was a man standing there looking at me. I didn't recognize him, so I continued to walk.

He started walking toward me and said, "Hi, Rebecca, how are you?"

The first thing that went through my mind was how did he know my name? Did I know this man? He didn't look familiar.

"Excuse me," I replied.

"How are you, Rebecca?"

"Do I know you?"

"We haven't met officially, but I know everything about you."

I just stared at him for a minute, trying to figure out who this man was.

"I think you have me mixed up with someone else." Then I started to walk away.

"I know you were born in Tignish, PEI. You have one brother and one sister. Your mom and dad died a couple of years ago. Then you went to live with your Aunt Debbie and Uncle Jeff."

At this point, I was getting extremely nervous, since he knew a lot of personal information about me and my family.

"How do you know that?"

"I knew your mother. I told her that if she moved you away from me, she and you would regret it for the rest of your life."

Shivers went down my spine, and before I could say anything, he turned around and walked away. I went after him but lost him in the crowd at the food court. How did he know my mom and me? What did he mean by that statement?

When I got back to the table, my friends said, "About time you got back. Where were you?"

"There was a line-up in the bathroom," I replied.

While my friends went to get another drink of pop, I told Nancy about the man.

"What did he look like?" she asked.

"I really couldn't tell, since he wore a black ball cap, sunglasses, and a black jacket. He did have a mustache and beard," I replied.

"Do you see him?" said Nancy.

"No, he's gone," I answered.

"He must have you mixed up with someone else," replied Nancy.

"I guess you're right," I said.

When I got home, Aunt Debbie noticed that something wasn't right with me, so she asked, "Are you okay?"

"Yeah, I'm just tired from shopping."

"Alright, if you need to talk, I am here for you."

"Okay."

I just went straight up to my room to think about what the man said. Then it dawned on me that if my parents knew him, they might have a picture of him from a party or gathering. If I could find a picture of him, Aunt Debbie might know who he was. I ran downstairs and asked if she had any pictures from my parents' house.

"All the photo albums are in a box in the closet, why?"

"I miss my parents a lot, and I just want to remember them."

She got the albums for me. I took them upstairs to my room to try to see if there was a picture of the man. I looked at each photo one at a time, but I couldn't find him in any picture. It brought up so much emotion that day all I could do is cry. I really missed my parents, especially my mom. I knew if she were still alive, she would be able to help me.

When I was almost finished the last book, an envelope with my name on it fell out. I opened it:

My sweetheart Rebecca,

I am so sorry for what is going to happen. I have made a terrible mistake about six years ago, and I believe you are going to pay the price. I wish I could go back and change the past, but I can't. If you can find it in your heart, please forgive me.

Love, Mom
XXXXOOOO

The date on the letter meant that I would have been four years old when my mom wrote it. Instead of finding answers to who the man was, now I had more questions. What terrible mistake did my mom make?

I tossed and turn all night and couldn't stop thinking about the letter and the man from the mall.

Chapter 5

It was two weeks before Christmas, and Aunt Debbie was out shopping while Uncle Jeff was in the kitchen making popcorn for us to eat during *Miracle on 34th Street*, my favorite Christmas movie, when there was a knock at the front door. I was closest to the door, so I got up and went to answer the door. Standing there was Sergeant Neilson.

"Hi."

"Hi, Rebecca, can I please speak with your Uncle Jeff?"

"Uncle Jeff, you're wanted at the door," I yelled.

I thought it had to do with who shot Monica.

Uncle Jeff came out of the kitchen and saw it was Sergeant Neilson.

"Hi, you have news on Monica's case?"

"No, I am sorry, I am here on other business. I am sorry to have to tell you this. Debbie was involved in a car accident tonight and is being rushed to the hospital right away."

"What! How badly is she hurt?"

"She was awake and knew what happened when they took her to the hospital. She told us when she was coming down Bakery Lane that she applied the brake to slow her down, but it didn't work. She lost control and went off the road. She has been taken to the Victoria General Hospital."

Enfield was a small community that didn't have a hospital. The nearest one was half an hour away in Halifax.

When he shut the front door and turned around, Monica was standing there.

In a shaky voice Monica asked, "Is Mom going to be, okay?"

"I am not sure right now. We will get more information as soon as we get to the hospital," Uncle Jeff answered.

We put on our coats and boots and drove to the hospital. When we arrived at the emergency department, a nurse took us to be with Aunt Debbie. The doctor informed Uncle Jeff that she had suffered a concussion, broke her right leg, and had three broken ribs. She would need to have surgery to fix her right leg. The doctor let us talk to her before taking her to surgery.

After a few hours, the doctor came in and told Uncle Jeff that the surgery went well. She would have to stay in the hospital a couple of days, and if everything went well, she could go home by the end of the week.

The nurse came to get us about an hour later and took us to her room to visit. When we went in, she was awake but very tired, so we only stayed a few minutes.

"Hi, I am so glad to see all of you," said Aunt Debbie. "I was so scared."

Uncle Jeff went over to the side of her bed, squeezed her hand, and asked, "What happened?"

"I was going down the hill on Bakery Lane, lost control of the car, and went off the road," replied Aunt Debbie. "It happened so fast; before I knew it, the car crashed."

"Mom are you okay?" asked Monica.

"I am a lot better now that I have you all with me," answered Aunt Debbie.

Monica started to cry. "Hey, honey I am going to be fine. I just need to stay in the hospital for a few days," said her mother.

When we came back to the hospital the next morning, we all drew a picture on her cast. Over the next few days, every night after supper, we went to the hospital to visit Aunt Debbie. It was the end of the week, and the doctor discharged her from the hospital that afternoon on the condition she would take it easy when she got home.

She would require help around the house, so Grammy Smith, Uncle Jeff's mom, came to stay with us until she healed. I was excited, since I liked Grammy's cooking better than Aunt Debbie's, but I would never tell her.

Grammy took Nancy, Monica, Billy, and I to the movies to get us out of the house. The weather had been minus 20, so we were unable to get outside to play, and we had a lot of energy built up. When we got home, Sergeant Neilson was at the house.

No one noticed that I was in the hallway and could hear what they were saying.

"The crime scene investigators looked at your car and found out that the brake line was cut, and the brakes couldn't get the fluid they needed. When is the last time you had your car in for service?"

"It was about month ago. I had the oil changed," replied Aunt Debbie.

"I will need the name of the garage you took it to," answered Sergeant Neilson.

"Do you think someone cut it on purpose?" asked Uncle Jeff.

"It appears that way," responded Sergeant Neilson. "How long have you been going to this garage?"

"It has been at least ten years," answered Aunt Debbie.

"You were out shopping, right, so what stores did you go to?" asked Sergeant Neilson.

"I was at the Walmart on Pine Hill Drive, Shoppers Drug Mart on Red Oak Drive, and finally at the bakery on Bakery Lane," Aunt Debbie replied.

"Is there anyone that you can think of that would want to hurt you?" asked Sergeant Neilson.

"No, no one that I know," answered Aunt Debbie.

"I will have the police patrol your neighborhood more for the next few days, and if you see anyone that doesn't belong, call me right away."

"Who would want to hurt Debbie?" asked Uncle Jeff.

"There were so many partial fingerprints on the car and under the hood, but there were no full fingerprints. If you can remember anything, please call me. I will be in touch with you after I have finished my investigation," replied Sergeant Neilson.

After the sergeant left, Aunt Debbie and Uncle Jeff decided they were going to get a home security alarm installed. Three days later, the security alarm was put in the house by the front door. It gave Aunt Debbie a little peace of mind.

A few weeks later, I was reading a book in the living room after supper when there was a knock on the front door. I opened the door and invited Sergeant Neilson into the house.

"You can sit in the living room while I get Aunt Debbie for you."

"Thank you."

I went into the kitchen to let Aunt Debbie know the police were here. When I returned to the living room, I said, "She will be right out. Did you catch the person that hurt Aunt Debbie?"

Before the sergeant could answer, Aunt Debbie and Uncle Jeff walked into the living room.

"Rebecca, please go downstairs with Grammy Smith and the other kids while we talk to Sergeant Neilson," said Aunt Debbie.

"But it is too noisy for me to read downstairs," I replied. "Could I just go into the dining room?"

"Okay, you go now," said Aunt Debbie.

I sat in the chair closest to the living room, luckily was the chair I always sat in, so I could hear what they were talking about.

"Do you have any leads on who cut Debbie's brake line?" asked Uncle Jeff.

"I went to the garage and talked to the manager. He hasn't hired anyone in the last three years," said Sergeant Neilson. "I asked him for a list of his employees' names, which he didn't have to give me, but he did. I ran all their names in our database, and nothing came up. I even went to each of the businesses to see if there was anything on their security cameras, and no luck."

"Does that mean there is nothing that you can do?" asked Uncle Jeff.

"I know this isn't the answer you want to hear, but you are right, there is nothing I can do," replied Sergeant Neilson. "We have no evidence or witness to who tampered with your vehicle. Have you noticed anyone out of the ordinary around the neighborhood?"

"No, I haven't," replied Aunt Debbie. "What about you, Jeff?"

"No," replied Uncle Jeff.

"That is good. If you do notice anyone, please call me, and try to have a good Christmas," said Sergeant Neilson.

Chapter 6

A few months later, it was so hard to get up that morning since it was the first day back to school after March break. I was used to sleeping in for the past nine days.

I must say that the day did go by faster than I thought it would. The next thing I knew, the bell rang for us to go home.

I saw Nancy walking home with her friends, a few hundred feet in front of me, and a car pulled up beside them to ask for directions. Nancy was the type of person who would always help anyone. She approached the car, and the guy rolled down the passenger window, shot Nancy in the chest, and sped away. Nancy immediately fell to the ground with blood running from her chest.

One of her friends started to scream, and the other one called 911 and yelled, "Help, help, my friend has been shot!"

I ran toward Nancy as fast as I could, but it felt like I was taking forever to reach her when a woman on the other side of the street ran across to help.

"My name is Emma, and I am a nurse. I am going to take off my sweater and put pressure on your wound. This is going to hurt, but I must slow down the bleeding. "

Nancy tried to say okay but could only mumble due to the pain.

"What is her name?" Emma asked.

"Nancy! She's, my sister!" I answered.

As Emma was pressing down on Nancy's chest, she kept asking her questions, trying to keep her conscious.

"Nancy, how old are you? Where do you go to school? Help is on the way. Look at me, Nancy, keep your eyes open. Stay with me."

Coincidentally, Sergeant Neilson was the first to arrive on the scene. I could tell by her expression that she was shocked to see it was Nancy who was hurt. A few minutes later, the ambulance took Nancy to the hospital.

I wanted to go with Nancy in the ambulance, but Sergeant Neilson thought it wouldn't be a good idea. After I gave her my statement, she drove me home.

On the way home, I asked Sergeant Neilson, "Is Nancy going to be, okay?"

"It is a severe injury. I am not sure, but she is well cared for with the paramedics."

I started to cry and remember thinking that I couldn't lose my sister. Why did sad things keep happening to my family?

We arrived home, and I ran into the house to tell Aunt Debbie what happened.

She yelled for Billy and Monica to come into the living room. They could tell from Aunt Debbie's tone there was something wrong.

"Nancy was shot on the way home from school. She is being rushed to the hospital, and we need to get there, so get your shoes on and get into the car."

"What happened?" asked Billy

"A car stopped to asked for directions and shot Nancy in the chest," I replied.

"Rebecca, why did they hurt Nancy?"

"I don't know why, Billy! The police are looking into it."

On the way to the hospital, Aunt Debbie realized she must call Uncle Jeff, so she calls him from the car. Uncle Jeff told her that he would meet them at the hospital right away.

We pulled into the parking lot, and before we all got out of the car, Uncle Jeff pulled in beside us, and we all rushed to the emergency room. A nurse came to take us to a family room to give us an update on Nancy's condition.

"Nancy was rushed up to the operating room a few minutes ago. It was touch-and-go when she arrived. We almost lost her, but we got her stable enough for surgery."

All we could do was sit there and pray that she would be okay while we kept looking at the door every few minutes, waiting for someone to enter to give us an update. I started to wonder why my family was always getting hurt.

First, Monica was shot in the front yard, then Aunt Debbie was in a car accident, and now Nancy was shot. I knew people got hurt and terrible things happened, but always to the same family? I started to feel that we were jinxed.

It was three hours later when the door opened and finally the doctor walked in. It was hard to read his body language to determine if it was going to be good or bad news.

"Hi, are you Nancy's family?"

"Yes, I am her Aunt Debbie, how is she?"

"Nancy is in serious condition. The bullet went through her chest and hit her heart. When Nancy was shot, she fell to the ground and hit her head on the curb, which caused bleeding in the brain. We repaired the hole in the heart, but she lost a lot of blood. As far as her brain injury right now, it is a waiting game."

"Is she going to be, okay?"

"Nancy is a strong young adult, but she has suffered tremendous injuries, and until she wakes up, we really don't know what her outcome will be."

"Do you know when she will wake up?"

"No. I am not sure."

"Can we see her?"

"Of course. I will have the nurse take you to see her. Remember, they say sometimes when a person is unconscious, they can still sense or hear you, so talk to her and encourage her to fight."

The nurse came into the family room and showed us to the ICU.

When I first walked into her room, I started to cry. I couldn't believe how many machines Nancy was hooked up to. I guess it really didn't hit me how bad my big sister was hurt until I saw her.

Uncle Jeff took my hand and led me outside to the hallway so I could gather myself. After a few minutes, I went back into the room and held her hand for a while.

"We better go home and get some rest," said Uncle Jeff. "Then we can come back tomorrow morning."

"Aunt Debbie, can I stay too?" I asked. "Just in case Nancy wakes up, I want to be here for her."

"I will have to check with the nurse to see if it is okay for the two of us to stay. I will be right back."

When she came back, she said, "The nurse said yes you can, but we have to stay in Nancy's room," said Aunt Debbie.

"I will not leave Nancy's side," I replied.

I gave everyone a hug then sat down on the chair beside Nancy and held her hand tightly. Aunt Debbie walked everyone out of the ICU then returned and sat in the other chair, just staring at Nancy.

Chapter 7

I remember talking to Nancy about all the fun we had over the years and how much I loved having her as my sister. I told her that we needed her in our lives, so she had to fight and come back to us.

The next thing I knew it was a few hours later; I must have dozed off. I would talk to her about the things we would do when she was all better, such as have a shopping day, go to the spa, sit at home, and watch our favorite movies. All I knew was that I wanted my big sister to live. I needed her. I fell back to sleep and woke up when Aunt Debbie tapped me on the shoulder.

It had been a week now, and Nancy still didn't wake up. I would go every day to visit her, and on the way, I would be excited, hoping today was the day she would be awake when I walked into her room. Then when I arrive and saw she wasn't awake, the more scared I became that she might not make it.

Sometimes I would read a book to her, other times I would just hold her hand. I would tell her all about my day and what was happening in our family. I wanted her to know that we loved her and were fighting for her. It just amazed me that with all the technology we had today, there was nothing the doctors could do for Nancy.

Now it had been two weeks since Nancy was shot, and Aunt Debbie called a family meeting around the kitchen table to tell us that the doctors wanted to discuss Nancy's situation. When our parents died, Aunt Debbie was appointed our guardian by the courts, and she could make any necessary decisions regarding our health and well-being. The meeting was scheduled for ten the next morning.

When we arrived at the hospital, we went to Nancy's room to see her and wait for the doctor to come. He wanted to take Aunt Debbie and Uncle Jeff to his office so they could talk.

"Wait!" I stood up and said with authority. "I might only be eleven years old, but this is my sister we are talking about, and I have the right to know what is going on."

Aunt Debbie, Uncle Jeff, and the doctor were shocked.

"Rebecca, you are right." Aunt Debbie turned to the doctor and said, "We will discuss Nancy's situation here with the whole family."

"Nancy's condition is what we call brain-dead. The damage from hitting her head on the curb and the loss of oxygen to her brain caused her brain to stop working," explained the doctor. "The machines are the only thing keeping her alive."

"Doctor, let me get this straight, you are telling us that she will never wake up, and if by some miracle she does, she will never be able to live without the machines."

"That is correct, Jeff. I am so sorry."

None of us could hold back the tears anymore. Uncle Jeff turned to Aunt Debbie held her as tight as he could while they both cried. Billy sat beside me and started to cry too. I put my right arm around him while my left hand held on to Nancy's, squeezing it for any sign of life. I tried to be strong for Billy, but I couldn't do it anymore. I started to sob and couldn't stop.

The doctor left Nancy's room to give us some time. After a few minutes, he came back.

In a shaky voice, Aunt Debbie turned to the doctor asked, "What happens now?"

"I realize this must be the hardest thing you will ever have to do, but you have to decide when to take Nancy off the machines. There is one more thing I would like for you to discuss and think about: if you want to donate her organs to help another child live? This is a lot to take in, and you don't have to decide today. You can go home and talk it over and let us know in a few days."

"When my sister asked us to be godparents, I never thought I would ever have to make this decision."

We all needed to have a break, so we went home for supper and to discuss what to do about Nancy's condition. I wasn't hungry, so I went downstairs to Nancy's room and sat on her bed while the rest of them had supper. I wanted to be close to her, and this was the place.

About hour later, Aunt Debbie, Uncle Jeff, and Billy came into Nancy's room.

"The doctor wants us to decide if we want to donate her organs to help another child live," Uncle Jeff said. "How do you feel about that?"

I could tell by Billy's expression that he was confused, and to tell you the truth, I didn't understand what was happening either, so I asked, "What do you mean?"

"Well, Nancy has kidneys, two lungs, and a liver that are in perfect condition and can be transplanted into another child's body whose liver, kidney, or lungs aren't working, so they can live a normal life."

Excited, Billy said, "Then why can't they give Nancy a new brain, so she can live?"

"The brain is the only organ in the human body that can't be transplanted," replied Uncle Jeff.

At that time, I still didn't completely understand the transplant thing, but I trusted Aunt Debbie and Uncle Jeff made the decision that was the best for Nancy.

The next morning, we all went back to the hospital to visit with Nancy one last time when the doctor came into the room and said, "Have you reached a decision?"

"Yes, we will let her go, so she can rest in peace and donate her organs to help another sick child," Aunt Debbie replied.

I couldn't believe there was nothing they could do. I had tears streaming down my face when I hollered, "No! No! They must save her! I need her!"

Uncle Jeff walked over to me, put his arms around me, and said, "They tried their best, but her injuries were too bad. I am so sorry."

Right before the nurses came into Nancy's room, I was holding one hand and Billy was holding the other, squeezing every few minutes, hoping she would squeeze back. She never regained consciousness, so we couldn't say goodbye to her.

The next thing I knew, the nurses were wheeling Nancy out of her room. That was the last time I saw her.

When we got home, Aunt Debbie asked us if we want to talk or had any questions. All I wanted was my sister alive. I didn't want to be around anyone, so I went into my room, sat on my bed, and cried for hours.

I remember thinking that I was only eleven years old and already lost both of my parents and my sister. Memories of my parents' death started coming back to me, and I couldn't sleep.

All our relatives started arriving within a couple of days, and the house was busy. I was getting tired of everyone hugging me and asking if I was okay. I wasn't. I felt like shouting, really, how do you think I am doing!

I realize now that they were just trying to be nice. They didn't know what to say, and there was nothing they could say to make me feel better.

*

It was the day of the funeral, and the church was packed. All the seats were taken, and people were standing at the back of the church and off to the sides. Nancy was a cheerleader, so the whole football team and all the cheerleaders were there, along with two-thirds of the grade 8 students.

It was so easy to love Nancy. She always had a smile on her face, would help anyone that needed it, no matter what, and was easy to talk to. There were several people that stood up and told a funny story or gave a wonderful speech about her. I didn't realize how many people she touched and how much she would be missed.

I knew that I would never get over her death. I would have to move on, but I would never forget what a wonderful big sister she was to me. She would allow me to go shopping with her and her friends at the mall, she would read me a story when I had a tough time falling asleep, and when our parents died, she held me all night while I cried. She was always there for me to talk to if I needed someone to listen. There wouldn't be a day that went by that I wouldn't think about her and how she didn't deserve to die.

A few days later, I was in my room looking at pictures of Nancy and my parents when I heard Sergeant Neilson's voice. I went downstairs and walked into the living room. "Did you catch the person that shot Nancy?"

"No, but I believe it was gang-related."

"Why do you think that?" asked Aunt Debbie.

"The crime scene investigators found a gun on the ground, so they dusted it for prints, but there were only partial ones. Also, the serial number on the gun was filed down, which means we couldn't get the number. Most of the guns we see like that are used by gangs and bought on the black market," replied Sergeant Neilson.

"How can you be sure that was the gun that shot Nancy?" I asked.

"The crime scene investigators tested the gun at the lab by firing it and comparing the bullet to the one that the doctors removed from Nancy. The bullets had the same marks on them, which means they were fired by the same gun," answered Sergeant Neilson.

"Why would a gang want to hurt Nancy?" asked Aunt Debbie.

"It wasn't that they wanted to hurt Nancy specifically. We believe it was a random act. Initiations to the gang — if you want to belong to the gang you have to hurt someone. The guys were driving around looking for someone when they saw Nancy," replied Sergeant Neilson.

"That isn't fair! Nancy didn't deserve to die!" I yelled as I ran upstairs to my room.

Chapter 8

It had been a year since Nancy's death, and we were getting ready for Halloween. This was Nancy's favorite holiday. She even liked it better than Christmas. I wasn't in the mood this year to go out trick-and-treating without her, so I helped Aunt Debbie hand out the candy. Of course, I would sneak a treat or two when Aunt Debbie wasn't looking. I couldn't help but wonder, if Nancy were still alive, what costume she would be wearing.

The only immediate family I really have left was Billy.

Today was the one-year anniversary of Nancy's death. The whole family went to her grave to place flowers by her headstone. All of us had tears coming down our faces. To me it was just like she died yesterday. They say time will heal all pain, but one year wasn't enough time.

Since Christmas was approaching fast, Aunt Debbie and Uncle Jeff knew it would be a challenging time for Billy, Monica, and I, so they decided to book a trip to Walt Disney World for us to get away during our March break. This was our big present, and we were excited. We had never been on an airplane before.

*

It was the middle of January, and after supper Aunt Debbie put some books about Walt Disney World and Florida on the table.

"Here is some information about our trip that is coming up fast. I want everyone to make a list of what they want to see and do. Then we will sit down and go over all the lists to ensure we see everything that we all want to see."

I was extremely excited, so right away I started to make my list, and getting my picture taken with Minnie and Mickey Mouse were on the top of my list. Also, I wanted to see the dolphin show at Sea World. Monica wanted to go to Disney's Animal Kingdom, Hollywood Studios, Epcot, Magic Kingdom Park, and Disney's

Blizzard Beach Water Park. Billy wanted to get his picture taken with as many Disney characters as possible, go on some rides such as the Teacups, Walt Disney World Railroad, Seven Dwarfs Mine Train, and many more.

Soon, I couldn't believe it was the day before our trip, and we were all excited. Aunt Debbie looked in each of our suitcases to ensure that we had enough clothes. We ordered in pizza that night and talked about what we were going to do and see in Florida.

We stayed at Disney's All Star Movie Resort. One of the perks was that the theme parks opened earlier and stayed open later just for the people that stayed on the resort. It was fantastic; we could go on the rides a few more times.

The week just flew by, but we did get to see everything and go on all the rides we wanted. It was our last night, and we decided to go and see the fireworks one last time at Magic Kingdom.

When we arrived at home, there was snow on the ground, and it was cold. We just left 30-degree sunny weather to minus 8. Why couldn't it be sunny and 30 degrees everywhere? We'd had a lot of fun and were exhausted. The best part of the trip for me was Universal Studios, going through the 3D shows; it was so real.

Uncle Jeff went through the mail and noticed an envelope with my name on it. I remember wondering who would be writing me a letter:

Dear Rebecca,

I saw that you had a wonderful time at Walt Disney World. When you were spinning in the Teacups, I couldn't help to notice how happy you looked. My favorite things were the fireworks at Magic Kingdom; they were amazing. If only life could be wonderful all the time, but you must know that sometimes bad things happen.

I was very puzzled and had a million questions. Who sent this letter? What did they want from me? How did they know what I did at Walt Disney World? The only way they would know is if they followed me there — but why?

Uncle Jeff could tell something was wrong by the confused look on my face.

"Monica and Billy, go upstairs and unpack your suitcase. Are you okay, Rebecca?"

At that point, Aunt Debbie looked at me.

"I don't know, someone was watching me on the trip."

"What are you talking about?" she asked.

I gave the letter to them to read. Right away, they knew I was scared and had good reason to be.

"We need to call the police," said Aunt Debbie.

They didn't want to alarm Monica or Billy, so Uncle Jeff called his mom to take them out for supper so they could tell her all about their trip. Billy wanted to know why I wasn't going, so he told him that I was sick and needed to sleep.

About an hour later, there was a knock. Uncle Jeff opened the door to the police.

He gave them the envelope and letter. After the police officer read it, he sat down on the couch next to me. "Did you tell anyone that you were going away to Florida?"

"Yeah, of course I told my classmates and friends. I was excited."

"Were they excited for you?" asked the police officer.

"Some were and others weren't."

The police officer looked at Aunt Debbie and Uncle Jeff. "Besides family, who else knew you were going away?"

"Just work. I had to get the time off," said Uncle Jeff.

"I just told our next-door neighbor, so they could get our mail for us and keep an eye on the house," replied Aunt Debbie.

"When you were away, did you see anyone paying a little too much attention to Rebecca?"

"I don't think so. There were so many people around," replied Aunt Debbie.

"The only thing on the envelope is Rebecca's name, and in the letter, there is no clue to who wrote it. It might be from a kid at school who was jealous she went on a trip and wished it was their family that went away," police officer said.

"But how did the person know we went on the Teacup ride and watched the fireworks?" asked Aunt Debbie.

"That is what most people do at Walt Disney," replied the officer. "I will patrol around the area over the next few days, and if you notice anyone strange, just call 911."

Chapter 9

For the following three years, everything was normal. I didn't receive any more letters, and we were just like any another normal family: wake up go to school or work, come home, have supper, and enjoy the weekends.

    I was fifteen years old, and like any other teenager I would rather be with my friends having fun than with my family. I knew that is normal for all teenagers, but now, looking back, I wished I spent more time with the family. If only we had a crystal ball and could see the future, life might be easier.

    I couldn't believe I was graduating from grade nine and in a few months, I would be in high school. As I was going through puberty, I missed Nancy increasingly more each day. I wished she were alive so I could talk to her, especially about boys. I knew that Aunt Debbie was there for me to talk to, but it wasn't the same. Aunt Debbie was like my second mom, and sometimes you just don't want to talk to your mom about boys.

    I was excited but nervous at the same time about going to a new school. The good thing was that my friends were with me. The first day was okay, trying to find my classes and the cafeteria. This school was larger than my junior high school, and there were double the students. Before I knew it, I knew exactly where to go.

    A month had already gone by, and it seemed like I had been in school for only a couple of weeks. It was Friday afternoon, and I was sitting in Math class, daydreaming about what I was going to do on the weekend when the 3:00 p.m. bell rang. It was the weekend, yeah!!!

    I went to my locker to get my jacket, and as I got closer, I could see an envelope sticking partway out. It wasn't addressed to anyone, so I opened the envelope:

Dear Rebecca,

In life, we have choices to make, and sometimes the choices we make have good consequences, but other times the outcome is bad. Now you have a choice to make either to stay at your aunt's house or to leave. If you stay, then some people will get hurt and/or die, but if you leave, everyone will be safe. Remember, the decision is yours, but if you tell anyone I will be forced to hurt them, I promise.

There were no clues as to who wrote the note, the same as a few years ago. I started to think about what happened to Monica, Aunt Debbie, and Nancy. Were they really accidents, or were they intentional?

I tossed and turned all night. I couldn't stop thinking about the letter.

That was all I thought about over the next few days. What should I do? How could I make such a major decision? No matter what I choose I was so scared that I was going to be the wrong one.

If I stayed, I took the chance that the person would make good on their threat. However, if I left, how I could be sure that the person wouldn't hurt my family?

I didn't want to leave, but more important, I didn't want any harm coming to my family. I felt so alone and didn't know what to do. I had no one to talk to, since if I did, I would be risking their safety. What did I do to this person that they were willing to hurt me and my family?

I thought about going to the police for help, but what if the person found out? The letter said if I told anyone, my family would be hurt. That was a risk that I wasn't willing to take.

All week, I had been trying to figure out how I could stay with my family without putting them in danger, and the answer is I couldn't.

That night, when Uncle Jeff came home from work, he told us that when he was crossing the street at the crosswalk, someone almost hit him. It was like they pressed the gas instead of the brake, and if he hadn't jumped out of the way, he would have been hit.

I don't know if it was a coincidence or if the person who wrote the letter was giving me a warning, but right then I knew what I had to do. I was afraid the person would follow through. If another member of my family was hurt or died and I could have stopped it by moving out, then I would never forgive myself.

I had decided that I had no choice but to leave to protect my family. I didn't want to leave, but their safety was more important than mine.

But where would I go?

I was afraid that Aunt Debbie and Uncle Jeff would come looking for me, so I knew I had to leave Nova Scotia.

*

It was Saturday. I told Aunt Debbie that I had a project due next week, and I had to go to the library. I knew I could use the computers there and research where I could go to live without her knowing.

It needed to be a place with lots of people, where I could blend in. I remembered one of my classmates telling me about her aunt and uncle that lived in Toronto. She went to visit them and couldn't believe all the people.

I looked up Toronto, Ontario, which was over 1,100 miles away and had over 2 million people; it would be hard to find me there. Also, if Aunt Debbie went to the police and reported me missing, it would be on the news in Nova Scotia but not in Ontario, since it was three provinces away.

Now that I had a place to move to, how would I get there? I couldn't afford a plane ticket, so I would have to take the train or bus.

I first looked up the train schedule. It would take twenty-nine hours to arrive in downtown Toronto. The ticket price would be $248.80. Next, I looked up the bus that would take thirty-six hours but only cost $211.50. If I took the bus, I could save $37.30 that could go toward food.

I decided to take the 8:30 a.m. bus on Tuesday morning, which would have me arriving in Toronto at 8:30 p.m. on Wednesday.

For the remainder of the weekend, I just kept wondering what I did to this person to make them not want me to be with my family.

After I paid for my bus ticket, I would have about three hundred dollars left from my savings that I had from babysitting the neighbor's children and my newspaper route for food. I knew that wouldn't last long, so over the weekend when no one was looking I went into the cupboards and packed some snacks.

On Monday morning before school, I went to the bus station to buy a ticket for the following morning. I realized that they might not sell me a ticket since I was a minor, so I decided to pretend I was Nancy. I went into my Aunt Debbie's dresser and took Nancy's birth certificate with me to prove that I was eighteen years old. The good thing about the birth certificate there was no picture on them, so I could get away with my lie.

I wrote a note telling my teacher that I was at an eye appointment. I hate to say it, but I was good at copying my Aunt Debbie's writing and signature.

That afternoon at school, I told my friends that I had a family thing and wouldn't be going to school tomorrow. This way they wouldn't be calling on me to walk to school with them. I knew if I told them, they would talk me out of it or tell Aunt Debbie what I was planning to do, and I couldn't take that chance.

That evening, I put Nancy's birth certificate back in Aunt Debbie's dresser.

In the morning, instead of packing my schoolbooks in my backpack, I packed some clothes, toothbrush, deodorant, hairbrush, soap, face cloth, towel, and a picture of my family. I hid my schoolbooks under my bed, so if Aunt Debbie looked in my room, she would think I was at school.

I was hoping by the time that Aunt Debbie found my letter on my bed, it would be after suppertime, and I would be far enough away:

Dear Aunt Debbie and Uncle Jeff,

I want to thank you very much for taking in Nancy, Billy, and I after our parents' death. I know you were mourning for your sister and brother-in-law, but you made the transition easy. I will always think of you guys as my second parents, and I need to protect you like you protected me for the past eight years.

Please don't try to find me, and one day hopefully when it is safe, I will contact you.

Love always, Rebecca

As I put the letter on my pillow, tears started to run down my cheek, so I went to the bathroom to wipe them away. At breakfast time, I couldn't help but look at everyone one last time.

"Aunt Debbie, can I have an extra sandwich today," I asked. "I have to stay at school late for a band meeting, and I get hungry around three."

"Sure, I will pack a little extra to get you through until supper."

Then I took my lunch and left the house. When I was at the end of the street, I couldn't help but look back at the house, hoping I would be reunited with my family one day.

On my way to the bus station, I went to a magazine shop that had maps and newspapers of different cities in Canada. I bought a map of the city of Toronto and a newspaper, so on the bus I could get familiar with the city and look for a job in the want ads.

As I was getting on the bus and taking a seat, I realized I had never been so scared.

Chapter 10

I finally arrived in Toronto. It was starting to get dark, and I knew I couldn't be walking around all night; and besides, I was starting to get hungry.

I looked up the street and saw a church. When I walked up the stairs, I was surprised that the door opened. I went in and sat down on the second last row of benches. I prayed that my family would be safe now that I had left.

I was tired, so I lay down and used my backpack as a pillow plus my jacket as a blanket. I must have been exhausted, since the next thing I knew, it was seven o'clock in the morning. I went into the bathroom to brush my teeth, change my clothes, and wash my face. When I came out of the bathroom, the priest was off in the distance. He saw me but didn't say anything. It was like he was confused that I was there.

Then I just turned around and walked out of the church down the street to McDonalds for breakfast. After I finished my sandwich, I went to Walmart to buy a pay-as-you-go phone so I could call some of the want ads in the paper. It turned out that I had to go to the stores, get an application, fill it out, return to the store, and wait for a phone call for an interview.

It was getting dark outside, so I headed back to the church. When I went in, the benches were all filled with people, and the minister was at the head of the church, giving a sermon.

The last time I was in a church was for Nancy's funeral. Actually, the only time I went to church was for a funeral.

After the minister was done, everyone stood up and left. I just sat there until there were only a few people remaining. Then I went into the bathroom until the church was quiet. I peeked out the door and didn't see anyone, so I went to the same bench as the night before to sleep.

A little while later, a man tapped my shoulder. "Miss, miss please wake up."

I jumped up and screamed, which startled the minister.

"I have to close the church. Do you have a home to go to?"

I looked down at the floor. "No."

"Is there someone that I can call to help you?"

I wiped the tears that were now streaming down my face and replied, "I have no one."

"Okay. Do you want to talk about anything?"

"No! I will be on my way, sorry." I stood up, put on my coat, grabbed my backpack, and walked toward the doors.

"Please wait," said the minister.

I turned around and stood there.

"You can stay here for tonight but starting tomorrow night you have to go to the shelter," he said. "It is about a fifteen-minute walk from here. I will write down the address, hours of operation, and give you a map on how to get there."

"Thank you very much," I answered.

I went back over to the bench, took off my coat, and lay down to get some rest. It took me a while to fall back to sleep. I was missing my family.

After I came out of the bathroom the following morning, the minister was there with the map of how to get to the shelter. I thanked him and left.

It was raining hard, so I went up to McDonalds for breakfast and stayed there most of the day. Every few hours, I would get a pop or muffin; I just spent enough money that they wouldn't kick me out.

It was my first night at the shelter, and I was awake every half hour. It was overcrowded and very noisy. Some of the people would talk in their sleep and others would holler. I had never been so frightened in my life. I knew that I didn't want to live in the shelter for long, so I started looking for a job the next day.

I had to leave the shelter by 8:00 a.m., so I would go to the mall and local stores to get applications for a job, and in the afternoon, I went to the park and filled them out. They wanted to know my address, but I didn't have a permanent address. What am I going to do I just put down a fake address and hoped they wouldn't check.

The one good thing I had going for me was that when I was little, my mom filled out the paperwork for me to get my social insurance number for when I wanted to start working. Aunt Debbie gave it to me a year ago when she came across it in a box.

*

It had been a couple of weeks, and no one had called me for an interview. I was getting afraid that I would have to live in the shelter for a long time.

I didn't realize a volunteer at the shelter had been watching me for the past week until she came over one day.

"Hi, my name is Suzanne," she said. "What is your name?"

"Rebecca."

"Where are you from?"

"I am from Victoria, B.C."

I didn't want anyone to know I was from Nova Scotia. I was trying to put as much distance between my family and myself to keep them safe.

"Why are you here at a shelter?"

"I had to leave home."

"Why did you have to leave home?"

"I don't want to talk about it. I am tired now, so I am going to try and get some sleep."

"I am sorry if I upset you."

She could see in my eyes that I was about thirty seconds away from crying, so she just got up, patted me on the back, and left me be.

The next day was typical: get applications in the morning and fill them out in the afternoon and return them the following morning.

Suzanne came over to me again at the shelter and asked, "What type of job are you looking for?"

"How did you know that I am looking for a job?"

"I saw you today at the park, filling out applications."

"Right now, I will take any job."

"How much school have you completed?"

"I have a grade nine education, but I do want to graduate from high school one day."

I don't know if she felt sorry for me or why she wanted to help me, but she called one of her friends that owned a gas station to find out if she had any job openings. I was already awake when Suzanne arrived at the shelter in the morning to tell me that her friend wanted to talk to me regarding a job.

"Why are you doing this for me?" I asked.

"I believe you are a good person, and you shouldn't be living in the shelter or on the street. You just need a little help to get on your feet."

The truth was that Suzanne needed me just as much as I needed her. Unfortunately, her daughter got involved in drugs and couldn't get off them. Three months earlier, she found her daughter dead on their bathroom floor from an overdose. She didn't want me to end up the way her daughter did, but she knew the chances were good of it happening the longer I stayed on the streets.

"Okay, thanks, I really do appreciate this."

Finally, I had a glimpse of hope.

"It is no guarantee you will get the job; you have to go through the interview process."

"I understand, but it is a lead to a potential job, and that is more than I have had in the past few weeks."

"What are you planning on wearing?"

"I have a pair of dress pants and a white top in my bag."

"I have a thought. Why don't you come to my house, where you can have a shower and wash your clothes?"

Let's face it, the last time I had a shower was a few weeks ago at my aunt's house. Every day I would go to the bathroom and washed up as best I could, but it wasn't the same as having a shower. I was nervous to go to her house, since I really didn't know her, but I had no choice. If I was going to have any shot at getting this job, I needed to take a shower and have clean clothes.

One thing I have learned is to follow my gut instinct, and it told me that Suzanne was a good lady.

"Okay, thank you."

Suzanne lived in a condo on a busy street downtown. There was a doorman at the front door who greeted everyone as they came in. I remember thinking this lady must be rich. There were ten floors, and Suzanne lived on the fourth.

Her suite had a big foyer with a hall tree for your coats and boots. To the left there was the laundry room and down the hallway before you get to the kitchen there was a storage room. The kitchen and living room were an open concept with a beautiful view of the park across the street. There was a full bathroom across from the kitchen and two bedrooms. One of the bedrooms was used as a TV room, and the living room was a sitting room for when she had guests over.

Suzanne showed me where everything was in the bathroom and gave me a housecoat to put on after my shower while I was waiting for my clothes to be ready. I forgot how good a shower can make you feel.

When I came out of the bathroom, Suzanne was sitting at the table reading a book. "There is an egg sandwich and bowl of soup on the table. I thought you might be a little hungry."

My eyes started to tear up, and for a minute it seemed like I was back home. That was why I had a good feeling about Suzanne; she reminded me of Aunt Debbie.

"Thank you."

I was starting to get low on money, so I only ate one meal a day. I was trying to make my money last until I found a job. I didn't realize it would take me this long to find employment.

Suzanne saw how quickly I ate, so she gave me a second serving. After I finished my food, I went into the bathroom to brush my teeth and get dress. When I came out, she had her shoes on and was ready to go.

I was so nervous; this was my first interview for a job, and I didn't know what to expect. All I knew was that I really needed this job to survive.

"Are you ready, Rebecca?"

"I think so."

"It is a fifteen-minute walk down the street, so we should go now."

When we arrived at the gas station, Suzanne introduces me to her friend, Jillian.

"Hi, Rebecca, let's go into my office and get started," Jillian said.

We sat down, and Jillian went over the duties of the job, hours, and the wage. She asked the usual questions such as do you have any customer service experience? Have you ever worked in a retail environment?

"I will be honest with you. I have no experience," I said. "This would be my first job, but I can tell you that I will work hard for you and be dependable. I know I am asking you to take a chance on me, but I know I can do this job."

"Okay, thank you for being honest. How can I get in touch with you?"

"You can reach me on my cell." I gave her the number.

"I will let you know in a few days." I shook her hand and thanked her for interviewing me.

Suzanne and I were walking down the street toward her house. "How did it go?"

"I'm not sure; that was my first interview. She told me I'll know in a few days."

We arrived at Suzanne's condo, and I turned to her said, "Thank you for setting up the interview." I shook her hand and walked across the street to the park.

Chapter 11

It was four days later, and I was in the park filling out more applications in case I didn't get the job at the gas station, when my phone rang.

"Hello?"

"Is Rebecca there?"

"Speaking"

"It's Jillian from the gas station. I would like to offer you the job if you are still interested?"

"Yes, I am extremely interested! Thank you very much."

"Can you start Thursday morning at nine?"

"Yes, I can, and again thank you very much."

After I got off the phone, I was so excited and couldn't wait until the shelter opened so I could tell Suzanne the great news.

For the rest of the afternoon, I decided to take it easy and just enjoy the park.

I arrived at the shelter right when they were opening the doors. I ran right over to Suzanne to tell her. She was so excited for me.

"Once again, thank you for asking Jillian to interview me."

"Sometimes in life we all need a little help along the way. I was thinking last night I have a spare bedroom. If you want, you can stay with me for a few months until you can save enough money to move out on your own. I would love to have the company, and you could sleep in a proper bed. What do you say?"

I thought about it for a few minutes. Not having to stay at the shelter would be wonderful. I could have a good night's sleep and not worry about anyone trying to steal the little bit of stuff that I had. As well, I knew that Suzanne would have food, and I only had a dollar to my name until I got paid. I felt like I had no choice but to accept her offer.

"Yes, I would like that, but how can I repay you."

"You can repay me by paying it forward. What I mean is someday if you come across a person that needs your help, you will be there for them."

"You have a deal."

We left the shelter at 7:00 p.m., and when we got to her house, she made me spaghetti and garlic bread. It was the best I ever had, and I am not just saying that because I was starving. No offense to my Aunt Debbie, but she couldn't make pasta; it was always overcooked.

I woke up the next morning and couldn't believe how well I had slept. After breakfast, Suzanne had to go shopping for a few things, and I was glad to accompany her. At the mall, she offered to buy me some new clothes for my job, but I couldn't let her. She had done so much for me already. I had three outfits to my name, so I would wear those until I received my first paycheck.

*

It was the night before I started my first job, and I had a tough time getting to sleep. I believed it was just the excitement and nervousness about starting a job.

Finally, it was time to get up and get ready for work. When I arrived, Jillian could tell that I was nervous but made me feel at ease. I learned how to use the cash register, how to do the lotto machine, and what chores I had to do on the day and night shift. The day went by fast, and I couldn't believe it was time to go.

"You did a respectable job today," Jillian said. "The schedule is posted every month in the staff room, and if you need a day off, let me know as soon as possible, so I can get your shift covered. I just added your shifts to the schedule. You can look at it before you leave."

I opened the front door and walked into the condo. Before I could get my shoes off, Suzanne asked, "How was your first day?"

"It was great! My feet are sore. I guess I'm not used to standing on them all day, and I'm tired. I have my schedule for the next month, so I will put it on the fridge, so you'll know when I work."

That night, I just took it easy and went to bed early. As each day went by, I felt more at ease and knew this job was good for me.

Chapter 12

I had been at this job for six months now, and everything was going well. I had saved enough money that I could move out of Suzanne's house and get my own place. Every payday, I would buy a few kitchen/bathroom items for when I moved into my own apartment.

    She helped me find the perfect bachelor apartment only a twenty-minute bus ride to the gas station, and most importantly, I could afford it. Suzanne took me to a second-hand store where I could buy a bed, kitchen table, and chairs, coffee table, and a dresser for a fair price.

    "Tomorrow is the big day. You move into your own place. How do you feel?"

    "I am sad and happy. I am sad since I am going to miss you and happy that I can provide for myself. Last night before I fell to sleep, I was thinking if I never met you, my life would probably be a lot different right now, and not for the better."

    "Well, you met me, and we aren't going to think about what could have happened. I got you a housewarming present."

    I was grinning from ear to ear when she brought out the big box all wrapped up. It only took me about ten seconds to unwrap it. I was in total shock. She got me a TV, and I was incredibly happy since I couldn't afford one.

    "Thank you very much."

    After breakfast, I packed up Suzanne's car and we headed over to my apartment. We spent the first few hours' cleaning everything, then we started unpacking my things when the second-hand store arrived with my furniture. They brought all the furniture in the apartment and set it up for me. By suppertime, the apartment was all put together and looking good, I must say.

    "Let's go out for supper. It's my treat to thank you for all your help."

Suzanne picked a diner just around the corner from where I lived. The food was homemade, and the prices were reasonable. After supper, she drove me to the grocery store so I could stock up. After a short visit, she left, and I had a shower then went straight to bed.

*

That night I had a dream that Aunt Debbie, Uncle Jeff, Monica, and Billy died. It felt so real that when I woke up, I was crying. My first thought was that the stranger didn't keep their promise.

Right away I knew I needed to go back to Nova Scotia to ensure my family was safe. I decided to take the train since it was little faster than the bus and I only had a few days off. The train left first thing Monday morning and arrived in Dartmouth, Nova Scotia on Tuesday at 1:30 p.m.

They had a new express train that would travel at night and take only twenty hours to arrive in Toronto since they didn't stop at every town. That would put me in Toronto on Wednesday afternoon at 3:00 p.m. in time for my 5:00 p.m. shift.

This was perfect. I could sleep on the train, and when I arrived back home, I went straight to work from the train station.

As soon as I arrived in Dartmouth, I took the bus to my aunt's house. I stood behind a big oak tree three houses down. At first, I saw Aunt Debbie sitting on the porch reading a book, Uncle Jeff was trying to rake the leaves while Billy and Monica were throwing them at each other.

I started to cry. They were happy tears because everyone was okay. I wished I just could go over and hug everyone and tell them I loved them, but I knew if I did, I would be putting their lives at risk again. That night on the train, I couldn't stop thinking about my family and how happy they looked. I just wished I could be part of that.

Chapter 13

I couldn't believe I had started working at the gas station a year ago. It was a slow day, so Amy decided to restock the shelves while I was at the cash waiting on customers.

Amy was working at the gas station part-time while she was studying nursing at the university. Over the past year, we had hung out and become friends. It felt good to finally have a friend again.

Amy went out back to get some more bread when she heard the door chime. When she came through the door to the store, she saw a guy pointing a gun at me, and he turned to look at her. Then I heard a bang and saw Amy fall to the floor. As soon as the gun went off, I looked at Amy in horror, while the man ran out the door and took off running down the street.

I grabbed the phone to called 911 while I rushed over to Amy. Right away, her medical training kicked in and she told me to put pressure on her wound.

"Ouch, that hurts!"

"I'm sorry but you told me to do it," I said.

"I know. You have to slow down the bleeding."

Amy was starting to feel tired, cold, and just wanted to sleep, but I kept getting her to recite the alphabet. I kept telling her to stay awake, that help was on the way. We heard the door open as the ambulance arrived.

"We are over here," I shouted.

Two guys with a stretcher came toward us. "My name is Stuart, this is Phil, and we are going to take safe care of you. What is your name?"

"Amy."

"Besides your shoulder, are you hurt anywhere else?"

"I don't think so, but I can feel something running down my back."

Phil lifted Amy's shoulder up and turned her so Stuart could look at her back.

"The bullet went through your body, and you feel blood going down your back."

"I am in pain, cold, and tired. Can I just go to sleep?"

"No, Amy, please stay awake. You are going into shock. Are you taking or allergic to any medication?"

"No."

"I am going to give you something for the pain."

"We are taking her to Toronto General Hospital."

"Okay," I replied.

I was shaking and scared, so I called Jillian to let her know what happened. She was at the gas station within twenty minutes. By that time, reporters were there taking pictures while the police were questioning me.

"Can you tell me what happened?"

"I was on cash while Amy was in the back room getting stock for the shelves. A man came into the store and pointed a gun at me. He demanded I open the cash register and give him the money. At that point, Amy came back into the storefront to see the guy pointing a gun at me. I believe Amy startled him, since he looked at her then shot her."

"So, it was a man. Could you tell what race he was?"

"He was a white man. I would saw in his twenties."

"How tall would you say he was?"

"I would say he was 5"8, just a little taller than me."

"Okay, good. Did he have any distinguishing marks on him?"

"What do you mean?"

"For example, did he have a tattoo, scar on his face, or any piercing?"

"He had his eyebrows and nose pierced but no other marks."

"Did he say anything else?"

"No, his hands were just shaky."
"Had you ever seen him before?"
"No."
"Thank you for your time. I will leave you my card, and if you remember anything else, please call me."
"I will."

Jillian could tell that I was too shaken up to finish my shift, so she called Suzanne to come and walk me home.

The next day, I checked my mail when I got home from work. There was an envelope just like the one that was in my locker. I started shaking so bad that I had to put the letter down on the table to read it:

Dear Rebecca,

It was clever of you to go three provinces away. I was watching the news about a gun shot at a gas station in Toronto when I saw you in the background. If it weren't for that, I would still be looking for you. It took me longer than I anticipated finding you.

Since you left your family, I will keep my promise and leave them alone. I see that you have your own place, and I just want you to know that I didn't have anything to do with Amy getting shot. Now, the accidents that your family had are another story. I was responsible for those.

How did I know that the person wasn't responsible for the shooting? Just because in the letter it said they weren't ...what if he/she were lying? If the stranger saw me on the news, what if my family saw it and came to Toronto to find me?

I decided to give the police officer that questioned me at the hospital a call, since the person in the letter confessed to hurting my family.

There was a knock on my door. I looked through the peephole to see the police officer.

"How did you get in?" I asked.

"A woman was leaving the building, so she held the door opened for me. I am a police officer. She probably thought it was safe to let me in."

"I guess you are right."

"Is there something you remembered about the shooting?"

"No, but I did receive this letter in my mailbox."

I handed the envelope with the note inside for the officer to read.

"What are you going to do?" I asked.

"There is nothing I can do. The note could have been written by anyone. There is no clue on who wrote the letter," replied the police officer. "Also, it says they aren't responsible for the shooting at your work."

"What about my family's accidents?"

"Unless you have proof that the person who wrote this note was responsible for your family's accidents, there is no crime."

After the police officer left, at that time I knew I made the right decision to leave my family, and I had to protect myself.

I put on my shoes and went to the hardware store to get two more deadbolts for my door. I was constantly looking over my shoulder to see if anyone was following me. The worst part about it was that the person knew me, but I didn't know what they looked like. All I knew was that it could have been anyone I passed on the street or that came into the gas station.

I remembered when I found the letter in the photo album from my mom that told me she told me she made a terrible mistake. If I could figure out what the mistake was, then maybe that would help me figure out who this person was and how to stop them.

Chapter 14

A few months had passed by, and I haven't received any more letters from the person, but I had a feeling it was far from over.

I liked working at the gas station, but I knew it wasn't the job that I wanted to stay at for the rest of my working life.

That weekend I went over to Suzanne's house to use the Internet and find out some information on how I could obtain my high school diploma. I couldn't enroll into high school full-time, since I had to work, but I could attend community college at night to finish the courses I needed. I printed off the application to the college and took it home to fill out.

On the application it asked what the last school I attended was, but I didn't want anyone to know, so I put down that I was home-schooled. After I mailed the application, I was nervous. If I wasn't accepted, what would I do?

About a month later, I received a letter back from the school stating that I would have to take a test to find out what grade I was at. Then they could help me choose the courses that I would need to take to receive my high school diploma. I called the school that afternoon to find out when I could do the test. It turned out that I could go in next Friday morning, which was perfect, since that was my day off.

Two weeks later, I received a letter in the mail stating that I only needed thirteen courses to complete my high school diploma, and it would only take me two years. My classes would be every Tuesday and Thursday night from 6:00 p.m. to 9:00 p.m. from September to June.

Before I could apply, I had to ask Jillian if I could have every Tuesday and Thursday night off. I was nervous to ask, so I decided to call Suzanne for her advice.

"Hi, Suzanne, can I ask you a question?"
"Of course."

"I'm thinking about finishing high school so I can receive my diploma. I would need to have every Tuesday and Thursday night off to attend classes. Do you think that Jillian will give me that time off?"

"I am not sure, but there's no harm in asking. What is the worst thing that can happen, she says no?"

"You're right. I will ask her tomorrow, thanks."

"Let me know what she says."

"Okay, I will talk to you tomorrow, bye."

My shift was over for the day, so I asked Jillian if she had a few minutes to talk before I left.

"Yes, go sit in my office, and I will be there in about five minutes."

While I was waiting, I was thinking, if she couldn't give me the time off, what was I going to do?

Jillian walked in the office, sat down in her chair, looked at me, and said, "How can I help you, Rebecca?"

"I would like to attend school every Tuesday and Thursday evening so I can finish my high school diploma. The classes will go from September to June, and it will take two years to finish. I can work any other time for you."

"I am proud of you for wanting to finish high school. Leave it with me, and I will see what I can do. When do you need to register by?"

"I have to register by the end of the month."

Jillian let me know the following week that with the help of the other employees she could give me the nights off that I requested. I was on cloud nine and couldn't wait to start classes.

I called Suzanne right away to tell her the good news. She was so happy for me and let me know that she was going out of town for a few months to visit her sister who had just become a grandmother.

I wished her a good trip and told her to call me when she got back.

Chapter 15

It was my first night of school. Since I wasn't sure if the five-thirty bus would get me there on time, I decided to take the one at five. It turned out that it was only a twenty-minute bus ride, so I went over to the cafeteria to get a drink.

When I arrived at the classroom, it was about half full. I went to the middle of the room to take a seat when I lost my balance and fell on my butt.

When I stood up and turned around, this heavenly guy was standing there. He was six-foot tall, brown eyes, light brown hair, nice natural tan, and a smile that lit up his face.

"Are you okay?"

Just when I thought he couldn't be any more perfect, he spoke with an Italian accent.

"Yes, just embarrassed, thank you."

"My name is Matteo. Is there anyone sitting here?"

"No."

That was all I could get out at the time.

"What is your name?"

I smiled and said, "Rebecca."

Then the teacher walked in, and the class began. I couldn't help it to look at Matteo, and a few times he caught me looking. I thought the three hours would drag on, but the class was over before I knew it.

"Goodbye, and I will see you on Thursday."

"Yes."

That was the first time I was nervous talking to a guy.

I was working the following night shift with Amy and there were no customers around, so I told her about the guy in my class. It was good to have someone my own age to talk to, especially about guys. I knew I could talk to Suzanne, but sometimes you just want someone your own age.

I couldn't wait until Thursday night when I would see Matteo. When I went into the classroom and took my seat, I started to wonder if he was going to sit next to me again. I was hoping he would.

Matteo walked into the classroom and sat in the chair beside me. "Hi, how are you tonight?"

"Good, thanks, and you?"

"I am good."

That class went by fast again, about which I was both glad and sad. I was glad because I was getting tired and a little sad since I wouldn't see Matteo until the following week.

Around a month later, after class when I was gathering up my books, Matteo turned to me. "Some night after school, would you be interested in going out for coffee?"

"Sure."

"How about next Thursday?"

"That sounds good to me."

Every time I started to do my schoolwork, I would get sidetracked by thinking about Matteo, which made it hard for me to concentrate. I finally manage to complete my homework for next week's classes.

Thursday night's class had just finished, and we decided to go the coffee shop just down the street from the school.

"What do you want to drink?"

"I've tried coffee and tea several different times, but I don't like the taste, so I'll have a Diet Pepsi."

He ordered a large coffee with one milk.

"You don't have sugar in your coffee?"

"No, I am sweet enough."

"That is for sure."

I couldn't believe I said that out loud, and I started to blush. The next thing, I knew it was 11:00 p.m. and we were still talking. He talked about where he grew up, what school was like, how many siblings he had, and my favorite subject: food.

It was a weird feeling of comfort, as if we had known each other for years. It just felt right being with him, and I could be myself. Besides, he could have read the phone book to me, and I would have enjoyed listening to his accent. Nothing was more romantic to me than a man with an accent, especially an Italian one.

When I was on my way to work the next morning, I was hoping Amy would be working so we could talk. I arrived at work to find out that I was with Beth for the day. However, in the afternoon Amy came into the gas station to see if I could switch a shift with her. She wanted to go away with her friends for the weekend. Of course, I agreed then told her everything about Matteo. I couldn't stop smiling.

"I believe you are falling for this guy."

"We just went out for coffee once. I am not falling for him. I am in lust with him."

We both started to laugh.

That night, Amy and I went out to the local bar for supper and a few drinks. It was time to unwind and have some fun.

*

It was Tuesday morning, and I was excited to see Matteo at school tonight. I guess what Amy said might be partially true. After school, we went out for coffee again.

This time Matteo wanted to learn more about me, which gave me a sick feeling in my stomach. I knew I couldn't tell him the truth, so I told him that my parents died when I was young and I didn't get along with my aunt who raised me, so I left the house. I don't know if he bought the story, but he didn't pry any more.

I quickly changed the subject to him and asked, "Why didn't you finish high school?"

"My mom got cancer a few years ago and couldn't work anymore. I decided to quit school and get a job to help support her.

She supported me all my life on her own, so it was time I took care of her. I was lucky, my aunt works for a construction company, and they needed extra help, so she got me a job there. My mom died last year, and I took that past year to deal with it. I decided it was time I get my life in order. It is what my mom would want me to do, so here I am."

"I am sorry for your loss."

Matteo just smiled and nodded.

Chapter 16

Now that I am busy with school, work, and homework, the time is just flying by. It was a custom for us to go to the coffee shop after school on Thursday nights. We were just getting ready to leave when Matteo asked me, "Would you like to go out for supper on Saturday night?"

I had been hoping he would ask me out on a date.

"Yes."

"I can pick you up at your house at seven if that works for you?"

"How about I meet you at the restaurant?"

Even though I had been getting to know him, I was still nervous telling him where I lived. I guess the last letter I received scared me.

"Of course, where do you want to go?"

"Do you like pasta?"

"You are asking me, an Italian, if I like pasta?"

"Well, when you say it like that, it does seem like a ridiculous question. Have you ever eaten at the Pasta House?"

"No, but I have always wanted to try it, so that would be perfect."

"Good. I will meet you at the restaurant."

We exchanged smiles then went our separate ways.

I wanted to call Amy as soon as I got home to tell her about my date, but it was too late, so I waited until the next morning.

"Amy, you aren't going to believe what happened. He asked me out on a date for this Saturday night. We are going to the Pasta House for supper."

"Oh, that is awesome. What are you going to wear?"

"I don't know. I don't have anything nice."

"What time do you get off work tomorrow?"

"At four."

"Okay, I am off tomorrow, so I'll pick you up after work, and we'll go shopping for a new outfit."

"That sounds good."

The following day, the gas station was busy. It was like everyone ran out of gas at the same time. I looked at the clock to see it was eleven, and the next thing I knew it was three. I loved those days when we were remarkably busy, and the time just flew by. I looked outside to see Amy waiting in her car.

When we got to the mall, we went to every dress shop until I found that special little black dress that made me feel confident. When I tried it on and looked in the mirror, I knew this was the dress for the dinner, and it was in my budget.

This was my first date, and I didn't know what to expect, so after shopping we went back to Amy's house to talk. Before I left, I told her that I would call her on Sunday to let her know how it went.

*

It was late Saturday afternoon, and I had to start getting ready for my dinner date with Matteo. I had butterflies in my stomach and realized when I wasn't with him, I couldn't stop thinking about him. At that time, I knew I was falling for him.

When I arrived at the restaurant, he had been already seated. The waiter showed me to the table, and when he saw me, he said, "Wow, you look beautiful."

I smiled and turned red, but inside I was happy. "Thank you."

He ordered a bottle of their finest wine.

"You look handsome tonight."

"Thank you. The first thing that I noticed about you was your smile. You have a beautiful smile."

"You know, that is funny, because the first thing I noticed about you was how your face lights up when you smile."

The waiter poured the wine in Matteo's glass for him to taste. When Matteo nodded, the waiter poured a glass of wine for both of us.

"Are you ready to order?" asked the waiter.

"Yes, Rebecca, you go first."

"I will have the chicken parmesan," I said.

"Make that two, please," added Matteo.

"Would you like an appetizer?" I asked.

"Do you like bruschetta?"

"I never had it before, but I am willing to try it," I said.

"It is diced tomatoes, onion, garlic, basil, olive oil, feta cheese on toasted bread. It is really good," said Matteo.

"It sounds great, you must really like it."

"Bruschetta was my mom's favorite appetizer, and every time we went out, she had to have it."

The waiter left the table, and I could see Matteo's eyes started to tear up when he talked about his mom. He really missed her a lot. I reached across the table and squeezed his hand to let him know he wasn't alone.

"Your mom was an incredible woman."

"How do you know?"

"She had to be to raise a caring and wonderful son. Any time you want to talk about your mom, we can."

While we were waiting for our appetizer to come, Matteo told me about a trip he and his mom went on when he was fourteen years old. They had so much fun.

"How old were you when your mom died?"

"I was only seven years old. I don't have a lot of memories of her."

The waiter arrived with bruschetta, and I was glad to get off the topic of my family.

"Do you like it?"

"Yes, I can see why this was your mom's favorite."

After we ate the bruschetta, the entrees arrived within a few minutes. We didn't talk much during dinner we were both too hungry.

When the waiter came over to take away the plates and asked, "Would you like dessert?" Matteo looked at me.

"Oh no, I am too full to eat another bite, but don't let me stop you, Matteo."

"No, thank you. Could we just have the bill, please?"

"I will be right back with the check."

While we were waiting for the waiter to bring the bill, Matteo asked, "Are you seeing anyone?"

My heart started beating fast. "No. Are you seeing anyone?"

I remember I was saying to myself, please say no.

"No, but I would like to start seeing you, if it is, okay?"

With a big smile I replied, "I would like that."

The waiter placed the bill down on the table and told us we could pay at the counter when we were ready.

"How much do I owe?"

"Nothing, I asked you out."

He walked me to my bus stop and stayed with me until the bus came. When he saw the bus coming down the street, he leaned toward me, and we kissed. It was just like I imagined — fantastic.

Matteo wrote down his cell number on a piece of paper and gave it to me. "Would you please call me tonight when you get home, so I know you arrived safely?"

"I will."

All the way home on the bus ride I couldn't stop smiling and thinking about the kiss.

I called Amy on Sunday afternoon and told her everything that happened. She was excited for me and suggested that we go on a double date sometime. I agreed that would be great.

After I got off the phone with Amy, it was three and Suzanne would be home in a couple of hours. I thought I should get up and tidy up the apartment.

She had just arrived home yesterday from her sister's, and I invited her over for supper to catch up on the news. I was by the stove when I heard a knock on my door. I thought the phone didn't ring, so who could this be? I went to the door and looked through the peephole to see Suzanne.

I opened the door. "How did you get in the building?"

"Someone was coming out, and they held the door open for me."

"How was your trip?"

"It was nice to get to spend some time with my sister. Her granddaughter is so precious. I have some photos of her on my phone. I had so much fun with her."

Suzanne handed me the phone so I could see the pictures.

"Aw, she is so cute!"

After I finished looking at the photos, I went to the stove to check on supper. "I hope you are hungry. I made a lot."

"Yes, I am. How is school going?"

"It's great. There is a lot of work, but I love it. I have some news to share. I am seeing a guy from my school."

"Tell me about him?"

"Well, his name is Matteo, and he is finishing his high school too. His mom took sick a few years back, so he quit school and went to work to take care of her. He has one brother that is older than him. His mom passed away a year ago. He is a nice guy, and I enjoy his company."

"I am happy for you, just be careful."

"I will. Supper is ready."

Chapter 17

Matteo and I went out on several more dates to the movies, restaurants, walking in the park, mini golf, and helping each other with our schoolwork.

I knew that I was falling for him, but was I putting him in harm's way? I couldn't help thinking if the stranger finds out, they might try to hurt Matteo.

On one hand, I knew I should leave him to ensure he was safe, but on the other hand, my womanly urges wanted him.

It had been six months, and he haven't made a move on me. I was beginning to wonder if he wanted to move the relationship forward. We had kissed and cuddled but nothing else. I wasn't sure if he was ready for the next step.

I decided to take Amy's advice and ask him.

After class on Thursday, we went to the coffee shop. My heart was beating so loud, I thought he could hear it.

"Matteo, I have a question to ask you."

"Okay."

"I was wondering if you are ready to take this relationship to the next level and be in a romantic relationship."

I should have waited until he was finished taking a sip of his coffee, since he started to choke.

After he stopped choking, I said, "If you aren't ready, that is okay. We can wait."

"No! No! I mean yes! Yes!"

"Now I am confused."

"Yes, I am ready to move this relationship forward. I was hoping you would ask."

"If you wanted to, why didn't you bring up the subject?"

"I was afraid it would be too soon, and I would scare you off."

"Okay. How about you come over for supper this Saturday night, and we will see where the night takes us."

"I will be there. What time?"

"How about seven?"

I wrote down my address on a piece of paper and handed it to Matteo.

I woke up on Saturday morning and went to the grocery store to get the food I needed for supper. I decided to make bruschetta, chicken breast stuffed with ham and cheese, roasted potatoes, vegetables, and for dessert an apple pie.

When the phone rang, I let Matteo in and quickly went into the bathroom to take one last look at myself. I just wanted everything to be perfect.

There was a knock, and when I answered it Matteo was holding a dozen of red roses.

"Thank you, they are beautiful."

"Just like you."

I put the roses in a vase and used them as a centerpiece for the table. How did he know I love the smell of fresh roses, or was it a lucky guess?

"Supper will be ready soon. How about I pour us a glass of wine while we wait?"

"That would be nice. Do you need any help?"

"You could open the bottle of wine."

"I can manage that."

We sat on the couch, sipped our wine, and talked about our day. I knew he was just as nervous as me, since I could see his hand shaking a bit at supper. While I was eating, I would look at his face, and a warm feeling would come over me.

"Do you want some more?"

"It was delicious, but I am going to save some room for dessert."

"Okay, I'll be right back, help yourself to the wine."

After we finished dessert, I cleared the table and said, "You can have a seat on the couch, and I will be there in a minute."

I put on some music and walked over to the couch. He stood up, put each of his hands on my cheeks, and passionately kissed me on the lips. It was a kiss that I will never forget.

While we were kissing, I caressed his chest with my hands. I could feel the ripples of his abs through the shirt. My hands started to undo his shirt one button at a time, until it was all undone. I placed my hands on his shoulder under the shirt and gently took it off. I took a step back to see his perfect six-pack, and I must admit my dreams didn't do him any justice.

He slowly walked toward me, always looking into my eyes. We started to kiss again while he softly touched my breast.

The only time he took his eyes off me was when we had to take out the hide-a-bed from the couch. It was so erotic.

While looking into my eyes, he picked me up, laid me down on the bed, and gently removed my top and bra. It was so intense. I could feel my underwear starting to get damp, and my nipples were hard as rocks. He started to suck on one of my breasts while his other hand rubbed my other breast. After a while, he switched breasts, and my hips started to move up and down.

At that point, he sat up on the bed and continued to look at me in the eyes, undid the button, and unzipped my jeans. In a soft, sexy voice he said, "Please raise your hips." I compiled with the request, and he took off my jeans, underwear, and of course my socks.

I remember thinking that this wasn't fair; I was completely naked, but he was only naked from the waist up. It was as if he read my mind.

He stood up took off his jeans, underwear, and socks. Before he lay down beside me in bed, I could see his whole naked body, and it was a masterpiece.

We started to kiss again, then he lifted his head looked deep into my eyes while he penetrated me deeper and deeper with every vigorous thrust after thrust after thrust.

I couldn't get enough of him; we went on for hours. It was like we were wild animals satisfying our sexual hunger.

Afterward, he held me, and we fell asleep in each other's arms. I never felt so safe and happy in my life.

I woke up first but didn't want to wake Matteo, so I sat at the table reading a magazine. I remember it was the best sleep I had in years. I was so happy I found a man that I was attracted to, who was a passionate lover, kind, and treated me great.

After a little while, Matteo started to stir, then I saw him open his eyes. "Why didn't you wake me up?"

"I couldn't. You look so peaceful. Did you have a good sleep?"

"It was excellent. Are you hungry?"

"Oh, yes, someone gave me a workout last night."

Matteo laughed. "How about I take you out for breakfast?"

"It sounds like a plan."

Chapter 18

There wasn't a day that went by that we didn't talk or see each other. It was like we were inseparable. It was either March or April of the following year, I can't remember the exact month, but I do remember what happened.

I spent the night at his house, and we were eating breakfast when he took my hand, looked into my eyes, and said, "I love you. You are the best thing that ever happened to me."

I was speechless for a few minutes. No one besides my family ever told me they loved me. I often wondered how it would feel to fall in love, and for me it was a nice, warm feeling.

"I love you, too."

Later that day, I left, and we decided to see each other the next day for supper. I didn't want the stranger to hurt Matteo, so by being with me he would be in danger. I knew had to break it off with him.

When I arrived home, I checked the mail to find a white envelope with just my name on it. I quickly ran up the stairs, unlocked my apartment door, went inside, and locked the deadbolts and door.

I opened the envelope and the note inside:

Dear Rebecca,

I see that you have a boyfriend, Matteo. I must say he is handsome. Could you forgive yourself if something bad happened to him?

After I read the note, a tear went down my cheek, and I knew that I made the right decision to end the relationship with Matteo.

He picked me up at 7:00 p.m., and we went to the local mom-and-pop diner for supper.

"Rebecca, are you okay? You seem distracted."

"I'm okay, just a little tired."

"I had a wonderful time last night, and I meant it when I said I love you," replied Matteo

A few tears started to trickle down my face. I knew I was letting a wonderful man go and whoever ended up marring him would be a lucky woman. He could sense that something was wrong.

"I also had a wonderful time, and I love you too."

For the rest of the dinner, he kept the mood light until we arrived back at my house.

"I know there is something bothering you. What is it? I don't want any secrets between us."

"Fine, there is something wrong. Could you please come upstairs to my apartment? We need to talk."

"That doesn't sound good."

"I don't know how to say, so I am just going to say it. I think we shouldn't see each other anymore."

The look on Matteo's face was one of shock. He couldn't believe what I just said. "Why? I thought we were happy. It seemed that way to me last night, or was that just an act?"

"No! I really do love you, but you can't be around me anymore."

"I don't understand. What are you talking about?"

"I never told anyone else, so I am just going to tell you. I love you very much, but there is a person that wants to hurt me, and I am not sure who they are or why. This person was responsible for killing my family."

I was trying to hold back the tears, but some went down my face. This was the one of the hardest things I ever had to do, let the love of my life go.

"I don't care. I want to be with you, and I can protect you."

"I can't live with myself if something happens to you. I love you too much, so I can't see you anymore."

"How do you know there is someone after you?"

I went into the closest, took down a box front the top shelf, and handed to Matteo.

"I received some letters from someone that is threatening me. I have kept them in this box. You can read them if you want."

I watched his face turn pale as he read each letter. When he was done, he just had a blank expression on his face for a few minutes. It was like he couldn't believe what he was reading.

"You don't have any idea who it is?"

"No! I don't know anything about the person. All I know is that anyone who gets close to me is at risk to be injured or worse. Please just let me go."

I leaned over and gave Matteo one last kiss. Then I stood up, opened my apartment door, and turned toward the kitchen. It hurt me too much to see him go.

I shouldn't have started a relationship with him, but I couldn't help myself. My inner urges got the best of me.

He called me three times that night, but I wouldn't pick up the phone. It would hurt too much to hear his voice. The only good thing was that we had finished school for the summer, and I didn't have to see him until September.

Chapter 19

Three weeks later, I was at work when Matteo walked in. I could see the pain I caused him in his eyes.

"I tried calling you, but you will not answer your phone. I need to talk to you. What time do you get off?"

"I don't know if that is a wise idea."

"I just need to talk to you, please."

"Okay, I am off at 7:00 p.m."

"I will be back. Thank you."

Usually, I couldn't wait until it was time to go home, but today I wanted time to stand still.

We took the bus over to his place, so we could talk.

"I am willing to take that risk. I am in love with you, and I want…"

I interrupted him. "But what if he hurts or kills you? It would be too hard to know that I was the cause of it. Think about it; how would you feel if you were responsible for getting someone hurt, or worse, killed?"

"It wouldn't be your fault. I am willing to take the chance to be with you. Anyway, I could walk out of that door and get hit by the bus. No one knows when their time is up, and I just want to be with you for as long as I am on this earth. Please give us a chance! You never know, the person may leave you alone once they realize you aren't by yourself."

I thought about it for a few minutes. Matteo did have a point; the person might leave me alone if they knew I was in a relationship.

"One condition: you promise me you will be careful when you go out."

"I promise I will be. It is getting late, so you should spend the night."

"Okay."

"You know, this was sort of a fight, and I heard make-up sex is awesome. Do you want to see if that is true?"

"You don't have to ask me twice. Let's go."

After we finished having sex, we just stayed in bed. It took me a while to fall asleep. I was still not sure if being in a relationship with Matteo was a smart idea.

When I woke up, Matteo was already in the living room, watching TV, since it was after nine. That was one good thing when we spent the night together; I always had a good sleep. I felt safe with him.

"Good morning, sweetie. Are you hungry?"

"Hi. Yes, I'm starving."

We went into the kitchen, where Matteo made eggs, bacon, home fries, toast, and juice for breakfast.

"My Aunt Isabella invited us for dinner on Friday night. I would like you to meet her and my brother. Will you go with me?"

"Sure, I would love to meet them."

*

I was nervous when we arrived at his aunt's house for supper, but after a few minutes she made me feel like one of the family. His aunt and mom looked a lot alike, which was why I think he loved going to her house.

His brother, Tony, was five years older than Matteo and didn't look anything like Matteo. I guess one took after their mom and the other after their father.

Aunt Isabella made a wonderful pasta dish with Caesar salad. It was so good, I had to have seconds. After dinner, we played cards for a little while then went back to Matteo's place.

"You never talked about your dad, why?"

"There is nothing to talk about. He was a deadbeat who left my mom after she gave birth to me. I guess he wanted a girl."

I could see that talking about his father still hurt him, so I quickly changed the subject.

"You're close with your family. They are wonderful, and I am glad I meet them. As you know from the letters, you can't meet my family."

"I understand, and that is okay. But you do have a family now — mine."

Chapter 20

In two weeks, it will be one year that we had been dating. During this time, the stranger hasn't tried to hurt Matteo and I haven't received any letters. Matteo was right, the stranger did leave me alone once I meet someone. I started to relax and enjoy my time with Matteo.

I planned a special weekend at a resort two hours outside the city, the Golden Gate cottages, to celebrate our first year together.

Matteo borrowed Aunt Isabel's car for the weekend; that way we could explore the area around the resort. We left at noon but didn't get to the lodge until 6:00 p.m. There were a few antique shops, a bakery, and a beach that we stopped at on the way.

After we checked into the lodge, the lady at the front desk said, "Rebecca, there is a letter here for you."

Matteo looked at me with a puzzled face. We went straight to our room so I could open the letter. It was different from the rest; it had my name on the envelope:

Dear Rebecca,

I can't believe how much you look like your mom. You know, we have a lot in common, and one day when we meet you will see what I mean.

I see that you are still working at the gas station, and you will be entering grade 12 in September. Good for you. Your mom would be so proud of you.

I took a picture of you both. It is in the envelope just in case you don't see it. I think that you guys make a cute couple. It would be devastating if something bad happened to him. I hope you have a wonderful weekend away and always remember I am close to you.

I started shaking and turned to Matteo. "What does the stranger mean, we have a lot in common? I am not related to them, so I would have nothing in common with a crazy person! The stranger took the picture last week when we were at the grocery store. This is what I was afraid of — the stranger threatening you. I need to talk to the lady at the front desk. I am hoping she got a look at the person and can describe what they looked like."

"Okay, let's go down to the front desk."

"Hi, someone dropped off a letter for me, Rebecca, this afternoon. By any chance did you get a look at them?"

"No, I wasn't here," the lady replied. "My shift just started at 5:00 p.m., and the day lady told me the letter was here for you."

"Oh, okay, thank you."

"Are there any security cameras on the front desk that possibly got a picture of the person?" Matteo asked the lady.

"No, I am sorry. Is everything okay?" the lady asked.

"Yes, thank you for your time."

We went back up to our room disappointed. I was stressed out, since I didn't know if the person was still at the resort, so we decided to order room service for dinner.

"Rebecca, I am going downstairs to see if they have a Ziploc bag, we can put the letter and envelope in. I have a friend that works in the police department. I can ask him to have the envelope and letter examined for a fingerprint or DNA. If we get a fingerprint, the person may have a record, and it would be in the system."

"But I touched the envelope and letter, so my fingerprints are on it. Also, the two people at the front desk touched the envelope. How will we know which fingerprints are the persons?"

"Good point. I am not sure. However, I believe it is worth a shot. We have nothing to lose. When we get home, I will call him."

"What if your friend asks why? What are you going to tell him?"

"We will have to tell him everything and let him read all the letters."

"Can we trust him?"

"Yes, I have known Bill all my life. His late wife, Ann, was my mom's best friend, and my mom was their maid of honor at the wedding. Bill was the father figure that I needed in my life. He took me fishing, taught me how to drive, and was there for me when my mom died. I trust Bill with my life."

The next day, we decided to go for a walk on the beach. Every time I saw someone, I couldn't help but think it was the stranger. At first, I didn't want to go out of the room, but Matteo insisted that we continue to live our lives.

"If we don't, then the person wins, and if something happens, we will deal with it at that time."

"That is easier said than done."

"I understand, but we have to try."

That night, Matteo lit the fireplace, and we watched a movie. It was very romantic. We were both quiet; the letter shook both of us up.

On Sunday morning, we just finished eating breakfast at the main lodge. On our way up to our room, Matteo looked at me. "I don't like that you live alone. I am not sure if you are ready, but I want you to move in with me, so I can protect you. What do you think?"

I thought about it. He was right. I wasn't ready to move in with him, but I was scared to live by myself.

"Matteo, I would love for us to live together, but remember in the letter the person threatened to hurt you. I don't know what I would do if something bad happened to you because of me."

"I told you before, I am willing take that risk to protect you. If something bad happens, it isn't your fault. You didn't do anything. It is this crazy person's fault."

I knew that there was no use in arguing with him, since he was stubborn as a goat and wouldn't take no for an answer. We arrived back in the city just after lunch. Before we returned the car to Aunt Isabella, we went over to my apartment so I could pack up some clothes for a few days.

We decided to move into his place, since it was bigger. The good thing about my lease was that it was a month-to-month, which gave us a month to move my things over to his apartment.

Matteo called his police friend and set up a meeting for that Monday night at the café down the street. I tried to relax the rest of the day, but I couldn't stop thinking about the letter.

*

It was Monday night. Matteo and I were walking down the street to the café. I was excited and nervous at the same time, eager to see if we could obtain a fingerprint to tell us who had been sending the letters. I was also nervous since I had to get someone else involved.

We walked into the café and Matteo said, "Bill is here sitting over at that table."

"How about you go over to the table while I get us a drink. What would you like?"

"A large coffee with one milk."

"Okay."

The café wasn't busy, so it didn't take long to get our drinks. I walked over to the table, and Matteo stood up.

"Bill, this is my girlfriend, Rebecca."

"Hi, it is nice to meet you."

"Hi."

"Bill, when we arrived at the Golden Gate cottages, there was an envelope waiting for Rebecca."

Matteo handed the plastic bag with the letter and envelope in it to Bill. He went outside to his car to get a pair of plastic gloves, opened the bag, took out the letter, and read it.

"Rebecca, do you have any idea who wrote this letter?"

"No, I don't know who or why the stranger is following me. This isn't the first letter I received. Here are the other letters I received over the years."

I told Bill everything: my parents' and Nancy's death; Monica and Aunt Debbie getting hurt; I showed him the letters that I received; about the man that talked to me in the mall when I was shopping for Christmas presents; the letter from my mom.

"I already lost my parents and sister. I couldn't bear to lose anyone else, so I moved away to Toronto. After a while, I took the bus back to check on my family, and they were all safe, so I knew I made the right decision. I don't know why someone is after me and what they want. Please don't talk to my family. I need to keep them safe! You have to promise me that you will not tell anyone," I said.

"My main concern is to keep Matteo, your family, and you safe. For now, I will not tell anyone, but one day we may need some more help."

"Bill, I was wondering if you could send it to the lab to see if there are any fingerprints or DNA on the letter or envelope," Matteo said. "If there is, then maybe the person may have a record and we could find out who is behind this."

"Normally, we can only send things to the lab if it is part of an open investigation. However, my sister-in-law works at the lab, so I will see what she can do for us. Did both of you touch the envelope and letter?"

"Yes, we both read the letter and touched the envelope," I replied.

"Then I will need both of your fingerprints so we can rule them out. We can go down to the police station now, and I can take them."

"Thank you very much. I appreciate all your help, but can we keep this just between the three of us?"

"For now, okay," Bill replied. "When I get the results, I will call you."

The next day after work, I gave notice to my landlord, and we moved my things out the following two weekends.

Bill came over to our apartment on Thursday night with the results. "There were several partial fingerprints but not enough to get a sample. I am sorry."

"I was hoping for a better result, but thanks for trying."

Since we moved in together, I felt safer. It had been an adjustment for both of us, learning each other's little quirks and routine.

Knowing that a stranger is out there watching your every move, and you don't know who the person is or why, can sometimes get you down. Matteo was good at reading my body language and knew when I need a hug or good laugh. Sometimes at night, if I couldn't sleep, I would watch him sleep, and for some reason it would relax me.

Chapter 21

We had been living together for nine months and would be graduating from night school next Wednesday. Suzanne told me that the two years would go by fast when I first started school, but I didn't believe her. Now, looking back, it did go by fast, and I was enormously proud of myself for the accomplishment. Three years ago, I would never have thought that I would obtain my high school diploma.

After the ceremony, Suzanne, Amy, Aunt Isabella, Tony, Matteo, and I went out for supper to celebrate our achievement. Everyone was proud of both of us.

That night when we got home, we were lying in bed, and I turned to Matteo. He had the biggest smile that I have ever seen and was staring at me. It made me feel so warm and happy inside.

"Can I ask you a question?"

"Of course, what is it?"

"I like working at the gas station, but I don't want to be there forever. For me to get a job that pays more, I will need more education. I was thinking about applying to college for next year. What do you think?"

"That sounds great."

"I will work any extra shifts I can throughout this year to save for my tuition fee, so I don't have to get a student loan. Also, I will work part-time on weekends while I am in school and full-time during the summer months."

Matteo said, "If you want to go to college, then you go, and as far as money goes, we will be fine. My boss told me that our IT person is moving away in two months, and he wants me to take over the position. I will be working with him until he leaves. I guess taking computers in school has paid off."

"Wow, that is awesome! I am so happy for you."

"Thanks. What would you like to study?"

"I have always liked working with numbers, so I am thinking about the accounting field. That way I wouldn't have to work weekends and nights, or at least not on a regular basis. It's a two-year program."

"We will get by, don't worry. If this is what you really want to do, then apply. Besides, that will be perfect. We can make plans to go away for the weekend without you having to get the time off."

"Exactly! Have I told you today that I love you?"

"I don't think so."

"Well, let me fix that. I love you so much."

"I love you too, and then you can take care of our finances."

I was so excited that the next day I went to the college to pick up an application for the following September. That night I filled it out and returned it the following day. The lady told me it would be a few months before I heard anything.

*

Over the following few months, it seemed like Matteo would just stare and smile at me more.

One day I said, "Is everything okay?"

"Yes, why do you ask?" replied Matteo.

"You are just looking at me a lot and smiling a lot."

He walked over to me, picked me up, twirled me around in circles, and gave me a soft kiss.

"Can't I admire a beautiful woman who makes me very happy?"

I just smiled at him and squeezed as tight as I could.

A few days later, I was having a difficult day, and when I arrived at home, he had a surprise waiting for me. The bathtub was filled with bubbles, candles were lit all over the room, soft music played in the background, and a glass of wine was waiting for me.

I enjoyed the bath very much; it was exactly what I needed. When I was done, he had supper all ready for us, and he even cleaned up the dishes after supper.

*

Four months later, Matteo was still acting funny by staring at me with a smile on his face, helping me more around the house, making me laugh more, and even tickled me. He wouldn't tickle me, since he knew I would do it right back to him, and he didn't like it.

At that time, I started to get preoccupied with waiting for a letter from the school. Every time I went to check the mail, I would get a scared feeling in my stomach. Before I opened the mailbox, I would look all around to see if anyone was watching. I would wonder, is today the day I am going to find another letter from the stranger?

I just arrived home from work, and there was no mail. I was relieved I didn't receive a letter from the stranger but upset that I had nothing from the school.

When I walked into the apartment, Matteo said, "Rebecca, I picked up the mail today and there is a letter for you from the community college."

I was so excited, I ran over to Matteo took the envelope out of his hand, opened it, read the first line, and yelled, "I got in! I got in! I will start this September."

He picked me up, twirled me around, and kissed me.

"Congratulations! We should go out for supper tonight to celebrate. Besides we haven't been out anywhere in the past couple of months. How does the BLU Ristorante sound to you?"

"I have to be honest; I am scared to go out. What if that stranger is watching us?"

"I understand, Rebecca, but like I said before, we still have to live and enjoy ourselves. We can't just stay in the apartment all the time and only go out to work. That isn't living."

"I know, but it's hard when I am always looking over my shoulder, wondering if the person behind or in front of me is the stranger. I will try to stop worrying so much, but it is hard for me."

The BLU Ristorante was a fancy restaurant, so we dressed up. I wore my little black dress while Matteo had a gray suit on. I must say, I love a man in a suit. He looked so handsome.

The restaurant wasn't that busy, so our appetizers didn't take long.

While we ate our entrees, we talked about how much money we needed to save for the accounting course that I would be taking. We also talked about the types of jobs I could apply for when I am done.

"When you were in the bathroom, the waiter asked if we wanted anything for dessert," said Matteo, "so I took it upon myself to us order dessert."

"What are we having?"

"It will be a surprise."

He had my curiosity piqued. Could it be cheesecake, chocolate cake, trifle?

The waiter brought over a plate that had four cupcakes on it, with a word on each cupcake that read, Will you marry me?

While I was reading the cupcakes, Matteo got down on one knee beside my chair, opened a ring box, and said, "I know that you are the one for me, and I want to spend the rest of my life with you. I love you very much and was wondering if you would marry me?"

I was in complete shock. We never really talked about marriage.

"Yes, I will marry you!"

Everyone in the restaurant around our table started to clap. It was so special. The ring had three diamonds and the band was yellow gold.

"That night when I walked into the classroom, the only person I noticed was you. I know there is someone watching us, and I don't care," Matteo said. "I just want to spend whatever time I have on this earth with you."

You couldn't take the smile off my face for the rest of the night. Then I realized that was why he was acting so funny the last few months. When we got home, I took him into the bedroom to show him how much I loved him.

When I woke up the next morning, Matteo was looking at me. "Good morning, Mrs. Rossi."

"I like the sound of that, Mr. Rossi. How about we invite Suzanne, Amy, Aunt Isabella, and Tony over for supper tomorrow night to tell them the good news?"

"Sounds great to me. I will call Aunt Isabella and Tony to see if they are free, and you call Suzanne and Amy."

It was decided that everyone would come to our house tomorrow night for a barbeque. We would supply the meat, and everyone else would bring a side dish.

Suzanne was the first one to arrive with a potato salad, Amy was next with a spinach salad, Aunt Isabella brought a carrot cake for dessert, and Tony had a bottle of wine.

After supper, we were all sitting in the living room talking when Matteo and I stood up and said, "We have an announcement…" At the same time, we both said, "We are getting married!"

Everyone gave both of us a hug. They were so happy for us, and the girls loved the ring.

"Amy, would you be my maid of honor?"

"Yes, of course I will."

"Thank you. Suzanne, you are like a mother to me. Would you walk me down the aisle and give me away?"

After she wiped the tears away, she said, "Yes, I will be honored."

"Tony, would you be my best man?"

"I would be honored too, bro."

"I will make your dream wedding cake," said Aunt Isabella. "Do you have a date in mind?"

"Well, I told Matteo my favorite time of year is fall, so I would like to get married either the end of September or October."

"It doesn't matter to me. Either the end of September or October works for me as long as I can marry you."

All I heard was all the women say, "Aw, that is so sweet."

"Then why don't we pick a date now?"

"Sure, let me pull up a calendar on my phone so we can look at the weekends next September and October," said Matteo.

When I was looking at the calendar, right away a weekend jumped out at me. "How about September 24?"

Matteo looks into my eyes. "That will be the day you become Mrs. Rebecca Rossi. We have a date!"

"Now the fun begins," said Suzanne.

For the remainder of the evening, us ladies talked about wedding plans in the kitchen while Matteo and Tony watched TV in the living room.

Eventually, everyone had left except for Aunt Isabella, who wanted to talk to us alone.

"Matteo, your mom had life insurance through her work, and she put me as the beneficiary. After I paid for her funeral expenses, I opened two trust accounts for your brother and yourself. I split the remainder between the two accounts at her request. She wanted to help pay for your wedding day. Here is the account information that you need to access the money."

Matteo was so overcome by emotion, he started to cry. I hugged him as tight as I could and told me that I loved him.

After Aunt Isabella left, Matteo asked, "Do you want to let your family know about the wedding?"

"I would love nothing better than to have my family at the wedding, but I am afraid if I invite them, the stranger will hurt them. The deal was I leave them, and the stranger wouldn't harm my family anymore. It's too big of a risk for me to take. Hopefully, one day you will get to meet them."

We had a little over a year to plan the wedding, which gave me something else to preoccupy me. Matteo wanted to be involved every step of the way, which was nice. Some men would say, "Just tell me where and when to show up and I will be there."

Our wedding was going to be small, only about sixty people, so we decided to have it at a beautiful country inn just fifteen minutes outside the city. If the weather was sunny, we were going to have the ceremony outside by the lake, and if it was raining, we would have it inside. The inn would provide the hors d'oeuvres while we were having our pictures taken, reception meal, tables, linen, centerpieces for the tables, and a cash bar that fitted into our budget.

One of Matteo's fellow workers just got married a few months before and gave us contact information for the DJ and photographer. Since they were referred to us by a previous client, we would receive a discount.

Since neither of us were churchgoers, we decided to get married by a justice of the peace. We met the lady for lunch to get the marriage license all filled out. She gave us two different scripts and told us to choose which one we wanted her to use at the wedding ceremony.

The flowers were going to be different shades of purple, gray, and white. There was a picture of a bouquet in a wedding book, and I loved the color of the flowers. I showed the florist the picture so they would have an idea of what I was looking for.

Amy's dress was plum-colored with short sleeves, floor-length, and a v-neckline with a slash around the waist that tied in back.

My wedding dress was sleeveless, a line dress with a sweetheart neckline, full-length with beads down to my waist with a long train. The dress below the waist was plain white, with a little flair at the end.

Chapter 22

It was the night before our wedding, and Suzanne stayed with me at the inn. We all know that the groom shouldn't see the bride until she walks down the aisle. I wanted to stay at the inn so we could use the room to get ready and have pictures taken.

We were sitting on the couch having a glass of wine, toasting my last night as a single woman, when I turned to Suzanne. "I want your honest opinion. Do you think I am making the right choice?"

"I believe you are. This is normal. It's the night before your wedding and you are having second thoughts. I went through the same thing the night before my wedding. I know that he loves you, will never hurt you, and wants to grow old with you."

I was really having second thoughts about putting Matteo in danger, but I couldn't tell Suzanne that without explaining everything. What if the stranger that was after me hurt Matteo — would I be able to live with myself?

When I woke up that morning, I realized after the afternoon I would no longer be a single woman. That made me excited and nervous at the same time.

Amy arrived at the hotel midmorning with breakfast, but I was too nervous to eat. About an hour later, the lady that was doing our hair and makeup arrived. She did Amy's hair and makeup first, then Suzanne, and saved me for last.

We had just finished getting dressed when the photographer knocked on the door to get pictures of us before the wedding. You know how some people are naturally at getting their picture taken and the camera loves them? Well, that isn't me. I always hated getting my picture taken, since I never liked the way, I looked.

It was a sunny day, perfect for an outdoor wedding. All the chairs had a white cover over them with a purple sash tied around them. The aisle was a stone walkway with flowers on both sides. There was an arch decorated with a white sheer over it and purple, gray, and yellow flowers going up the sides and on top, which was used for the altar.

Suzanne walked me down the aisle, and when I first saw Matteo, I couldn't believe I was marrying this wonderful person. When I arrived at the altar, I could see a tear running down his cheek, so I wiped the tear away and smiled at him.

As the justice of the peace started the ceremony, I looked into Matteo's eyes and mouthed "I love you." After she was finished with the ceremony, she told all the guests that we wrote our own vows to each other.

"Matteo, you can read your vows," the justice of the peace said.

"Rebecca, you are my lover, best friend, and better half. From the time we met, I have grown and become a better person. I believe in you, the person you will grow to be, and the couple we will be together. I will dream with you, celebrate with you, and walk beside you through whatever our lives may bring."

She turned to me. "It is your turn, Rebecca."

"Matteo, when I first met you, I had a comfortable feeling that I never experienced with anyone else. I knew this was worth investigating, and along the way I fell in love with you. I love you because you make me laugh; I love you because you are there for me when I need a shoulder to lean on; I love you because you have a huge and honest heart; I love you because you accept me for the way I am."

"Matteo, please repeat after me," said the justice of the peace. "I, Matteo, take you, Rebecca for my wedded wife, to love and cherish, for better or worse, for richer or poorer, in sickness and in health. From this day forward."

"It is your turn, Rebecca. Please repeat after me. 'I, Rebecca, take you, Matteo, for my wedded husband, to love and cherish, for better or worse, for richer or poorer, in sickness and in health. From this day forward."

"May I please have the rings," she requested. "As you put a ring on each other's hand, I want you to repeat after me: this ring is my sacred gift to you, a symbol of my love, a sign that from this day forward and always, my love will surround you, with this ring I thee wed."

She looked at Matteo. "You may kiss your bride."

There was a table to the side of the stage where we signed the marriage licenses while the DJ played a song.

After the song, the justice of the peace said, "It is my pleasure to introduce Mr. and Mrs. Matteo Rossi."

Everyone stood up and started clapping while we walked down the aisle, followed by Amy and Tony. When we went out to the hallway, I looked at Matteo. "We did it! We are married."

"Yes, we are. This is the best day of my life."

There was a beautiful spot for us to take our wedding pictures down by the lake while our guests enjoyed cocktail hour inside the inn where the reception was being held.

When we went into the reception room, the DJ announced us, and everyone cheered.

There were two speeches, one by Aunt Isabella and the other by Suzanne. After the speeches were done, Matteo and I thanked everyone for attending our special day and cut the wedding cake. We were having our first dance while the inn put the wedding cake on trays for Matteo and me to serve our guests.

We were serving the cake when we heard the first gunshot. The wine glass in Aunt Isabella's hand shattered, and wine was running down her hands. It looked like blood.

I screamed, "Aunt Isabella, was your hand hit?"

She just stared at her glass in shock and couldn't say anything.

We threw the cake on the table while Matteo rushed over to Aunt Isabella. The bullet didn't hit her; it only broke the glass.

Everyone was screaming. Some of the guests were able to run out of the room while others had to take cover under their tables. People were pushing each other out of the way trying to find cover.

We didn't know who was shooting. All we knew was they were in the room with us.

Within a few seconds, we heard a second shot. I notice that Matteo was acting funny.

"Are you okay?"

"No, I have a burning sensation in my stomach. I am going to pass out."

One of the staff members was able to get to the emergency door to open it, trying to get as many people to safety as possible. I saw a waiter with a gun running out the door, but I couldn't leave Matteo's side. I had to start applying pressure to his wound.

As tears were coming down my face, I hollered, "Matteo, can you hear me? Please say something or squeeze my hand!"

He didn't move or say anything. I knew he had lost a lot of blood.

Bill rushed over to Matteo and me. "Is he breathing?"

"It is very shallow."

"I am going to do CPR until the paramedics get here. They are on their way," said Bill.

"Matteo, you can't die. I need you. Please fight, follow my voice."

As I was watching Bill perform CPR on him, I realized my wedding day could also be the same day I became a widow.

It took the ambulance ten minutes to arrive. The paramedics were able to get him breathing before rushing him to the hospital. I went with him in the ambulance while Tony and Aunt Isabella followed behind in his car.

When we arrived at the hospital, they had to cut off his tuxedo and rushed him into the operating room. When I was sitting in the family room waiting for news on Matteo's condition, I realized who had done this, but I didn't tell the police. I had no direct evidence that anyone was after me, except for the letters that had no fingerprints on them. Whoever this person was, they were smart enough not to leave any evidence.

The door opened to the family room. I was hoping it would be the doctor or nurse, but it was Bill.

"How is Matteo?"

"I haven't heard anything since he went into surgery."

"Is there anything I can get for you?"

"No, just pray for Matteo."

"I will. Are you up to answer a few questions?"

"I guess."

"Did you hear a gunshot?"

"Yes, two shots. The first shot hit Aunt Isabella's glass and the second hit Matteo."

"Do you know where in the room the shots came from?"

"No. After the first shot, everything was so chaotic."

"Was there anyone there that you didn't know?"

"No, we knew all the quests that were there. They were either Matteo's family or our friends. The only people we didn't know where the people that worked at the inn, the photographer, and the DJ. We hired the photographer and DJ based on referrals from people we knew."

"Did you see anyone acting suspicious during the evening?"

"No, but when the emergency doors opened and people were rushing out, I saw a waiter with a gun, running. I couldn't go after him; I had to help Matteo."

"Could you describe what he looked like?"

"I only saw him for a few seconds."

"Anything you noticed would be a help."

"He was white, wore glasses and a waiter uniform like the others, and had brown hair. Do you think this is the stranger that has been leaving me the letters?"

"He may be the stranger."

All I did was put my hands over my face and started to cry.

At that point, I couldn't talk anymore. I was numb all over. I sat there with a blank expression, my eyes red and mascara running down my face. It was so quiet in the room; you could hear a pin drop. Bill stayed with me until Matteo's family arrived.

When Aunt Isabella and Tony walked into the family room, I could tell they were scared by their expression. Aunt Isabella rushed over to me and put her arms around me. She hugged so tight, that I couldn't breathe.

"Did you hear anything on his condition?" asked Tony.

"No one has been in yet! I am so scared."

Matteo's friends and more relatives started to arrive at the hospital.

An hour later, the doctor came into the room and walked toward me. I guess it wasn't hard to figure out who Matteo's wife was, since I was the only one in a wedding dress with makeup running down my face from crying.

"Rebecca, the bullet put a hole in Matteo's stomach then entered his pancreas. The acid from his stomach leaked into his abdomen, which has caused a serious infection that could go through the rest of his body. He lost a lot of blood, but we were able to repair his stomach and removed the bullet from his pancreas. We are aggressively treating the infection with antibiotics."

"He is going to make it, isn't he?"

"We are doing everything we can, but until the infection is cleared, it is hard to say what the outcome will be."

"You mean he can die from this infection?"

"I just want to prepare you for the worst, but yes."

Aunt Isabella squeezed my hand and said, "Everyone please pray for Matteo."

"When can we see him?"

"He is now in the recovery room but should be in the ICU soon. I will have the nurse let you know when you can see him."

The nurse came into the family room. "Hi, I can take you to see Matteo's room now, but only two people can go in at a time."

I asked the nurse to make an exception this time and allow Aunt Isabella, Tony, and myself to go in at the same time. I explained to her I thought it was good if he had all his immediate family with him.

She agreed.

I remember walking into the room while he was still sleeping. I walked over to the side of his bed reached down for his hand, lifted it up, kissed, and squeezed it. I was hoping that he would squeeze back or open his eyes, but he didn't.

After a little bit, I went out to the waiting area to give everyone an update on his condition and tell everyone that he was sleeping. Some of his relatives gave me their phone numbers in case his condition changed during the night, and others said they would be back in the morning.

Aunt Isabella and Tony stayed at the hospital with me until one in the morning. At that time, they were getting tired and needed a break, so they left. I told them if his condition changed, I would call them right away.

Of course, I stayed with him throughout the night; after all, it was our wedding night. A nurse gave me a pair of scrubs so I could get more comfortable. I loved my wedding dress, but after ten hours I needed to change. I dozed off for an hour here and there, then around three, Matteo woke up.

"Hi, honey."

"Matteo, I love you so much. How are you feeling?"

"I love you too." And the next thing, I knew he fell back to sleep.

I must have dozed off too, since the next I knew, the doctor woke me up when he came into Matteo's room. I looked at my phone and realized it was eight in the morning.

"Hi, Rebecca, how are you?"

"I have been better."

"The nurse told me that Matteo woke up around 3:00 a.m. this morning but was only awake for a few minutes. That's normal. I will check back later to see if he is awake. The best thing for him is to get as much rest as possible while is body is fighting the infection. You should try to get some rest too."

At 9:00 a.m., Aunt Isabella and Tony arrived back at the ICU to visit Matteo. I filled them in on how the night went. About ninety minutes later, Matteo woke up again just as his doctor was walking into the room.

"Hi, Matteo, how are you feeling?"

"I have pain in my abdomen, I feel sick to my stomach, and I am exhausted."

"I will have the nurse give you something for the pain. Just try to get some rest."

He was only awake for about thirty minutes, then he went back to sleep. But it was enough to put a smile on all our faces. At that point, I knew he was going to make it.

Early that afternoon, the nurse came into the room to inform us that more family and friends were waiting in the family room.

When Aunt Isabella, Tony, and I walked into the room, among them was Suzanne with a bag of clothes for me. Aunt Isabella gave everyone an update on Matteo's condition while I went over to sit next to Suzanne.

"Hi, I thought you might want a change of clothes."

"That was nice of you, thanks."

"Do you want to go downstairs to the cafeteria for a break?"

"Sure. I am just going to the bathroom to change, and I will be right back."

Before I went back into the family room, I took the scrubs to the nurse and thanked her.

While I was downstairs with Suzanne, it gave Matteo's other family members a chance to see him. We must have been gone for a couple of hours.

When we came back upstairs to the family room, Aunt Isabella and Tony were sitting watching TV.

"Is everything okay with Matteo?"

"Yes, we just needed a break," replied Aunt Isabella.

"Okay, I am going to take Suzanne in to see him," I said.

"We will stay here," said Tony.

After a while, Suzanne and I returned to the family room, where Aunt Isabella and Tony were. For the remainder of the afternoon and early evening, between Aunt Isabella, Tony, Suzanne, and I, we took shifts sitting with Matteo, two at a time.

Visiting hours were over, so Aunt Isabella, Tony, and Suzanne left for the night while I went to stay with Matteo.

He woke up a few times throughout the night, but to me he wasn't improving. He was still tired and not hungry, so the following morning the doctor ordered some blood work to see if the infection was improving.

Aunt Isabella and Tony arrived at the hospital, and I filled them in on Matteo's condition.

A little over an hour later, the doctor walked into the room. "Hi, I have the results of the blood test. The medicine is working, and the infection isn't spreading."

I let out a big sigh of relief while Tony cheered and Aunt Isabella said, "Thank you, good lord."

"How long will he have to stay in the hospital?" asked Tony.

"He will need to stay for ten more days. We have to ensure that the infection is all gone before we can send him home, but he should make a full recovery."

I knew that I couldn't take the following ten days off from work, so between Aunt Isabella, Tony, Suzanne, and I, there was always one of us at the hospital by Matteo's side.

*

It was three days later, and I couldn't believe how strong Matteo was getting. The color was coming back in his face, and he was awake more. They moved him from the ICU to a regular hospital bed, which meant he was on the mend.

The doctor came into his room in the afternoon and asked, "How are you feeling, Matteo?"

"My stomach is sore, but I am feeling better."

"You will be sore for a few days," replied the doctor. "Later on, this afternoon, I will have the nurses get you up to walk around and eat some food."

"How does that sound?"

"Good."

After lunch, the nurse came in and said, "It is time for you to get up and go for a short walk."

When he stood up, he started to feel dizzy, so he sat back down. The nurse told us that was normal and to sit back down for a minute or two. He was able to walk out to the nurse's station and back again.

The next day, Matteo's relatives came in to visit him, and the nurses made him walk around a few more times. By the time visiting hours were over, he was tired, and it didn't take him long to fall asleep.

Over the following week, Matteo was getting stronger and stronger every day. It was about midmorning when the doctor came into his room.

"I talked to the nurses. You have been doing well all week, and there is no sign of infection in your body. How are you feeling?"

"I feel good. I just want to go home and sleep in my own bed."

"Okay, I am going to discharge you this afternoon. Please follow up with me or your family doctor if you have any discomfort."

"Thank you, Doctor."

I shook the doctor's hand. "Thank you, Doctor for saving my husband's life."

"You're welcome."

Later that afternoon, the nurse came into the room. "Your discharge papers have been signed by the doctor, so you are free to go."

We were on our way to the elevator when a nurse came running toward us, saying, "Rebecca, wait, Rebecca! This was dropped off to the nurse's station this afternoon when you went to get some lunch. Sorry about not giving it to you earlier."

"No problem, thanks."

As soon as I looked at the envelope, I had a sick feeling in my stomach. I told Matteo I would open it when we got home. When Aunt Isabella was driving us home, I kept looking behind us to see if anyone was following us.

Chapter 23

We arrived at home, but I couldn't open the letter, my hands were shaking too much. Matteo opened the envelope, took out the letter and read it to me:

Dear Mrs. Rebecca Rossi,

You looked so beautiful in your wedding dress, and the ceremony was wonderful. I hope you enjoyed the chicken that I served you. I am glad that Matteo will make a full recovery. You could have been a widow just hours after being married. Life can be short, and you never know when tragedy will strike.

I started to cry, and I couldn't stop. Matteo whispered in my ear while he was hugging me, "Everything is going to be okay."

My face started to turn red, the tone of my voice changing. "How can you say that! Someone just shot you at our wedding reception! It isn't going to be okay. What if the stranger tries again and is successful? I don't know if I can live with myself knowing you died because of me. I am trying to protect my family and you. I have already buried too many of my family members, and I don't want too burry anymore, especially you."

"Shhh." He put his finger to my mouth. "I am going to call Bill to come over, and we will show him the letter."

The following morning, Bill came over to the apartment and Matteo showed him the letter.

"On Tuesday I am going to Halifax, Nova Scotia, to attend a conference. While I am there, I will investigate Monica, Aunt Debbie, and Nancy's cases to see if something was missed. I will let you know if I find anything," said Bill.

"If you don't mind, could you go by the house to see if they are all safe?"

"Sure."

"I really appreciate this, thank you."

"You're welcome."

"Bill and Matteo, please excuse me I am going to lie down. I have a terrible headache."

"I will check on you later, honey, try to get some sleep."

*

A week later, Bill returned from his conference in Nova Scotia. He came over to our house the following evening to discuss what he had found out.

"The person who committed these crimes ensured they didn't leave any evidence. There were too many fingerprints on the envelopes that were partials. The letters had no prints on them besides yours and Matteo's. The person must have worn gloves," said Bill. "I even took the sketch that was done up in Nancy's case and put it through the RCMP's database; I have a friend that works there. There were no hits. This tells me that the person doesn't have a record, and they are singling you out for some reason."

Bill could tell by my expression that I was disappointed.

"I was hoping that you could shed some light on why people around me are getting hurt."

"When I went over to your Aunt Debbie's house, I noticed there was a house for sale just down the street, so I knocked on her door. The door opened, and it was your Aunt Debbie. I told her I was thinking about buying the house down the street and was wondering how the neighborhood was. She invited me in."

"How is she?"

"She is doing well. I talked to everyone, and they are all healthy and happy. At least the stranger has kept their word and left your family alone."

"I am so happy for that, thank you."

"The only thing I could say is that the person is punishing you for something your mom did. What did she do and why are the million-dollar questions? Be careful whenever you are out, either together or separately. Also, if you notice any suspicious cars or people in your neighborhood, call 911 first, then call me."

Matteo walked Bill to the door so he could lock the three deadbolts behind him. He came back over to the couch where I was sitting. "A penny for your thoughts."

"I am going to register for a self-defense class so I can learn how to protect myself."

"That is a great idea. Do you want me to take it with you?"

"Sure, if you want, you can."

"I will."

The following morning, I registered us to take classes on Tuesday and Thursday evening from seven to eight for the next eight weeks to complete level 1. Altogether, there were five levels, each taking about eight to ten weeks.

Chapter 24

Over the winter and spring, I took as many shifts as I could to save money for my tuition, so I didn't have to take out a student loan. The only two nights that I couldn't work were Tuesday and Thursday because of my self-defense class.

I liked working at the gas station, but Matteo didn't like me working the night shift. He did feel safer now that I had been taking self- defense classes but thought it would be the perfect opportunity for me to leave work so I could concentrate my efforts on my schoolwork. We were lucky that he had a decent job, so we could get by on one salary for a couple of years.

I was nervous to tell Jillian that I was quitting. She gave me a job without knowing me. The only reference I had was Suzanne, who had only known me for a few weeks. If it wasn't for Jillian and Suzanne, I wouldn't have been able to attend night school or haven't meet my husband.

I wanted to give Jillian more than the typical two weeks' notice, so I gave her three months' instead. She was happy for me that I wanted more out of life but sad to be losing a great employee. She knew she could always count on me to show up for my shifts, and if she needed someone to come in on short notice, I would most of the time.

It was a week before school started, and I had one hour left on my last shift at the gas station when everyone that worked there came into the store.

I looked around and with a confused look said, "What are you guys doing here?"

Before anyone could reply, Jillian came out of the back room carrying a big chocolate cake. "You didn't think we were going to let you leave without having cake and ice cream."

I started to laugh. "The cake looks delicious. Let's eat."

Jillian handed everyone a slice of cake and a scoop of ice cream.

"It was a pleasure to work with you, Rebecca," said Jillian. "We all wish you the best of luck in your future. Please come in to let us know how you are doing. We wanted to get you a present to start you off in school on the right foot."

I opened the gift, a beautiful pen and pencil set.

It was very overwhelming, and I choked up. "Thank you, how can I not succeed with this beautiful gift!"

As I walked out of the gas station store for the last time as an employee, I waved goodbye, and a tear came down my face. I was going to miss everyone.

*

It was now the middle of October, and I had just finished writing my midterm. I haven't been feeling that good lately; it was just my luck I had caught the flu that had been going around the school. I had a doctor's appointment on Monday, so if I didn't feel any better by then, I would talk to him.

When I walked into my doctor's office, I felt like I was going to throw up.

"Hi, Rebecca, what can I do for you today?"

"I need a new subscription for my birth control. Also, could you look at my ears, throat, and lungs? I don't feel good."

After the doctor was finished examining me, she said, "Explain how you don't feel good?"

"I feel like throwing up all the time, my breasts are sore, and I am tired."

"How long have you been feeling this way?"

"About a little over a month."

"Have you had your period this month?"

"Actually, now that I think about it, I don't think I did."

"You might be pregnant, so I want you to have a blood and pregnancy test done at the hospital. While you are here, I am going to check your blood pressure."

"I will go tomorrow first thing in the morning to get the tests done."

"Are you still doing your self-defense classes?"

"Yes."

"You are going have to stop them until after the baby is born."

"Oh, okay."

"Good, on the way out book an appointment for the end of next week."

On my way home, I thought about it. What would Matteo think? We never talked about when we would start our family; I thought it would be best when I was back in the workforce full-time. Before I got too far ahead of myself, I would wait for the test results.

I tossed and turned all night, thinking about what Matteo would say if we were expecting. I got up and made breakfast for him, like I did every Friday, since I had no school. Today it seemed like it took forever for Matteo to leave for work, but I was just anxious to have the pregnancy test done.

I arrived at the hospital, and of course the lab was busy. I had to wait thirty minutes before I could take the test. Now, that may not sound like a long time, but when you must hold your pee, it is.

The following week, I arrived at the doctor's office with my stomach full of butterflies, palms sweating from being nervous, anxious to get my test results back.

"Hi, Rebecca, I have your test result back. Congratulations, you are pregnant. Are you happy?"

"It isn't the ideal time with me in school full-time, but the truth is I am happy."

"Great, I want to check your blood pressure…that looks good. I want you to start taking your prenatal vitamins you can get at any drug store. No drinking, get plenty of sleep, and eat healthy. Do you have any questions?"

"When is my due date?"

"Let's figure it out. You are approximately two months along, so that would make your due date July 15."

"A summer baby!"

"I would like to see you in a month, so while you are here, make your next appointment and congratulations."

I was smiling from ear to ear on the way home, and nothing could have brought me down. I was so excited and happy, just nervous to tell Matteo, hoping he would be happy too.

I knew I couldn't keep this a secret make longer, so I decided to tell him tonight. I heard his key in the front door and got extremely nervous as he walked in.

"Oh, my favorite dish, turkey dinner! Are you buttering me up for something?"

A big smile came on my face, and I said, "Me! Butter you up for something? I don't know what you are talking about."

Matteo started to laugh, wrapped his arms around my waist, and kissed me.

"Supper will be ready in a few minutes."

He went to change into his relaxation clothes, washed up for supper, and came back into the kitchen.

"How was your day?" asked Matteo

"It was good. How was yours?"

"It was good, just a regular day. Is there something I can do to help?"

"Sure, you can set the table while I put the finishing touches on supper."

It was perfect timing; the table was set, and supper was ready.

"Let's eat."

"Supper tastes delicious."

"Thank you. You know, I didn't discuss with you if you wanted a family before we got married. I guess I just assumed you did."

"Yes, I do want to have children. To be exact I would like to have two, a girl and a boy."

"Well, you know the guy's sperm determines the sex of the baby, so you will have to tell your buddies you want a girl and a boy. I was thinking that after I finished school and obtain a job in my field, we could start a family. What do you think?"

"It would be great. That way we both are settled in our careers."

I could feel my heart beating like crazy, but I knew I had to tell him.

"You do have a point, but sometimes life has surprises."

Matteo looked at my smiling face and then realized what I was trying to tell him. "Are you pregnant?"

"Yes, we are pregnant."

He stood up, came over to me, took my hand to help me up, picked me off my feet, and twirled me around. I was a little lightheaded from the spinning around. I took a deep breath and relaxed now that I knew he was excited.

"Thank you for making me a daddy."

"You also had a part in this. I know it isn't the best time, but the baby is on his/her way. I realize that money is tight now with only one income, but I can get a part-time job to help out."

"No, you concentrate on school and the baby. I will ensure we have enough money for the bills. Don't worry, everything will be okay. How many months are you?"

"I am two months along, and the baby is due on July 15. I have to stop my self-defense classes, so I am going to call to see if I can get a refund on level 4, since I just started it last week."

"I want to be involved as much as possible, so I am going to go to every appointment you have. If we can't get a refund on the classes, don't worry about it."

"I am so glad to hear that. I could use the support."

"I want to make love to you right now."

"Then what are we waiting for? Let's go."

*

Now that I was four months along and everything was good with the pregnancy, we decided it was time to tell the family the good news. Aunt Isabella, Tony, Suzanne, Amy, Matteo, and I went out for supper at our favorite restaurant, the Pasta House.

Matteo had to work late, so we were the last ones to arrive at the restaurant. Everyone had a drink, and knew they wanted to eat, so we looked at the menu right away.

While we were waiting for our food to arrive, Matteo couldn't hold the news in any longer. "We are going to have a baby!"

I looked around at everyone, and their jaws could have hit the floor. Just like us, they were all surprised about the news.

"Congratulations! When are you due?" Asked Aunt Isabella.

"July 15," I replied.

Suzanne said, "How are you feeling?"

"I feel sick, and I use the bathroom a lot," I replied.

"After a couple of months that will taper off until the end of the pregnancy," said Suzanne. "Then it will seem like all you do is use the bathroom."

"Are you going to find out if it is a girl or boy?" asked Amy.

"I want to know, but Rebecca wants to wait and let it be a surprise. I just don't know what color to paint the nursery," answered Matteo.

"We can paint the nursery with neutral colors such as yellow, green, and even blue can work for either a girl or boy," I said.

"I am so happy for you. I hope you have a girl," said Amy.

"I hope it is a boy so I can take him fishing," Tony said. "I would like to make a toast to Matteo, Rebecca, and soon to be my nephew/niece, congratulations, and may your life be filled with happiness."

Everyone raised their glasses and took a drink.

Aunt Isabella said, "Matteo, your mom is in heaven looking down on you today with immense pride at the husband you have become and the father that you will be. I know she wishes she could be here with us but will always be in our hearts."

Matteo stood up, went over to Aunt Isabella, and gave her a hug. "Hear, hear, I will toast to that," I replied.

*

I was seven months pregnant and suddenly woken up by a sharp pain in my stomach. I was lying on my side and thought the baby didn't like that position, so I moved to lie on my back.

It felt like I just got back to sleep when I was woken again by a sharp pain in my stomach, but this time it was more intense. I rubbed my stomach with my hand and moaned, "Ooh, that hurt."

Matteo turned over to me and said, "Are you okay?"

"No, I think I am in labor!"

He jumped out of bed, "Labor…but your due date isn't for another few months!"

"I know, but if it isn't labor, then I don't why I am in pain. I'm scared."

Matteo squeezed my hand. "Let's get you to the hospital."

When we arrived at the hospital, I was feeling sick to my stomach and started to throw up. The nurse put me in a wheelchair and gave me a bucket. Matteo told her that I was only seven months pregnant.

Everything was happening so fast. Within minutes the nurse had us in a delivery room with the fetal monitor on my belly.

"How is the baby?" I asked.

"I am not sure. I am going to get the doctor," said the nurse.

While the nurse was out, I had another contraction. Matteo helped me breathe through the pain.

The doctor came into the room, listened to the fetal monitor, and said, "The heartbeat is shallow, and the baby is in distress. The baby will have to be delivered now!"

I looked over at Matteo, and I could tell that he was just as scared as I was. We held each other's hands tightly.

"But she is only seven months!" said Matteo.

"The baby needs to be delivered now. We have to do a caesarean," the doctor said.

The nurses took off the fetal monitor and wheeled me into the operating room. A few minutes later, Matteo came into the room wearing a mask and gown. The nurse put a sheet over the top of my chest so I couldn't see what was happening. I could feel my belly being tugged, but it didn't hurt.

"The baby is out," said the doctor.

I couldn't hear the baby crying. I looked at Matteo said, "Look over the sheet and tell me what is happening."

"The cord is around the baby's neck, and the doctor is trying to cut it off," said Matteo.

Then suddenly, I felt very weak and passed out.

Chapter 25

When I opened my eyes, I was relieved to see Matteo sitting in a chair looking at me. I could see the worry in his eyes disappear as I woke up.

Weakly, I said, "How is the baby?"

"Our son is in the Neonatal Intensive Care unit."

"We have a boy." I started to cry.

"Yes. Do you still want to call him Ryan?"

I nodded.

"Well, then, it is settled. His name is Ryan."

He continued to tell me that Ryan was in serious condition. His lungs aren't fully developed, so he couldn't breathe on his own. He was hooked up to machines that were giving him medicine to help his lungs develop stronger.

All I wanted to do was stand up, run down to the NIC unit, hold Ryan as tight as I could, and whisper in his ear, "I love you." However, I didn't have the strength to get out of the bed, so I prayed to the good lord to please take care of my son.

"What happened? The last thing I remember was you telling me the cord was wrapped around the baby's neck."

"You started to hemorrhage, so the doctors put you to sleep to fix the bleeding. I was afraid I was going to lose you."

"I am very tired and need some rest, so you go down to be with Ryan. Please tell him that I love him and will see him very soon."

Matteo leaned over the bed, kissed me on my lips, and said, "You get some rest, and I will be back soon. I love you."

After he left the room, I couldn't hold back the tears anymore. I just broke down and cried. He was so strong holding it all together for me. I just felt that I had to do the same for him. I was just overwhelmed by everything that happened. I went from being happy to praying for my son to live. I was so terrified for Ryan.

When I woke up, Suzanne was sitting in the chair by my bed. She gave me an update on Ryan's condition and showed me some pictures that Matteo took of him. This was the first time I would see my baby boy. When I saw, him I started to cry. He was hooked up to a lot of machines. I knew then he had a long road ahead.

Suzanne thought it would make me feel better if I could see Ryan, so she left the room to ask the nurses if she could take me to the NIC unit. The nurse agreed it would be a great idea. Suzanne came back into my room. "If you want, I will take you in a wheelchair to see Ryan?"

"Yes, please."

Suzanne wheeled me to the NIC unit and Matteo was outside the unit waiting for us. Unfortunately, she couldn't go in and see the baby, since only immediate family were allowed in the unit.

Matteo wheeled me into Ryan's room and moved back the chair he was sitting in, so I could get a closer look at the baby. I took one look at him and couldn't believe how small he was. When the nurse saw, me she came over to see if I had any questions.

"Can I touch his hand?"

"Of course," said the nurse, "we encourage you to caress his hand and talk to him."

I held Matteo's hand with my left hand and with my other hand carefully caressed Ryan, telling both how much I loved them. We were a family, a sick family but nevertheless a family, and I was incredibly grateful for this moment.

"When will Ryan be able to go home?" I asked the nurse.

"Ryan is going to be in the hospital for a few months. He needs to be able to breathe on his own and weigh at least five pounds before he goes home," replied the nurse.

*

It had been a few days since my surgery. I had to stay in the hospital for another few more days to ensure I was better. Matteo took the following two weeks off to be with me and the baby.

Between Suzanne, Aunt Isabella, and Tony, they would take turns coming to the hospital every day to see if there was anything we needed.

Three days later, the doctor told me that I was well enough to go home. I had mixed feelings; on one hand, I was glad to be healthy again, but on the other hand I was leaving the hospital without my son.

Over the next three months, either Matteo or myself was at Ryan's bedside as much as possible. It was starting to take a toll on us. We were exhausted from working, going to school, doing homework, studying for tests, and then spending as much time as we could at the hospital with Ryan.

It was starting to put a strain on our marriage. If Matteo wasn't at work, then he was at the hospital by Ryan's side. As for me, I was going to school, doing my homework, studying for tests, attending group meetings for projects, and any spare time I had I was at the hospital with Ryan. Then at night, we usually never got home until after nine. We would just have a quick bite for supper, since we were too tired to make a meal. It was like we were both on autopilot, just trying to get through it.

Chapter 26

Today was a special day: Ryan was coming home. I couldn't believe how big and strong he was. Looking at him, you would never know that he was three months premature. Over the past few months, there were times when I wasn't sure he would make it.

I couldn't sleep; I was so nervous. All I wanted to do is watch him sleep to ensure he was okay. The birth of a child is truly a miracle, and there is nothing you wouldn't do to protect your little miracle.

I was glad it was summer, since I didn't have a babysitter; I still had time to find one before I returned to school in September. With the earlier arrival of Ryan and not being sure if he was going to make it, the last thing on my mind was a finding a babysitter.

One option for me was to take a semester off and return to school in January. That way I would have more time to find a suitable babysitter. However, that meant a delay in me returning to the workforce, and with a baby, a second income would be nice.

I woke up at two in the morning to a crying baby. I changed his diaper, fed him, and about an hour later he was back asleep.

I tried to go back to sleep, but I couldn't, so I went on the computer in the living room to look for daycares in our area. I wasn't sure how much it would cost, but I was surprised how expensive they were.

The next thing I knew, I could hear Matteo's alarm clock going off. He came out into the living room and looked at me. "How long have you been up?"

"I woke up at two to feed Ryan but couldn't fall back to sleep."

"What are you doing on the computer?"

"I am looking for a daycare in our area."

"Any luck?"

"I have a few numbers, and I will call them later today to see if they have any spots open. What do you want for breakfast?"

I figured since I was up, I could have breakfast with him before he went to work.

"I would like to have an English muffin with peanut butter, please."

I made each of us one, and we sat at the kitchen table talking about the different daycares that I found on the Internet.

Shortly after, Matteo went to work, and Ryan woke up.

It was around midmorning, and I just got Ryan down for his nap when my phone rang. It was Suzanne at the front door. I forgot she was coming over for a visit. I could only imagine what was going through her mind when she first saw me. My hair was messy, eyes bloodshot from being on the computer, dark circles under my eyes from lack of sleep, still in my pajamas, and a dazed look on my face.

I looked through the peephole to ensure it was her. I opened the door and she stared at me. "Rough night?"

"I have been awake since two."

"Is Ryan down for a nap?"

"Yes, I just put him down about five minutes ago."

"You go, have a nap, and I will take care of Ryan when he wakes up."

"That would be awesome. Thank you."

I walked into the bedroom and was asleep before my head hit the pillow.

I emerged from the bedroom three hours later; I guess I was tired. Suzanne was playing peek-a-boo with Ryan on the couch. They were both laughing.

"It sounds like you two are having fun."

"Yes, we are. Do you have a daycare spot for Ryan in September?"

"No, that is why I was up last night looking for daycares in the area."

"I have an idea. I will come over babysit Ryan for you. That way you can concentrate on your schoolwork and not worry if he is okay. What do you say?"

"Suzanne, are you sure? That is a lot of work."

"I would love to, and remember I did have a daughter, so I know a thing or two about taking care of a child."

"Of course, you do. I will talk to Matteo tonight about it, and I am sure he would have no problem with that. What about your job at the shelter?"

A big smile came over her face. It was like she has a second chance at raising a child, and I would take the help.

"I will give them one month's notice. Besides, my family needs me now, and that is more important."

My face lit up in a huge smile.

After a few hours, Suzanne went home, and I felt like a heavy weight was just lifted off my shoulders. However, was I putting Suzanne in danger? What if the stranger tried to hurt Suzanne since she was babysitting Ryan?

Matteo checked the mail on the way home today, and when he came in the apartment, his face was white. Right away, I got a bad feeling in my stomach. He handed me a letter that was addressed like the others, just my name on the front.

In a frightened voice Matteo said, "Open the letter!"

I franticly opened and read it:

Dear Rebecca,

Congratulations on becoming a mommy to a beautiful baby boy. One of the most important jobs is to safeguard your child, just like I am your protector. Remember, a child is a precious thing to lose. If you were a boy, Ryan would have been your name.

"What does that mean the stranger is my protector, and if I was a boy, Ryan would be my name? They would have no say in what my parents wanted to name me. He is crazier than I thought."

"I am going to see if I can take a couple of weeks off to be at home with Ryan and you."

"That will make me feel better. Also, Suzanne offered to babysit Ryan starting in September while I am in school. Should we take her up on the offer?"

"We need to tell her about the letters and everything else, and then she can make her own decision if she still wants to babysit. If she doesn't, then we will figure something out."

"But that is someone else the stranger can hurt."

"I don't believe we have any other choice."

"I can offer to bring Ryan over to her house each day for her to babysit there. She has a doorman, which can give a little more protection than here. I will call her later tonight."

I sat on the couch with my hands over my face, shaking my head and wondering when this would stop. I would never say this out loud to Matteo or anyone else, but sometimes I wished I was never born.

"Matteo, could you take care of Ryan on Tuesday and Thursday evenings so I can go back to finish level 4 and 5 of my self-defense classes?"

"Of course, I will. I was thinking it would be a great idea if we learned how to shoot a gun."

"What, shoot a gun? I don't want a gun in the house!"

"I know, but you might need to use it for protection. I would feel better if you knew how to protect yourself and Ryan if I am at work. I can see if Bill will take us to the shooting range."

Over the next couple of weeks, Bill took us to the shooting range several times to teach us how to shoot. I was surprised on how quickly I learned and how natural it felt to hold a gun. It made me feel more powerful, in control of my life, and I knew if I had to, I could protect my family.

Chapter 27

People told me that my life would change when I had a baby, but I didn't realize how much until Ryan was born. A year had already gone by, and this weekend was when we were going to have the party for family.

I decided to make a turkey dinner with all the fixings and of course birthday cake for dessert. Suzanne and Aunt Isabella arrived in the afternoon to help me prepare the vegetables then play with Ryan.

After we ate our dinner, I lit the candles, and we sang happy birthday to Ryan. He tried to reach for the candles; I believe the flames had his attention. I gave Ryan his own piece of cake on a plate, which he had all over his face, in his hair, and on the floor.

I remember that Amy was quiet that evening, which was uncharacteristic. While everyone was in the living room having tea or coffee and relaxing, she came into the kitchen to help me clean up.

"Amy, is everything okay?"

"I received a job offer that is in my field, but I have to move."

"Where is the job?"

"Vancouver Island. I must start my job in a month. The company is going to fly me out on Monday for five days so I can look for a place to live."

"Oh…that is great that you have a job but sucks that you have to move away. You worked hard in school and deserve this job. Think of it as an adventure or a new chapter in your life."

"I know, but I am going to miss you and your family, especially my nephew, Ryan. You have become like a sister to me."

"I am happy for you but sad that you are leaving. I'm going to miss you a lot, but we can keep in touch online. Also, you or I can fly out for a visit."

Later that evening, when everyone left, I told Matteo that Amy was moving to the other side of the country in a month. Then I realized that my stalker didn't hurt Amy, so maybe everything would work out.

*

The last year just flew by with Amy leaving, school, and life in general. I was graduating from my accounting program this Friday afternoon.

Aunt Isabella came over to the apartment to babysit Ryan while I went to the mall with Suzanne shopping for new clothes to start off my career.

I finally arrived at the mall and ran inside to see Suzanne window-shopping at a kid's store.

"Hi, Suzanne. Sorry I'm so late. I missed the first bus. I can't wait to get back into the workforce and start saving for a house. It has been tight with one income, but now it will all be worth it, I hope."

"I am sure it will be. Have you started to look for a job?"

"Yes, I did apply to a few, but I didn't hear anything yet."

"Sometimes it takes a couple of weeks before you hear anything. Just keep applying to jobs and something will come along."

I couldn't believe the clothes I bought, plus I didn't spend that much money. Every store we went in had sales on.

"I didn't realize how tiring shopping can be. My feet are sore. Do you want to get a snack at the coffee shop before going home?"

"Yes, that will be great. I can tell by your face that you are happy."

"I am the happiest that I have ever been, thanks to you."

"Me! It was you who did it, not me."

"Yes, but you believed in me, which gave me the confidence that I needed."

After lunch, we did a little more shopping then decided to head home for the day.

When I got home, Matteo had already started supper.

"Hi, how was your day shopping with Suzanne?"

"It was great. The stores were having huge sales, which means I got more for my money."

"I am glad you had fun. You got a call from Emma at Thompson Food Brokers. She wants to interview you for a job."

My eyes lit up like a Christmas tree, I was so excited. I picked up the phone and called her right away. "There was no answer, so I will have to call her first thing in the morning."

I called Emma at 9:00 a.m. and we set up an interview for Thursday morning at ten.

The night before the interview, I must have tried on five different outfits when Matteo said, "Relax, you look professional and perfect for the job. Emma will be crazy not to hire you. Remember, you can do this job. I believe in you."

"How did I get so lucky to have you as my husband?"

"I am the lucky one. Look at the beautiful woman I get to spend the rest of my life with, and you have to put up with me."

On my way to the interview, I was going over in my mind what I wanted to say. I disliked interviews, I got nervous and had a tough time trying to sell myself, even though I knew I could do this job and would be perfect for it. The one good thing was that in the last month of school we did do some mock interviews to help prepare us.

After the interview, I went to a coffee shop just a few minutes away to call Matteo.

"Hi, how did it go?"

"I'm glad that is over with, but I believe I did well. I answered all their questions, and they seemed pleased with my answers. Emma told me they will be making their decision by the middle of next week, and I will be notified either way. Now it's just a waiting game, the hardest part of this entire process."

"I hear you. Now just go home, relax for the rest of the day, and I will see you after work."

*

Already it was Wednesday. As each day went by and I didn't hear anything, I had less faith that I got the job. Just as I was going to get on the job bank, my phone rang.

"Hello."

"Is Rebecca there?"

"Speaking."

"Hi, it is Emma from Thompson Food Brokers. I would like to offer you the job if you are still interested?"

Right then I wanted to scream "Yes" right into the phone, but I knew that wouldn't be professional.

"Yes, I am."

"Good, how about you start this Monday morning at eight thirty?"

"That sounds great. Thank you and have a good weekend."

"You too, see you Monday."

As soon as I hung up the phone, I started jumping and screaming with joy. My life was starting to come together. I had a wonderful man who loved me for me and wanted to grow old together, I had a wonderful son that I adored, and I would be working in my field of study.

My hands were shaking so much, it was hard to dial Matteo's phone number.

"Hi, I got the job!"

"That is great, congratulations! How about we go out for supper, and you pick where we go."

I decided that we would go to a Chinese restaurant for a change. On the way to the restaurant, I kept looking over my shoulder to see if anyone was following me. I loved going out with my family for a nice supper, but I could never really relax.

Anyone that came over to the table, including the restaurant staff, I would always wonder if they were the stranger.

Chapter 28

I had been working at Thompson Food Brokers for three years now, and life was great. Ryan was four years old and growing like a weed. Every day, he was looking more like his father.

All I could think about all day at work was what Matteo said last night. He surprised me by talking about having a sister or brother for Ryan. It wasn't that I was against the idea, but that was another person we had to protect from a crazy person.

I called Matteo that afternoon at work, and neither one of us wanted to cook supper tonight, so I picked up a pizza while he stopped for Ryan. When I arrived home, I checked the mailbox, which was empty.

After we ate supper, I helped Ryan put on his pajamas, then we played a game. It was Ryan's turn to pick the game, and he chose Go Fish. We played for an hour, then I read Ryan his bedtime story.

When I came into the living room, Matteo had the TV on but was staring at an envelope with just my name on it.

"Where did you get that?"

"Ryan and I were home first, so we checked the mail."

"My hands are shaking too much, can you please open the envelope and read the letter."

He nodded his head:

Dear Rebecca,

I saw Matteo and Ryan a few days ago at the mall. I can't believe how fast he is growing up, but I think he looks more like Matteo than you. To me the worst thing a parent can go through is the death of a child. Before long, I will tell you who I am.

We both just sat on the couch and stared at each other in shock for a few minutes.

"What are we going to do?" I asked.

"I don't know. I am going to call Bill."

Bill just got off work, so he dropped by our house on his way home. Matteo showed him the letter.

"The stranger is threatening Ryan, what can you do?" I asked.

"There is no evidence that the stranger is going to hurt Ryan. The letter is just asking you a question," Bill replied. "We don't even know who is writing these letters."

"So, we just wait and see," I answered.

"I know it isn't the answer you were looking for, but anyone could have written the letter. It isn't signed, but I will take it to the lab to see if there are any fingerprints."

"Can you do me a favor?" asked Matteo.

"What is that?" replied Bill.

"Take us back to the shooting range to have some practice. It has been a while since we shot a gun."

"Yes, that sounds like a great idea."

*

A few months later, it was our fifth wedding anniversary and Aunt Isabella was babysitting Ryan so we could have a romantic evening. Matteo told me that he was taking Ryan over to Aunt Isabella's house and would be back in about an hour or so.

I went into our bedroom to put on a red lace teddy, Matteo's favorite. Then I put on my favorite perfume on my wrists, neck, and between my breasts. I touched up my hair, makeup, and opened a bottle of wine. I knew that Matteo would be home anytime now, and I wanted him to be surprised.

It had been an hour since Matteo left when the phone rang. It was Aunt Isabella asking me when we were going to bring Ryan over to her house. I told her that Matteo left an hour ago and should be arriving anytime. I thought that he might have stopped at the store to get some treats for Ryan. I tried calling Matteo's cell, but he didn't answer.

Half an hour later, I called Aunt Isabella to see if Matteo made it to her house. He didn't. At this point I was getting anxious when there was a knock on my door. I forgot I was just wearing the teddy and answered it.

At first Bill was taken aback by the way I was dressed, then he said, "Maybe you should go and put something else on." When I returned to the living room he said, "You should have a seat, Rebecca."

I couldn't talk; there was a lump in my throat. I tried to say, "What happened?" but the words wouldn't come out. I guess I was afraid of what Bill was going to tell me.

"There was a car accident. I am deeply sorry; Matteo and Ryan have died."

"What are you talking about? No! No! It can't be them."

I heard the words but couldn't believe it. I kept thinking, there must be a mistake. I just sat on the couch staring into thin air, wishing I would wake up from a bad dream.

After a little while I asked, "How did the accident happen?"

"The eyewitnesses said, 'The car hit a puddle of water, started to hydroplane, lost control and hit the median head on.' There is no way anyone could have survived."

"How do you know it was Matteo and Ryan? It could have been someone else."

"I know the license plate and model of his car. I will have their dental records sent to the morgue to confirm it was them."

"I need to see them. Take me to their bodies."

"Believe me, you don't want to see them. That isn't how you want to remember them."

"I need to see it was them and not somebody else."

"You can't tell by the bodies; they were so burnt. I will take you to the car so you can ensure it was Matteo's vehicle."

When we arrived at the scene, I saw Matteo's car was scorched, and from the condition of the car I knew that no one could have survived. Then I looked to the side and saw two white blankets covering two bodies, a big one for an adult and a smaller one for a child. I fainted, and Bill caught me before I hit the ground. A few minutes later, I came to and started to cry uncontrollably, saying, "No! No! It's not fair."

In a matter of seconds, my family was taken from me. I wanted to look under the blankets to confirm it was them, but I knew I would never be able to get that image out of my head.

In between sobs I said, "Bill you need to take me to Aunt Isabella's house."

"Of course, let's go."

When I walked into Aunt Isabella's house, she looked at me and knew something was wrong. She saw my eyes were bloodshot and glossy from crying, plus I was with Bill. The plate of cookies she was carrying to the table dropped to the floor, and the glass shattered everywhere.

"There was an accident. Matteo and Ryan have died."

I went over to put my arms around her and squeezed as tight as I could. Bill explained what happened, and we all sat there and cried. While she was on the phone with Tony, I called Suzanne to let her know what happened. Right away, they both came over to Aunt Isabella's place to be with us. I didn't want to be alone, so I stayed at Aunt Isabella's house for the night.

In the morning, Aunt Isabella called all their relatives to inform them what happened. Suzanne went over with me what I needed to do over the next few days. I had never planned a funeral, so I was grateful for her help.

In the afternoon, the doorbell rang, and Aunt Isabella opened the door. "Hi, Bill. Please come in."

"Hi, this is Detective Johnston. He has a couple of questions for Rebecca."

"Please have a seat, and I will tell her you are here," said Aunt Isabella.

I walked into the living room. "Hi, Rebecca, I am Detective Johnston, and I am investigating your husband and son's accident. How was Matteo's driving?"

"I thought he lost control of the car and it was an accident. He was a good driver and wouldn't take chances with Ryan in the car."

"How was your marriage?"

"It was great. We are in love. We just had our fifth anniversary."

"What was your husband's frame of mind?"

"Are you asking me if he was depressed?"

"Yes. Could it be possible that he wanted to cause the accident?"

"No! Not at all! My husband and son just died, and you are accusing my husband of suicide!"

"Where were you at the time of the accident?"

"I can't believe it that you would think I had something to do with the accident! I was home waiting for my husband. He was bringing our son over here for a sleepover so we could celebrate our anniversary. You can verify my story with Aunt Isabella."

I was so angry with Detective Johnston for implying that I had something to do with Matteo and Ryan's death that I had to leave the living room before I hit him. I had stood up and walked toward the hallway to go upstairs to the bedrooms when the detective said, "The dental records confirmed it was Matteo and Ryan's bodies that were in the car. I am sorry for your loss."

Tears started to run down my face. I nodded then left the room and went upstairs.

*

Since it was Saturday, I couldn't let Emma know what happened, so I left a message on her office phone informing her that I wouldn't be at work for several weeks.

On Monday, Suzanne helped me write the obituary, which was in Wednesday's edition of the newspaper. It was decided that we would have viewing at the funeral home from 2:00 to 4:00 p.m. and 7:00 to 9:00 p.m. on Thursday, and the funerals would be Friday at 11:00 a.m.

After that was done, my phone rang. It was Emma telling me how sorry she was and to take as much time as I needed.

On the morning of the funeral, and I was numb all over. I have never felt as empty and alone in my life as I did that day. I just lost my entire world. They say that you never completely get over a death of a child or spouse; you just learn how to move on. At that point, I didn't want to move on; all I wanted was to be with my husband and son.

I couldn't believe how many people came to the funeral. Tony did the eulogy for Matteo, and I did Ryan's. When I was partway through, I had to stop to collect myself.

At the reception, everyone had nothing but wonderful things to say about Matteo. His boss told me that if there was anything I needed, to let him know. Also, he informed me that all his employees had life insurance and I would need to come into the office to sign the paperwork.

Everyone had left except for Aunt Isabella, Tony, Suzanne, Bill, and me.

"Rebecca, let's go home," said Aunt Isabella

"I am going to my house tonight. I just want to be by myself," I replied.

"Is that a wise idea? You did have a very emotional day," said Bill.

"I don't know for sure, but it is what I need to do," I replied.

"Okay, I will drop you off," said Bill.

On the drive to my house, I didn't speak a word. I was tired of talking. All I really wanted to do was drink and pretend that Matteo was at work and Ryan was either at Aunt Isabella's or Suzanne's house.

When we arrived at my house, Bill said, "If you need anything, call me, and I will be over tomorrow to check on you."

I nodded, got out of the car, and opened the door to my house. When I turned around to lock the door, I waved to Bill.

The following morning, Bill came over to the house to check on me to find me drunk. "How are you?"

I slurred, "Not good. I told Matteo this may happen, and he still wanted to get married. How would you feel if the two most important people in your life are dead because of you? Why are people around me dying?"

"I got the report from the accident back. It turns out there was nothing wrong with the car. He lost control and crashed into the medium. We have no proof that the stranger that is sending you the letters is responsible for this accident."

"I know that the stranger did this. Matteo and Ryan were threatened in the last letter just a few months ago."

"I know that he loved you very much, and he didn't want to live his life without you."

I just sat on the couch and cried while Bill held me. At that point in time, I didn't want to live. I thought about committing suicide, but I knew that Matteo wouldn't want that. I just didn't know why dreadful things were happening to me.

"Rebecca, tomorrow morning I need you to be sober. You must go to Matteo's work to fill out paperwork for the insurance money. There is more paperwork that you need to fill out for the government, and we must go to the bank. I will go with you and help you fill out all the necessary forms."

"Okay! But when I get back, I am having a drink."

A few hours after Bill left, there was a knock on my door. I looked through the peephole to see my next-door neighbor. I opened the door, and she said, "I believe this belongs to you. It was in my mail slot."

She handed me a white envelope with just my name on it. Right away, I got a sick feeling in my stomach. I said, "Thank you," then shut the door.

I put the envelope on the kitchen table and just stared at it for a while. It was just like the other letters I received from the stranger, and I was petrified to open it. Finally, after a few more drinks, I got the courage to open the letter:

My dearest daughter Rebecca,

I realize that two of the most important people in your life have died, but is drinking really the answer? As your biological father, I feel it is my duty to tell you this behavior is unacceptable.

Your father, Fred.

Chapter 29

I called Bill right way to tell him that I received another letter, and within half an hour he was at my apartment.

"Bill, you aren't going to believe this — the stranger thinks he is my father! I can't believe it; this guy keeps getting crazier and crazier."

I gave the letter to Bill to read.

I couldn't stop crying. I broke down from the guilt.

"I knew that I shouldn't have married Matteo. The night before the wedding, I had a feeling that something bad was going to happen to him."

"You can't blame yourself. You were completely honest with Matteo, and he married you knowing the risk involved."

"But what about Ryan? What did he do — nothing. He didn't deserve to die."

"You are right. He was innocent, but there is nothing you can do that will bring him back and blaming yourself doesn't solve anything. Are you hungry?"

"No, my stomach is to upset. All I want to do is sleep and cry."

"Okay, I am going to order in a pizza."

"I am afraid I am not going to be much company."

"That is okay. I am going to eat my pizza, watch TV, and sleep on your couch. I just want you to know that I am here if you need me."

I went to bed, but I couldn't sleep. Every time I closed my eyes, I would see Matteo and Ryan crying for help.

The following morning, Bill said, "Rebecca, we have some information now about this man by the name of Fred claiming to be your father."

"But he isn't my dad! Brent was my dad that died when I was a young child."

"What if your mom did have an affair with Fred and wasn't sure who your father was?"

"Okay, let's say that was true. So, what if my mom had an affair, what does that have to do with him wanting to hurt me?"

"I don't know."

"If what he is saying is true, then why would he want to hurt me since I was a child?"

"That could explain what your mom meant by making a terrible mistake and wishing she could go back to change it."

"I know that Fred was the one responsible for the car accident. Why doesn't he just kill me instead of hurting other people? It's like a game to him."

"You were from a small town, right?"

"Yes, Tignish, PEI, why?"

"I am going to call the police station to see how many Fred's live in Tignish. There shouldn't be that many, and if we are lucky, I may be able to obtain a picture. I will be back shortly."

A few hours later, there was a knock on my door. I looked through the peephole to see Bill. I opened the door and said, "Hi, come in."

"There were three Fred's at the time your mom was living in Tignish. One had passed away and two of them are in their seventies, so I don't believe it was them."

"So that puts us back to where we started."

As Bill was opening his computer he said, "Not exactly. I expanded the search to include the nearest city, Charlottetown, and found three more Fred's that would have been around your mom's age. One I have a picture of and the other two I don't, but I do have their last name. Do you recognize this man?"

"No, he doesn't look familiar to me, but honestly, I didn't get a good look at the man. He was wearing sunglasses and a ball cap. I do remember that he had a black mustache and beard. Why couldn't you get pictures of the other two?"

"They didn't have a police record."

"Okay, what are the other two's last names? I am going to search on the Internet to see if I can find a picture or information about them."

"They are Smith and LeBlanc."

"I will search Fred Smith first…let's see…there are numerous hits for Fred Smith. This is going to be harder than I thought."

"Well let's narrow down the search to Fred Smiths that are in their late thirties and earlier forties. That would be your mom's age group if she was alive today."

"Okay, now that is more manageable. Just wait I have something here…a news story about a Fred Smith that was a police officer who was shot in the back while on duty. Due to his injuries, he had to quit the police force. That would explain why he is good at finding me; it was part of his job."

"I never thought it could have been an ex-police officer. I only ran the name Fred for convicted criminals. Is there a picture of him?"

"No."

"Do you want to search for any Fred Smith?"

"Yes…okay there are a few, but they are either too young or old. There were none around my mom's age."

"I will go to the station tomorrow to try and obtain a picture of Fred Smith when he was a police officer. Then I will come over to show you."

"Okay, that sounds good."

The next afternoon Bill arrived at my apartment. "This is Fred Smith."

He didn't look familiar to me, but I got a cold chill down the back of my neck. One thing I have learned is to trust my gut. It was saying this was the man.

"Do you have an address for him?"

"The last address on file was in Tignish. I called the local police to see if he still lives in the area, but he moved away. Also, I found out that he is married, or at least was."

"I wish I had a picture of Mom and him so I can be sure I have the right Fred Smith. Do you know where he is living now?"

"No. I pulled up all the Fred Smith's pictures in the police database but no match. I will reach out to the other police departments across the country to see if we can locate him."

*

About a week later Bill let me know he had no luck. It was so bizarre, just as if Fred dropped off from the face of the earth. There was no trace of him. The only way he could be surviving is either he changed his name, or he came into some money that would allow him to live off the grid.

Chapter 30

It had been a couple of weeks since the deaths, and it was time to go back to work. When I first walked into the office, everyone I saw hugged me, or squeezed my hand, or told me if I needed anything to let them know. I could feel myself starting to lose control, and tears were coming down my face. I knew they only meant well, but I wished no one said anything about the deaths.

I was at my desk working when I noticed Eddy, an employee from the warehouse, walking toward me. "It's lunch time. Do you want to get out of the office for a bit?"

"Yes."

He decided to go to Wendy's drive-through just down the street then drive to a nearby lake to eat lunch.

Eddy knew that when I had a lot on my mind, I liked to go to the lake and stare at the water. He was a good friend and that was exactly what I needed now. I knew I had Bill to lean on, but he was also grieving. Sometimes I felt bad when I broke down in front of Bill, since he tried to be strong for me.

We just sat there and ate our lunch without saying anything. When we arrived back at the office after lunch I said, "Thank you, I really needed to get out of the office."

"Anytime," said Eddy.

*

Over the next two years, Bill kept searching for Fred but couldn't find anything. It was as if he vanished into thin air.

I just went to work, ate when I felt like it, and drank myself to sleep each night. Then got up and did it all over again. I felt that I had nothing to live for and blamed myself for the deaths.

The following week, Eddy asked me if I wanted to go out for supper with him on Friday night to Chicken 'N Ribs Restaurant.

I knew that Eddy liked me, but he respected that I was married and never made a pass at me. However, in the past year he had made a couple of passes at me, and I didn't react to them.

Eddy loved to drink, and I think that was what attracted me to him. At that point in my life, all I wanted to do was drink and have fun.

I wanted to feel alive again by having the touch of a man on me. I choose Eddy, since I knew he liked me, and if I decided to change my mind partway through, he would stop. He wouldn't push me to continue. I trusted him, and to me that was important, so I accepted his invitation to supper on Friday night.

When I woke up Friday morning, I took a shower, washed my hair, groomed myself, and put on jeans with a T-shirt. When I was on my way to work, I thought to myself that this would be the first time that I had sex since Matteo. Honestly, I wasn't sure how I would react.

The workday was over, and we went to the local bar a few streets from the office. We had a couple of beers before we ate supper. Then Eddy suggested we go and get a case of beer to take back to his house.

After we went to the liquor store, we stopped at the corner store to get some chips and munchies for later in case we get hungry.

We pulled into a driveway of a semidetached house.

"This is my house. Come in and I will give you a tour."

The house was a bungalow with two levels. On the first level there were the kitchen, living room/TV room and half a bathroom. The lower level had two bedrooms, laundry room, and a full bathroom.

"You have a wonderful home."

"Do you want to play cards while we have some beer and talk?"

"That would be nice."

While we played cards and drank some beer, I found out that Eddy was divorced with two kids, a girl and boy. He had the children every second weekend. He also had a cabin in the woods, where he loved going on weekends.

As he was talking, I was thinking about ripping his clothes off and having wild sex with him. I thought about reaching over and kissing him a few times but stopped myself. I guess I wasn't sure exactly how he would react.

After the fifth beer, I did get the courage to lean over and kiss him on the lips. Eddy looked at me and smiled. I stood up, took his hand, and walked to the couch. We sat there and started kissing.

Eddy knew his way around the female body. He was touching all the right spots. The next thing I knew, we were naked on the couch moaning like two wild beasts in heat. Don't get me wrong, I enjoyed the sex with Eddy, but that was all it was, just sex. I was in love with Matteo, and I believe that was the difference.

*

Over the next few months, Eddy was more like a drinking buddy with benefits to me. I enjoyed spending time with him, but I wasn't falling for him. I am not sure, but I think he was falling for me. Every time he saw me, he would smile, and the guys in the warehouse expressed concern that he was getting emotionally attached to me. The last thing I wanted to do was hurt him.

It was a Friday afternoon, and I was at my desk working when my boss asked me into her office. She sat me down, told me that she could smell alcohol on my breath, and asked if I was drinking at lunch. I told her no because I didn't want to lose my job. She told me that I have a drinking problem, and like any other alcoholic, I denied it and got angry. I stood up, grabbed my chair, and threw it across the room. Then I just stood there in shock.

At that point I knew I needed to get some help. I didn't like the person I was becoming. I knew I wasn't doing great, but I didn't realize how it was affecting my job. She gave me the phone number of a therapist I could talk to.

I didn't remember anything past leaving work at the end of the day. When I woke up, I was in Eddy's bed, naked. I felt so sick to my stomach that when I stood up, I almost passed out. I sat back down on the bed for a few minutes then stood up again. When I came downstairs into the kitchen, Eddy was reading the newspaper and having a beer.

"Good morning. Are you hungry? I can make breakfast."

"No thanks, the smell of food is going to make me want to take sick. How can you have a beer first thing in the morning?"

That was when I knew I had to stop drinking. I left Eddy's house and arrived home around eleven in the morning.

Chapter 31

First thing Monday morning, I called a therapist. I had weekly sessions, which helped me with the grieving process. I told her that I was feeling guilty for not being in the car with them. The therapist helped me face the pain and gave me ways to deal with it. Of course, I didn't tell her that there was a man stalking me that I believed is responsible for killing Matteo and Ryan. I figured the less people knew, the safer they were until Fred was caught.

I pray every night that Bill will find Fred but no such luck so far.

Since I was on a self-destructive path, Suzanne, Aunt Isabella, and Tony tried to help me, but I wouldn't listen. I couldn't go or do anything without having alcohol in my system. After a while, they stopped calling and visiting me. I didn't blame them; you can only try to help someone so many times, but they have to make the first step.

I especially wanted to mend my relationship with Suzanne, since she was like a mother to me. She took me under her wing and made sure I was okay. I really don't know what would have happened to me if I didn't meet Suzanne.

I called Suzanne, Aunt Isabella, and Tony to see if they would agree to have lunch with me. and to my surprise, they all agreed.

"Hi, everyone. I'd like to apologize for the hurtful things I have said and for not returning your calls. I will be honest; I don't remember what I said the last time we talked. I was so drunk. I know that isn't an excuse, but it is the truth. I didn't mean to push you away. The pain was so bad, I just didn't know what else to do."

"I accept your apology, but I just want you to know that you can always talk to me, no matter what the situation is," said Suzanne. "Also, usually when you talk to someone, it always makes you feel better."

"I realize that now, thanks to my therapist."

"Rebecca, you will always be part of this family; after all, you are my nephew's wife. Matteo loved you more than life itself, and he would want you to be happy."

I wiped the tears away from my eyes. "I just felt guilty that I am still alive and that I should have been in the car that day."

"We are glad that you weren't in the car," replied Suzanne.

"You know, I am a really lucky girl to have wonderful people in my life."

"Rebecca, you remember that next time when life gets you down," said Aunt Isabella.

I smiled. "It's a deal."

Then we sat at the restaurant for the next few hours, catching up on what I missed in their lives. It was just like old times.

There was another person that I had to make amends with, and that was my boss. I now realized that I could have been fired for showing up to work with alcohol on my breath.

After my last session, when I got back to the office, I went into Emma's office to thank her for making me get help. I told her that I really appreciated her giving me a second chance and that I was deeply sorry for throwing the chair.

Chapter 32

It had been a little over a month since the last time I took a drink, but I still felt sick in the morning. I knew that it couldn't be the alcohol since it doesn't stay in the bloodstream that long. I had also noticed that my breast was sore, and my appetite increased.

I knew there was a chance that I could be pregnant, but if I was, what was I going to do? Did I do harm to the baby from drinking the past few months? How could I protect the baby from whoever was trying to harm me? What was I going to tell Eddy?

I didn't realize how much Eddy drank until I got sober. I had to distance myself from him. I knew if I continued to be around him, I would go back to drinking. I told him I couldn't hang around with him right now; it was too hard for me to be around alcohol.

I had been longing for something good to happen to me and having someone to take care of was what I needed right now. However, I was nervous since I had been unable to protect Ryan. How could I be sure I could protect this child? If this child had the same outcome that Ryan, I didn't know if I could live anymore.

I decided before I got ahead of myself, on the way home from work that night, I would stop at the drug store to pick up a pregnancy test. While I was waiting for the test results, I was wondering what I was going to do if it came back positive.

If I told Eddy, then he would step up to the plate and want to marry me, but I didn't want that. I loved Eddy like a special friend but not as a husband.

At that point in my life, I didn't want to be around alcohol; I was afraid that I couldn't stay sober. I know this sounds bad, but I just wanted to have sex and a few good laughs with Eddy. I wanted to feel alive again, and he accomplished that.

Since I didn't want Eddy to know about the baby, and we worked at the same company, I had to find a new job.

I did start to think about attending university, getting a degree, that way I could apply to better-paying jobs. After Matteo died, I received money from the life insurance, and I could use that money to pay for university.

I needed to talk to someone, so I decided to take Suzanne up on her offer and called her. She sounded overly excited that I asked her for help instead of going to the bottle. She had to run an errand, then she would be over.

When she showed up, I opened the door, and right away she gave me a hug and said, "I thought you might need that."

"Yes, I did. You always know what to do, and that is why I need to talk to you. When I was drinking, I missed the touch of a man, and it had been two years since Matteo died. I needed to feel alive again, so I had a friend with benefits. His name was Eddy, and I met him at work. Well, it turns out that I am pregnant."

"You're pregnant! How do you feel about that?"

"It isn't exactly what I planned, but I am happy. Eddy will always hold a special place in my heart, and I love him, but I am not in love with him. Does that make sense to you?"

"Yes, I understand what you mean. Does he know about the baby?"

"No, and that is the way I want it. Eddy is a nice guy, but he likes to drink a lot, and that is what attracted me to him. I don't want to be around someone who wants to drink a lot. This baby is my way of staying on the right road. I can't stay at my current job, or Eddy will find out that I am pregnant. I can find a new job, or I was thinking about going to university to obtain my degree. I can use the money that I received from Matteo's life insurance. What do you think?"

"First, I do believe that Eddy has the right to know about the baby. Second, obtaining more education would be an asset to you."

"I want to do an accounting degree, since I am already working in that field, and I like it. I am going to see if some of my courses from community college can be transferred to university. As far as Eddy is concerned, I am not going to tell him, and I would appreciate it if you kept this bit of information to yourself."

"I disagree with you, but I will keep your secret. Congratulations on the baby."

"Thank you."

"Are you going to tell Aunt Isabella or Tony about the baby?"

"Not yet. I am not sure how they will feel about it, especially when the relationship was casual."

"You don't have to tell them everything, just that you are expecting a child and the relationship didn't work out. If they ask any more questions, just tell them you don't want to talk about it."

"Okay, I will tell them."

My phone rang, and I looked at the number. "Speaking about Aunt Isabella…"

It turned out that Tony's company was relocating to United States, so he was moving. Aunt Isabella wanted to have a surprise going-away party next Saturday night at her house. She asked me for Bill's number so she could invite him.

After I got off the phone, Suzanne's phone rang. The way she was talking, I could guess it was Aunt Isabella inviting her to Tony's party. When she hung up, I said, "Let me guess, Aunt Isabella inviting you to the party?"

We both laughed.

"Please promise me that you will not say anything about me being pregnant. This party is for Tony, and I don't want to ruin it for him; besides, I have to confirm with my doctor."

"You haven't been to the doctor yet?"

"No, I just took an over-the-counter pregnancy, test and it came back positive. I am going to call Monday morning for an appointment."

After about an hour, Suzanne went home, and I went on the computer to print off the application for university. It turned out that I could transfer my courses from the community college. I was pleased.

I hated Monday mornings; they were so hard to get up for, but I knew it was going to be a busy day at the office. It was mid-morning when I remembered to call Dr. MacRae's office. It turned out another patient just cancelled their appointment for Thursday morning.

At lunch, I copied my transcripts from community college, my high school diploma, and the accounting program I took. I put them in the envelope along with the application and mailed to the university. Patience was never a strong suit of mine, so waiting to see if I got into the school would be hard.

It was Thursday morning; I registered with the doctor's receptionist and was waiting to get in to see him. Surprisingly, it was only a fifteen-minute wait before I was called into his office.

Dr. McRae walked in said, "Hi, Rebecca, how can I help you?"

"I believe I am pregnant."

"What makes you think that?"

"I haven't had my period for the past two months, my breasts are sore, my appetite has increased, and I took a pregnancy test, which came back positive."

"It does sound like you are pregnant, but I am going to send you to the hospital for a pregnancy test just to confirm."

"Doctor, I am scared. I took Matteo and Ryan's deaths extremely hard and have been drinking a lot. I stopped drinking about a month ago, but I am nervous that I might have done some harm to my baby. How can I know for sure that the baby is, okay?"

"We normally don't send a patient for an ultrasound until the mom is about five months along, but in your case, I think you should get one right away just in case there is something wrong with the baby. Then you will have time to make your decision go through with the pregnancy or terminate it."

"What if I harmed the baby? What kind of mother am I?"

147 | Page

"Rebecca let's not get ahead of ourselves. Let's see what the ultrasound shows. My reception will call you with the appointment."

What if I had done harm to the baby just because I wanted to drink? How was I going to handle that? If I knew I was pregnant, I would have stopped drinking. I didn't plan this baby, but I was glad he/she is here, and I could only hope that I didn't do any damage.

I started thinking about what Suzanne said, that Eddy had a right to know about the baby. I felt bad but thought this was best for everyone. If he did know about the baby, that was someone else I had to protect.

I had just finished getting ready for Tony's party when Bill called to say he was on his way to pick me up. We had to be there by six since Tony was due to arrive home at six thirty. We were all hiding with the lights out, and when Tony turned the lights on, we all jumped up and yelled "Surprise!"

He was so shocked, it made him speechless, which was a hard thing to do. Aunt Isabella had invited all his friends, people from his work, and the family. It was a wonderful time, and the food was incredibly good. The one good thing about being a recovering alcoholic is no one asks why you aren't drinking.

In the car on the way home from the party, I looked at Bill. "I have to tell you something."

"Did you get another letter?"

"No." Then I took a deep breath.

"Rebecca, no matter what it is, I will help you as much as I can."

I knew that I had to tell Bill that I was pregnant, but I was scared to. I wasn't sure if he would feel that I had a relationship too soon.

"Okay, I am pregnant."

I looked at his face to see what his expression would be, but I couldn't tell.

"Are you happy?"

"I didn't plan this, but I am happy it happened. This has given me new hope and something to keep me off the alcohol."

"Well then, congratulations, and I am happy for you."

*

On Monday, I received a phone call informing me my ultrasound would be next Wednesday afternoon.

I tell you that wasn't easy. I had to drink a lot of water, and I felt that I was going to pee my pants all the way over to the hospital. After the test, they said that I could go and use the bathroom. It seemed like I was in the bathroom forever, but it felt good.

That night, I went with Aunt Isabella to the airport to say goodbye to Tony. We agreed to keep in touch with each other through email and Skype, but it is easier said than done. At first, we would email and Skype every week. Then it would be every two or three weeks, and so on.

Life gets in the way, or at least that is what happened with Amy and me. We agreed to the same thing, but now we only emailed each other every three or four months.

Before Tony went through security, we hugged, and I had a feeling this would be the last time I would see him in person.

On the following Monday, I received a phone call from Dr. McRae's office telling me that he wanted to see me on Thursday. My heart started to pound, and I was extremely nervous about the results.

Chapter 33

When I arrived at the doctor's office, I went in to see him right away.

"Hi, Rebecca, how are you feeling?"

"I am very nervous, is the baby, okay?"

"Yes, there seems to be no damage to the baby. However, we will not know for sure until the baby is born. I believe that you are almost four months along."

I let out a big sigh and started to cry.

"I will see you in a month for a check-up. You can make the appointment on your way out."

"Thank you. From now on, I will take care of myself."

About three weeks later, I received a letter from the university stating that I was accepted into their accounting program, starting in January. They gave me credit for the courses I took at the community college, which meant I could finish the degree in two years if I didn't take summers off.

I had to call Suzanne right away to tell her the good news and invite her out for supper. It was decided that we would meet at the Chinese restaurant tomorrow night for supper. When I arrived at the restaurant, she was already seated.

"Hi, how are you feeling?"

"Good. I had an ultrasound, and the doctors confirm that my due date will be mid-May. I have another favor to ask you."

"That is wonderful, a spring baby. How can I help you?"

"I am going to need a babysitter for when I am in school, and when I return to the workforce. You are a good judge of character, so will you help me interview some possible sitters?"

"I don't need to interview anyone. I have someone already picked out."

"Who?"

"Me, of course. Do you really think that I would let a stranger take care of my grandchild? I know I am not the real grandmother, but I think of you as my daughter and would like to help you. Besides, I babysat Ryan."

"I think of you as my mother. You have helped me so much, and if you are sure you want to take this on, I would be grateful. I can rest knowing that the baby will be well taken care of."

"Well, then it is settled. I will babysit."

While we finished our supper, we talked about the baby, me starting school, and when I would be leaving Thompson Food Brokers. Every time we talked about the baby; Suzanne's eyes would light up. Then I realized she needed us as much as we needed her.

I decided I would keep working until the end of December to get some more money. At that point, I would be five months along and could wear big sweaters to hide my belly.

*

It was my last day at the food brokers, and I had mixed emotions. I was sad about leaving but also happy to start a new chapter. It was about mid-afternoon when Emma asked me to come to her office. When I walked in, everyone started cheering and clapping for me. There was a cake that said, good luck in university.

Emma made a beautiful speech and presented me with a picture to put on my wall. I started to cry. I wasn't sure if it was the hormones from the pregnancy or I was just overwhelmed by the kind words of encouragement from everyone.

After we had the cake, I went back up to my desk to pack up my personal items when Eddy came over.

"Hi, now did you think you were going to go before I could say goodbye?"

"I guess not."

"Good luck in university. I know you will do great."

"Thank you for being a good friend to me."

"It was more than just friends to me."

"I know. I am sorry, but I am not ready for anything more."

"At least could I call you once in a while to catch up on each other's lives?"

"Sure, that would be nice."

Eddy gave me a hug and went back to the warehouse. I went around saying goodbye to everyone, especially Emma, who helped me get my life back on track, then I left Thompson Food Brokers for the last time.

*

It was Sunday night, and I was getting ready for my first day at university when I started to have doubts about leaving the workforce. Was I really making the right decision for my baby? Leaving a full-time job to pursue my education with no guarantee that I would get a job when I graduated, that was scary. However, if I wanted a job that pays more money, than I had to get more education.

I was sitting on the couch watching TV when my phone rang. I haven't talked to Aunt Isabella in the last few months. I believe the last time was when we said goodbye to Tony at the airport. She wanted to let me know that she was moving down to be with Tony.

I understood why; you see, she could never have children. Matteo and Tony were like her children, and she couldn't get over Matteo's death. She told me there were too many memories here, and she needed a fresh start.

*

When I arrived at university, I had to find my classroom, which didn't take as long as I thought it would. I took a seat in the second row. I knew since I was paying for my education, I was going to do everything possible to ensure I would pass.

I sat down in the second chair on the right-hand side of the room. There was no one sitting in the first chair, but there were books on the table. A few minutes later, a young guy came in sat in the first chair and introduced himself as Larry. He was only eighteen years old, and it was his first time leaving his home province of Newfoundland.

Over the next three months, we got to know each other. He loved to party but always ensured his studies were done first. He loved his family very much and wanted to succeed at university to help his parents financially. He talked about his childhood and had wonderful stories to tell. I would sit there and listen to him, sometimes not sure what he said due to the accent, but I could tell how close he was with his family.

Larry was incredibly competitive, which was good, since it kept me on my toes and made me study harder. He always wanted to get a higher mark on test, quizzes, and papers than me. Sometimes he would, and other times I would, which made him a little mad. I would just laugh at him.

When I started to show, he got excited. Later, I found out that his sister was seven months pregnant when she died from a brain aneurism. One minute she was standing in the kitchen talking about baby names, and the next moment she was on the floor, unconscious. By the time the EHS arrived at the hospital with her, she was already gone, and the baby didn't survive.

Larry took on the role of being my coach during the pregnancy. He came to every Lamaze class, went to all my doctor's appointments, and even read a book about the delivery process.

One day in class, I started to have contractions, but it was early. My due date wasn't for another three weeks.

I was standing in front of the class with my group giving our presentation, and I had to present my part next. All I could think about was to get through the next five minutes without anyone knowing. I didn't want to let down my group; we worked so hard on this project.

As I was presenting my part of the project, sometimes I would raise my voice when I had a contraction, trying to hide the pain, but the professor noticed something was wrong.

The professor said, "Rebecca, are you in labor?"

"Yes, but I have to finish my part. I will be done in a minute."

Then all you heard in the classroom was a gasp, and all the guys had a look of terror on their faces. I don't know if they thought I was going to give birth at once.

"You are done now," said the professor. "I am going to call an ambulance for you."

"Thank you." I sat down on the chair. "Larry please call Suzanne and Bill to let them know I am in labor and on my way to the hospital."

Larry rushed over to me with a big smile and said, "Now focus on your breathing. "

He would breathe with me and hold on my hand so I could squeeze it through the contractions.

Within a few minutes, the ambulance attendant was at my side, asking me questions. I answered in between the contractions. When we arrived at the hospital, my doctor was already there. He had just finished delivering another baby.

Dr. MacRae came into the birthing room. "Hi, Rebecca, I am going to put the fetal monitor on your stomach to see how the baby is doing."

"Is everything okay? I am not due for another three weeks."

"Everything sounds fine, the baby is just eager to meet you, Mommy."

The doctor smiled, and then I knew the baby was going to be okay. I took a deep breath and closed my eyes. It made me remember when Ryan was born and how much I missed him and his daddy. In a little bit, I was going to be a mommy again, and I was happy but scared.

"Okay, Rebecca, it's time to push and meet this little one. Now, with all your strengthen, bear down and push as hard as you can."

Larry was on my left, and when I started to push, I dug my fingernails into his hand while he was encouraging me. This went on forever — okay, not forever, but it seemed like it did.

Larry could tell that I was starting to get tired, so he inspired me to continue to push. "You got this, Rebecca. You can do it! I believe in you!"

"Okay, let's take a little break," the doctor said. "I can see the baby's head, just one more good push and that should do it. Are you ready, Rebecca?"

I was so weak that I couldn't talk, so I just nodded and pushed as hard as I could with every bit of strength I had left. I pushed and pushed until I could no longer push. At last, the baby's head was out.

"You have a baby girl."

Larry looked at me with a big smile. "You did it, Mommy! I knew you could do it."

"Is she healthy…why isn't she crying?"

"The nurses are just clearing her nose, throat, and checking her over."

Then, within a second, I heard the best noise ever: my daughter crying for the first time. The nurses cleaned her up, wrapped her in a blanket, and handed her to me.

"She is a healthy and beautiful baby girl," the doctor said. "Congratulations."

She seemed like the most beautiful little girl in the world.

It was about half an hour later that I was in a private room with my daughter when Larry walked in.

"Hi, Rebecca, how are you feeling?"

"I feel better now the delivery is over."

"Can I hold the baby?"

"Of course, you can."

He just seemed so natural with the baby, and that's when I knew he would make a wonderful father. I hoped someday he would find the right person and have a baby.

"I called Suzanne and Bill to let them know baby and mommy are doing great. They will be over shortly."

"Thank you for helping me through the delivery."

"You are welcome. Did you decide on a name for the baby?"

"I think so — Abigail. What do you think?"

"She looks like an Abigail." I never understood what he meant by that, but he liked the name.

Suzanne and Bill walked into the room when Larry introduced them to Abigail.

"Suzanne, do you want to hold the baby?" asked Larry.

"Of course. Hello, Abigail, I am your Nanny."

Then Suzanne looked at Bill said, "Do you want to hold Abigail?"

I could tell that Bill was nervous, so I said, "It is okay if you don't want to hold the baby. I understand."

"I am just nervous holding babies until they can hold their head up."

The next day, I was discharged from the hospital, and Suzanne was there to help me at home with the baby.

I still had three weeks of class before the course was over, but I didn't want to have an incomplete on my transcript, so I asked the professor if I could do the work from home and just come to the classroom to write the final exam. I was lucky that she said yes, and it wasn't one of my core courses. Thanks to Larry for making a copy of his notes for me and handing in my assignments, I passed the course.

It was the middle of August when I went down to check the mail and noticed an envelope with just my name on it. I quickly ran upstairs and opened the letter:

My dearest daughter Rebecca,

Congratulations on the birth of your daughter. What did you name her? Oh yes, it was Abigail. I hope she doesn't have the same fate as Ryan. I see you are furthering your education. Your mother would be so proud of you.

Your father, Fred

I called Bill right away, and he could tell by my tone that something wasn't right. He came over to my apartment right after work and read the letter.
"What am I going to do in September when I have to return to school? How can I protect Suzanne and Abigail?"
"Rebecca, calm down. We will figure something out. Suzanne has a doorman, so why don't you take the baby to her house? If you like, I can drive you in the morning, and you can take the bus home in the afternoon."
"I would feel better with the baby at her house, since it is more secure and in a better neighborhood. I will call her tomorrow to ask her."
It was now September, and I was returning to school full-time. I would drop off the baby at Suzanne's house on the way to school and pick her up on the way home on Mondays, Wednesday, and Fridays. I didn't have any classes on Tuesdays or Thursdays, which gave Suzanne a break, and it allowed me to spend time with Abigail.
It was weird to be at university without Larry. He left my life as quickly as he came into it. His father suffered a heart attack, and he had to leave school to go back to Newfoundland to help his

mom. Deep down, I knew I would never see Larry again, but I was thankful for having him help me through my pregnancy.

Chapter 34

It had been two years since I was in the work force, and now that I had graduated with my degree, I had to find a job. I had applied to several jobs over the past two weeks and received a call for an interview on Monday for an accounts payable position with Sara's Furniture. I knew I would have to start at the bottom and work my way up to an accountant position.

I arrived at the company ten minutes before my interview, took a deep breath, and went in. I was incredibly nervous. In an interview, you are supposed to sell yourself, and I wasn't good at that. The interview took an hour, and they say that if it is more than forty-five minutes, it is a good sign.

The company had two divisions, furniture, and real estate. The company owned and operated three furniture stores within the metro region. On the real estate side, the company had both commercial and residential buildings that it maintained.

I was told that I would know if I was the successful candidate by the end of the week. This was one of the longest weeks of my life. Finally, Friday came, and I was anxious waiting for the phone to ring. It was eleven in the morning when it rang. It was Jamie from Sara's Furniture stating I was the successful candidate if I was still interested in the position. Of course, I told him I was, I would start my new job in two weeks.

*

I will not forget the first day I started at Sara's Furniture. It was the start of my new career. I was nervous and didn't know what to expect. There were six of us in the accounting department: Patty and Charlotte's duties were the accounts receivable. Margaret did the purchasing of the furniture. Jamie was the accountant, and Grace and I were responsible for the accounts payable.

The past month, I learned a lot at work about the job and the employees. Jamie was a good boss, but when he was in a bad mood, you knew to stay away. Grace knew her job very well, since she had been doing it for twenty years, but she treated me as her employee and not her coworker. Margaret, Charlotte, and Patty were like me; they worked hard but liked to have some fun.

They wanted to know about my personal life, such as did I have any siblings, children, was I married, etc. I had to be careful on what I told them, since I didn't want them to become targets.

I told them I was a single mom with a daughter that was a year and half old. I was an only child, and my parents died when I was young. I was raised by my aunt who passed away a few years ago, so the only family I had was my daughter.

*

Seven months after I started working at Sara's Furniture, I was finally feeling like I belonged. Sometimes I would wonder what it would be like to have a normal life. I mean not having someone trying to hurt you or someone else in your life.

I was lucky that Suzanne would babysit for me when I wanted to go out with the girls from the office. I didn't go out often, but occasionally I needed to let loose. Sometimes we would go out for supper, to the movies, or out on the town. When I was out with the girls, I forgot about my problems. It was like I was living two lives.

It was time for us ladies to get together for a night out. We went to a local bar for drinks and dancing. I was up on the dance floor with Margaret when a man came over to the table, gave Charlotte an envelope with my name on it, and asked her to give it to me.

When I came back from the dance floor, Charlotte handed me the envelope and said, "This is for you."

I opened the envelope, which was just like the others:

My dearest daughter Rebecca,

I see you are having an enjoyable time dancing on the floor with the ladies at the bar. I just want you to know I will always know where you are at, always. You can't hide from me. Take care of your friends; it would be a shame for something bad to happen to them.

Your father, Fred

I turned to Charlotte. My face was white as a ghost. I shakily asked, "Is he still here?"

She looked around the bar said, "No. Are you okay?"

"Did he say anything to you?"

"Just please give this to Rebecca. Then he handed me the envelope and left."

"What did he look like?"

"Average, brown hair and eyes, 5 feet 7 inches about, and he had a mustache. Who is he?"

"I believe it is my ex-boyfriend who doesn't want it to be over."

"Are you sure you want it over?"

"Yes, he cheated on me."

"I understand."

I had to say something, but the truth was I really didn't know who he was. He claimed to be my biological father, and if that were true, why did he want to hurt anyone I cared for? Usually, fathers protect their children from pain, but he wanted to cause me pain.

Bill has been searching for Fred over the past several years with no success.

I was too scared to go outside in case Fred was out there waiting for me. I knew I wouldn't be able to hear Bill because of the noise, so I texted him that a man gave Charlotte an envelope while I was on the dance floor.

He texted me back. Are you and the ladies, okay?

Yes, but I am scared.

Stay inside the bar, I am on my way, and I will drive all of you home.

Thank you.

I finally had a brief description of what the man looked like, unless he got someone else to deliver the envelope to me, which would be my luck.

Within twenty minutes, Bill arrived at the bar. He pretended he just dropped in for a drink when he noticed me. I introduced him to the ladies and told them he was a friend, which technically that was true. I didn't mention that he was a police officer. I felt the less they knew, the better off they would be.

The ladies invited him to join us, which worked out perfectly. I gave him the letter to read while the ladies and I danced.

When I was on the dance floor, I could see Bill talking to a staff member. I could see that he went back to the table, so I told the ladies I needed a break while they continued to dance.

I asked Bill, "Who were you talking to?"

"The supervisor. I wanted to know if they have a camera in the bar, and they do. He told me I can come back in the morning when the manager is here to view the tape."

For the rest of the night, I only sipped my drink and constantly looked around at any guy that resembled the description that Charlotte gave me. It was last call at the bar, so the ladies ordered another drink.

Bill drove each of my friends' home to ensure they made it home safe.

We were on the way to my house when I looked at Bill. "Do you think you could get a sketch artist to sit down with Charlotte to do a drawing of the man that gave her the envelope? I just want to see if it resembles the Fred Smiths that I have a picture of."

"I know someone. I can talk to him."

"Do you mind asking him?"

"No, I will call him tomorrow."

"Okay, and can you let me know if he is on the tape?"

"Of course, I will."

The next afternoon, I was playing with Abigail when Bill called to tell me there wasn't a clear picture of him. I was bitterly disappointed.

*

It was Monday morning, and we were all sitting by the window for a morning talk session. Some offices have water coolers to talk around, but we had a window. After about twenty minutes, we all went to our desks to start work.

It was about half an hour later when my cell phone rang. "Hi, Bill."

"Hi, my friend will do the sketch for you."

"That is awesome!"

"I just have to tell him the time and place."

"I will talk to Charlotte to see if she will do it, and I will let you know."

"Okay, I will wait for your phone call."

After I hung up, I walked into Charlotte's office. "Can I talk to you?"

"Sure, what can I do for you?"

"Would you be able to describe to a sketch artist what the man looked like that gave you the envelope on Saturday night?"

"Are you sure everything is, okay?"

"Yes, I just want to ensure it isn't my ex-boyfriend."

"I guess, but remember I had a few drinks, so my memory might be a little off."

"That is okay, just do the best you can. Are you free on Monday or Wednesday night?"

"I can do it either night."

"How about Wednesday night you come over to my place, and I will cook us supper."

"That works for me," said Charlotte.

I went back to my desk to call Bill right away. "Charlotte said yes. She is going to come over to my place on Wednesday after work, and I am going to cook supper for us while she talks to your friend."

"I will call him to let me know the time and place."

It seemed like Wednesday would never end. I just wanted to see if I had the right Fred. He knew what I looked like, and I wanted to know for sure what he looked like. Finally, the day was over, and we were on our way to pick up Abigail before going to my apartment.

We were only at my place for about five minutes when the phone rang. It was Bill and his sketch artist friend. "Hi, please come in."

"Logan, this is Charlotte, Rebecca, and her daughter Abigail," said Bill.

"Hi, nice to meet you," he replied.

"How does this work?" asked Charlotte.

"I will ask you questions about his face and make the sketch from the answers," said Logan. "Then I will get you to look at the sketch, so you can tell me if it looks like the guy that you saw at the bar. If something needs to be changed, for example, the hair should be shorter, you just let me know, and I will make the change."

"Okay."

After I gave them something to drink, Bill and I went into the kitchen to get supper started. My apartment wasn't the big, so I could hear Logan and Charlotte talking.

"I am sorry, Bill, do you want something to drink?"

"A glass of Diet Pepsi, please."

"What shape would you say his face was, Charlotte?" asked Logan.

"Oval."

"Tell me what you remember about his face."

"He had short, straight, dark hair, brown eyes, and a mustache."

"Okay, did he wear glasses?"

"No, but he hadn't shaved for a few days."

"Were there any other distinguishing marks on his face or neck such as tattoos, a birthmark, scar etc.?"

"No, not that I remember."

It took about forty-five minutes for the sketch artist to show Charlotte a picture. "Does this look like the man?"

Charlotte looked at the picture and said, "From what I can remember, you know, I was drinking, I believe this is the guy that gave me the envelope."

"Okay, we are done. Rebecca and Bill, you can come into the living room."

When I walked into the living room, I said, "That is perfect timing. Supper is ready."

Logan handed me the sketch. "Thank you for the offer, but I have to be going."

"Okay, thank you for coming over and doing the sketch. It was nice to meet you."

"Logan, I will walk you out. I will be right back," said Bill.

"Charlotte, help yourself to the food," I said.

Bill came back into the apartment to have supper with Charlotte, Abigail, and myself. My daughter kept looking at Charlotte, and when she looked at Abigail, she would quickly look away. It was like a game to my daughter. This was the first time they had met.

After supper, we relaxed for a little while before Charlotte had to go home. I thanked her for talking to Logan.

I went into my bedroom to obtain the picture of Fred Smith that Bill got me so we could compare it to the sketch. I put them both side by side on the kitchen table and stood back.

"To me they look like the same man. What do you think, Bill?"

"I would have to agree with you. I believe we know who the stranger is now."

"Does he look familiar to you?"

"I don't know if he was the man from the mall when I was ten years old. I was shopping with Nancy and my friends when I had to go to the bathroom. When I came out, a man with a ballcap, sunglasses and a beard and mustache was standing there. He gave me the creeps. He knew where I was born, who my parents and siblings were, that my parents died, and I lived with my aunt and uncle. It has to be him!"

"I am going to leave now and let you get Abigail to sleep."

"Thank you for asking Logan to sketch a picture and cleaning the kitchen while I gave Abigail a bath. You are a good friend."

Chapter 35

It was a sunny April morning, and I was on my way to work when I put my foot on the brakes and nothing happened. The car wouldn't stop. There was no indication that the brakes were getting bad, so what was happening?

I know I shouldn't be on the phone while I was driving, but I didn't know what else to do. I picked up my phone, called Bill and frantically said, "Help me! I am putting my foot on the brake, and I am not slowing down. I am going down Green Street, which is one big hill, and I am picking up speed. What do I do?"

"Just keep driving straight. Is there is anyone in front of you?"

"No."

"I am going to radio in for help to be sent to you. I am on my way, just keep on the phone with me."

"Hurry," I cried. "There is a car in front of me now, and I am catching up to them very quickly. What do I do?"

"Are there any cars coming in the lane toward you?"

I veered the car over the yellow line, so I could see. "No."

"Then use the other lane to pass the car."

"Okay…I passed the car." I felt relieved. "I am coming up to another car, so I am going to do the same thing."

"Good idea."

"I can't go into the other lane; there is a steady stream of cars coming toward me! I am getting closer to the car in front of me…there is no time…I am going to drive my car into the ditch."

It all happened so fast. Somehow, I managed to turn the steering wheel so that the back end of the car took most of the impact.

Bill heard the crash through the phone. "Rebecca, hang on, I am on my way. I am calling for help."

Within a few minutes, Bill ran to my door and opened it. "Rebecca, are you okay?"

"Yes, but I can't feel my leg."

"Just stay still until we can get you to the hospital to see what your injuries are."

"Bill, call Suzanne and let her know what happened."

"I will call as soon as you are on your way to the hospital."

Luckily, I could talk and tell the EHS people what was hurting me, so when I arrived at the hospital, they did an ultrasound of my abdomen and x-rayed my legs.

Suzanne arrived at the hospital with Abigail when I was waiting for my test results. We were talking while I was playing with the baby when the doctor walked into the room and said, "You are an incredibly lucky girl. The only injuries you have are a broken leg, three sprained ribs, and a concussion. We are going to keep you for a few days be on the safe side."

"I will keep Abigail for as long as you are in the hospital," said Suzanne. "Do you mind if Bill lets me into your house so I can get a few things for the baby?"

"Yes, of course, you can go into my house. Are you sure about keeping Abigail while I am in the hospital?"

"Yes, I wouldn't have it any other way. I am going to take Abigail home now to feed her lunch and let her have a nap. We will be back this afternoon."

She handed the baby to me so I could give her a hug and kiss goodbye.

After Suzanne left the room, Bill told me that he was having my car towed to the crime lab so they could look at it.

"I just have a funny feeling that this was no accident, but I am hoping I am wrong."

"I have that feeling too."

"I promised Matteo that I would protect you as much as I can. Now, you don't worry and get some rest. Suzanne or I will be here when you wake up."

I just smiled at Bill and closed my eyes.

I woke up from my sleep to the sweet sound of Abigail saying, "Mommy, Mommy." Suzanne was trying to keep her busy so I could rest.

"How are you feeling?" Suzanne asked.

"I am going to be just fine, especially now that I have my family with me."

I told Suzanne about my injuries and that Bill was going to stay with her for the night. She didn't want Bill to stay; she told me she would be fine with the baby. I knew she would be, but I was petrified that the man would try to hurt her or the baby while I was in the hospital.

I pleaded with her, telling her that if I took a turn for the worse, she could come to the hospital without waking up Abigail. Finally, Suzanne agreed to let Bill stay for the night.

Over the following few days, Suzanne would bring Abigail to visit a few times each day. I didn't realize how much I would miss being with my daughter.

The following morning, the doctor came in to examine me and told me that I could go home that afternoon. I had to come back in six weeks to have my cask removed and check my ribs to ensure they healed.

While the doctor was preparing the discharge paperwork, Bill arrived with a clean outfit for me to wear home.

Monday morning, Bill was at my house to drive me to work, since I couldn't drive for six weeks. When I got to work, everyone wanted to know how the accident happened. I told them that I lost control and went into the trees, which was true.

A few days later, when Bill picked me up at the end of the day, he said, "The crime lab finished looking at the brakes on your car, and they were tampered with. The brake line was cut with the intention for the brakes to fail when you tried to use them, causing a crash. I believe it was Fred who did this. He wanted you to die."

"I agree with you. Is there any evidence that Fred cut the brake line, such as his fingerprints?"

"They checked for fingerprints, but no luck. I would suggest that you should put a camera on your car in case Fred tries again. If he does, then we will have the proof we need to arrest him."

"That sounds like a great idea. If I buy one, could you set it up in my car for me?"

"Yes, I will."

"I know this is my problem, not yours. You are trying to keep a promise to a friend, to keep me safe, which you have, and I am very thankful for. However, if you want you can walk away now and stay safe. I don't want what happened to Matteo to be your destiny. I couldn't bear that, and the longer you are around me, the more you are at risk."

"I intended to keep that promise. I will try to protect you and Abigail for the rest of my life."

"You are a loyal friend, but if you change your mind, I will understand."

He just smiled at me and gave me a hug.

*

Six weeks had gone by, and I couldn't wait to get the cast off. I missed driving and being independent.

I was grateful to have such wonderful friends that helped me out a lot over the past six weeks. Between Suzanne, Bill, Charlotte, and Margaret, they helped me get my groceries, cleaned my house, drove me to and from work, and took care of Abigail.

"How are you feeling?" asked the doctor.

"I am doing great. My ribs don't hurt anymore, and I can't wait to get this cast off."

"I am going to take the cast off, then we will take an X-ray and go from there."

It felt good when the cast came off; it was very heavy, and now I could scratch my leg. The doctor came in with the X-ray and said, "Your leg looks great. Now I want you to stand up and put some weight on it. Does that hurt?"

"No, it just feels weak."

"That is normal due to the lack of use in the muscle over the past several weeks. If you have any issues with the leg, then come back, otherwise take care."

I thanked the doctor and walked out of the hospital.

A few days later, when I got home, I checked the mail. As soon as I saw the envelope, I knew who it was from:

My dearest daughter Rebecca,

How are you feeling? I am so glad that your leg has healed. As your father, I felt you had to be punished for going to the police. It wouldn't take too much to intentionally cut the brake line. It would be a shame if you were driving with Abigail in the car and the brakes failed again. Both of you mayn't be as lucky to survive the crash.

Your father, Fred

As always, I called Bill immediately. He came over right away to read the letter.

"I knew it was him! The only people that knew about the brakes were the crime lab, you, and me. The accident never made the newspapers."

"You are right. I am going to get the letter and envelope check just in case. You never know, he may get careless, and we could catch a break. Also, I will talk to my boss to see if we can release the sketch of Fred Smith on the news as a suspect in a crime. We may get lucky, and someone might recognize him."

"I am going to give a picture of Fred to my super just in case he shows up here."

"Also, give her my cell number and tell her to call me right away, night or day."

"Okay, I will."

After Bill left, I went downstairs to my super's apartment to give her the picture.

Every time I got one of these letters, it put me on edge for a few weeks. All I wanted to know is why? Just because my mom wouldn't leave her husband for this man. Was that my fault?

A few days later, Bill informed me that his boss was going to release Fred Smith's sketch to the news and issue a warrant for his arrest across Canada.

Chapter 36

Abigail was reminding me every day that her fourth birthday was coming up. I think she was excited. I gave her the option could go out for supper or have supper at home. She decided we would go out to supper to her favorite restaurant, which was McDonalds. Suzanne and Bill came along with us to celebrate her big day.

After we ate our meal, Bill took Abigail into the playroom to play with the toys while Suzanne and I talked. I had to deal with a lot over the years with my family getting hurt, having to move away from them, and the death of my husband and child, but I wasn't ready to hear what Suzanne had to say.

She told me that she had stomach cancer and only had a few months left to live. I just stared into space and tried to digest what she just told me. After a few minutes, I took her hand, squeezed it, and let her know I was there for her.

"What can I do to help you?"

"There is nothing anyone can do. The cancer spread into my liver and lungs."

I tried to stay strong for her, but I couldn't stop the tears from coming down my face. In my eyes, Suzanne was my mom, and I wasn't ready to lose her.

She told me that Bill already knew. He was the one that took her to the doctor's appointment.

Once the lump in my throat went away, and I could talk, I said, "I want you to come and live with me, so I can take care of you. I will find another babysitter for Abigail."

The truth is that she was all alone, and I didn't want her to spend her last few months alive by herself.

At first, she wasn't on board with moving in since she didn't want to be a burden on me. I said that is what family does, take care of each other. I told her it would be my honor to take care of her. I knew one thing: I would have been worse off if I never met her.

I could see the relief in her face when I said, "Okay then, it is settled. You are moving in with us this weekend."

Bill helped me pack up Suzanne's place and move her things into my apartment. Suzanne was on a year-to-year lease, which just renewed last month. I explained to her landlord the situation with her health, and he agreed to let her out of the lease.

That night, after Suzanne and Abigail went to bed, Bill told me that his partner's wife ran a daycare from their house, and he could see if she had any openings. I thought that would be perfect for this year. The following year, I could put her in the Excel program at her school.

My only concern was putting her and the other children at risk by taking Abigail there. Bill sat down with his partner and his wife to explain my situation. He didn't tell them everything, just what they needed to know, but he did give them a picture of Fred as a precaution.

In a few days, Bill took me over to his partner's house to introduce me to his wife, Mary. We talked for about an hour, and she showed me around the daycare, which was exceptionally clean. She gave me her price and told me that there was one spot left, which I could have.

The price fit into my budget. Also, Abigail was old enough to tell me if something was wrong.

I accepted the spot and asked if I could start taking Abigail next week. She smiled and said, "Of course."

Over the next few months, Suzanne was getting weaker and weaker. She tried her hardest to fight, but the cancer spread throughout her body. The doctor told me that she was going to die any day.

I didn't want her to die alone, so I asked my boss, Jamie, for a leave of absence from work. After I explained the situation, he agreed the best thing for me was to be with my mom.

As each day went by, I could see her slipping away. The next few weeks were hard, not knowing if today was going to be the last time I got to talk to her. When she was having a nap, I would go in to check on her, and she looked so peaceful.

I will never forget that day. It was a Thursday morning when she reached for my hand. I squeezed it tight to let her know that she wasn't alone. She smiled at me and took her last breath. I kept holding her hand for about half an hour. I don't know why, but I couldn't let go. I guess I wasn't ready to say goodbye.

I stood up, wiped the tears off my face, kissed her head, and then called the doctor to let him know she had died. The doctor told me he would make the necessary calls.

I thought that since I knew she was dying, it would be easier for me when it happened, but I was wrong.

When her body was removed from the apartment, I called Bill to let him know she passed away.

Then I went over to the babysitter's house to get Abigail. When we arrived home, I sat her down and explained to her that her grandmother, Suzanne, had died. I put it in words that she would understand, but she was only four years old and didn't get what was going on.

A few days later, we had a service at her church for her friends and us. I couldn't believe it — the church was packed. I never quite realized how important she was to the community until I prepared her obituary. Not only did she volunteer at the shelter where I meet her, but she also volunteered at the Children's Hospital reading books and playing games with the children and at the local food bank.

Some of the people that she helped from the shelter and children's hospital were there to pay their respects. I talked to a few of them. They said they didn't know where they would be today if she didn't come into their lives. It put a smile on my face to know that a lot of lives were better because of her.

A few days later, I was reading the cards from her funeral, and I came across one that sent shivers down my back. It was in an envelope with just my name on it:

My dearest daughter Rebecca,

I am so sorry for your loss, Rebecca. I know Suzanne was like a second mom to you. The service was a wonderful celebration of her life. Do you ever wonder what your funeral would be like? I will try to make it as tasteful as possible.

Your father, Fred

    Bill came over that evening for supper to see if we needed anything. After Abigail went to bed, I showed him the letter.
    "Why do I have to die!"
    "Rebecca, look at me. I am going to do everything possible to keep you safe and alive. Please trust me."
    For the remainder of the night, I just sat on the couch and watched TV. I didn't say anything.
    A week later, Suzanne's lawyer called me at work to set up an appointment, since Abigail was in her will. He came over to my apartment to tell me that she left some money in a trust fund for Abigail's secondary education. For her to access the funds, I had to sign for the release, and the check had to be made out to the university or college.

*

Today was the first-year anniversary of Suzanne's death. After I picked Abigail up from daycare, we took flowers to put on her grave. Afterward, we went out for supper and bought a thank-you gift for Mary, since this was Abigail's last week at daycare.
    She was going to start primary next Thursday. The past five years just seemed to fly by. She was ready to go, but I didn't know if I was ready to let go. I decided to take the first day of school off and take her myself. That way I could meet her teacher and the

Excel leaders. I could also have a look around the school to make me feel better.

When we arrived at the school, we went into the Excel room and meet the leaders. They showed us around the classroom and told Abigail where she could put her school bag and jacket when it was cold outside. About twenty minutes later, the school bell rang for the children to line up in the hallway by their classrooms.

I went into her classroom with her to meet the teacher and look at her desk. After a couple of minutes, she told me that I could leave, but I wasn't ready. She was settling in very nicely, and I was the one having a tough time letting go.

Before I left the school, I had a meeting with the Excel leaders and the principal to show them a picture of Fred.

"If you see this man, call 911 right away and lock the doors," I said. "He has been stalking me for a while but hasn't harmed Abigail. Just in case he shows up here, I want you to know what he looks like. Please share this picture with the rest of the teachers."

"Do the police know about this?" asked the principal.

"Yes," I replied.

"Okay, I will ensure that all the teachers see this picture."

"Thank you," I said.

*

The fall went by so fast, the next thing I knew it was the night of Abigail's Christmas concert. Bill came with me, and we were sitting five rows from the stage when her class came out. I remember her putting her hand over her eyes to try to find us. We stood up for a minute so she could see where we were.

The class was singing "Frosty the Snowman" and "Jingle Bells." She would sing a few words, yawn, sing a few more words, and yawn again. This went on the whole time her class was singing, but in her defense, it was 7:30 p.m., which was passed her bedtime.

I just found out recently from Bill that his wife had passed at Christmas time. They tried to have children, but it didn't work out for them. He had no siblings, and his parents were deceased.

He would spend Christmas with Matteo and his mom until she passed away. After that, Matteo and Bill didn't want to celebrate the Christmas season.

I asked Bill if he would like to spend Christmas with Abigail and me instead of being alone. He agreed.

It was Christmas Eve, Bill, Abigail, and I just got back from driving around looking at the Christmas lights. Abigail was so excited for Santa Claus to come she was bouncing off the walls. It was time for her to go to bed.

I was going to wait a little while to ensure that she was asleep.

A few minutes later, Abigail yelled from her bedroom, "Did Santa Claus come?"

I chuckled to myself. "No, he can't come until you are asleep."

"But I am sleeping, Mommy."

This time Bill and I couldn't help but laugh. "Abigail, if you are sleeping, then you can't talk."

"But I really am sleeping."

This went on for about half an hour, then it was quiet. I went down to her room just to make sure that she was asleep before I started to put together her toys. This is what Christmas is all about: the children's excitement.

*

It was now the end of June, and school was out for the summer. Bill came over for supper to give Abigail a present. While she was playing with her new toy, Bill informed me that he had an address for Fred Smith.

"How did you get his address?"

"I went to the Register of Motor Vehicles, showed them my police badge, and told them I needed an address for this man because he was a suspect in a crime."

Right away, I wanted to go over to confront Fred and ask him why me? What did I or my mom do that was so terrible, he wanted to hurt the people that I loved?

"That is great news. Can you watch Abigail while I go and pay Fred a visit? I want this to be over with now."

"I know you do, but I am not letting you go over there by yourself. I am coming with you, so I can call for backup in case we need it."

I was relieved that Bill wanted to come. I was really scared to go by myself.

"Let me see if Joleen, the lady up the hallway, can babysit Abigail for a few hours. I will be right back."

About ten minutes later, Joleen loved to talk, I returned to my apartment to let Bill know that she would be happy to look after Abigail.

On our way over to Fred's place, I was so nervous, I couldn't even speak. We arrived at the building and luckily someone was coming out, so we just went in. I knocked on his apartment door, but there was no answer, so I knocked again.

As the door opened, I got more butterflies in my stomach, but it wasn't Fred, so I said, "Is Fred here?"

"No, he moved out two days ago. Who are you?" asked the superintendent.

"I am an old school friend of Fred's," said Bill. "We just reconnected a few weeks ago, and he invited me over for a visit. Did he say where he was going, or did he leave a forwarding address?"

"He just told me that he was leaving the country to deal with a family emergency," replied the superintendent.

The super opened the door so we could come into the unit. From what I could see, he just had the basic furniture.

"What about his stuff?" I asked.

"He told me that I could give it away or sell it. You can look around and take whatever you want. It will be less for me to deal with," answered the super.

Bill looked around the living room, bathroom, and kitchen, while I went into the bedroom. When I opened the closet door, there was something that looked like a piece of paper on the floor that caught my eye. I bent down to pick it up to see it was the back of a picture. When I turned the picture over, I couldn't believe what I saw. I immediately put it in my purse.

After a few minutes, we thanked the super and left the building.

On the way home in the car, I said, "We have the right Fred."

"How can you be so sure?"

"I found this picture on the closet floor. He must have dropped it and didn't notice when he was packing his things."

"Were there any other photos?"

"No."

A tear started to come down my face when I looked at my mom. It had been a long time since I saw her picture, and I missed her a lot.

"Maybe he is telling the truth that you are his daughter."

"Just because my mom knew him doesn't mean he is my father. My mom and he might have only been friends. I am glad that he's gone. I can have a normal life that doesn't require me to look over my shoulder all the time. I just wished my family members were with me."

"I am going to continue to search for Fred, so when I find him, I can bring him to justice for the murders he did commit. That way you can have some closure."

"Okay but please be careful."

We arrived back at my apartment to see Joleen and Abigail playing a game. They were laughing and having so much fun. After the game was over, I tried to give her some money for babysitting, but she wouldn't take it.

After Abigail went to bed, I let out a loud sigh of relief that it was finally over. I was so happy.

Chapter 37

Over the next six years, life was simple but great. Go to work, come home, ensure Abigail's homework was done, plan family vacations, and enjoy the weekends. It was like we were a normal family again. It took me a few years until I stopped looking over my shoulder all the time.

My daughter was going into grade 7 in September and informed me that she wanted to come home on her own from school. I thought about it and decided it was time to give her some independence, especially since I didn't have to worry about a crazy man stalking me.

Abigail had to stay at school for lunch, since she didn't have enough time to come home, eat lunch, and return to school before the bell rang.

It was a week before school started when Abigail and I were out shopping for clothes, school supplies etc. We were having a wonderful mother daughter day.

After I pulled into the parking lot of our building, Abigail asked for the mail key. She loved to check the mail for me.

"What is in the mail today?"

"The phone bill, power bill, a letter for you, and an envelope for me!"

She loved opening mail, so occasionally I would buy a card and send it to her.

After we went into the apartment, she handed me the mail and opened her card. She smiled from ear to ear. "Aw, thanks, Mom."

"You are welcome."

I sat on the couch and opened the phone and power bill to see how much they were. Then I saw the envelope with just my name on it, and right away my heart started to pound, and my hands were sweaty. I frantically opened it:

My dearest daughter Rebecca,

How long has it been? I believe it has been over six years since I sent my last letter to you. I have been out of the country handling some family business. I saw Abigail and you shopping at the mall this afternoon. She is growing into a beautiful young lady. It would be a shame if something bad happened to her.

Your father, Fred

I was sitting on the couch, staring into space, when Abigail came out of her room. "Mom, are you okay? Your face is white as a ghost."

"What?"

"Mom, are you alright?"

I shuffled the papers so she couldn't see the letter. "Yes, I am not feeling good."

"Can I go to the movies with Jennifer and her family? They are going to pick me up and bring me home after the movies."

"Okay, bring me my purse, and I will give you some money. When are they picking you up?"

"In about an hour."

I called Bill right away asked him if he could come over in about an hour.

Abigail left to go to the movies. Within a couple of minutes, there was a knock on my door. I went over and looked through the peephole and saw Bill.

"How did you get into the building?"

"Abigail let me in on her way out."

"It isn't over!"

"What isn't over?"

"This letter was in my mail today."

I handed the letter to Bill.

I was so overwhelmed with worry that I started to cry. Bill squeezed my hand. "We will get through this."

"What am I going to do? I already told Abigail that she could walk home after school by herself. What if he hurts her on the way home? I couldn't handle burying another child; that would destroy me."

Bill was quiet, and I could tell by his face that he was thinking when he said, "Does the lady up the hallway, Joleen, still teach at the elementary school?"

"I think so, why?"

"You could ask her if she would mind driving Abigail back and forth to school, since the elementary school is next door to the junior high school."

"It would solve the problem of her walking home by herself. At least that way I'll know she will be home safely, and if she needs anything she could go to Joleen for help."

After Bill left, I sat on the couch and watched some TV while I was waiting for Abigail to get home. I thought, that would put Joleen at risk without her knowing— was that fair?

Abigail arrived home after the movie, and I said, "How was the movie?"

"It was good."

I remembered not long ago when I would ask Abigail a question and I would get a half-hour detailed description. I guessed this was the start of the teenage years.

"I was thinking about asking Joleen if she would drive you back and forth to school. What do you think?"

"Cool."

*

A few days later I ran into Joleen in the laundry room and asked, "Do you still teach at Astral Elementary School?"

"Yes, why?"

"I was wondering if Abigail could catch a ride with you in the morning and after school?"

"Yes. I can't believe that Abigail is going into Grade 7 in September. Where did the time go?"

"I know, she is growing up fast. Are you sure you don't mind?"

"No, I am going there anyway, and it would be nice to have someone to talk with on the way."

"There is just one more thing. If you see this man around the school or the building, please call 911 right away."

"Yes, of course. Who is he?"

"It started a long time ago; he was stalking me but then stopped for six years. The other day I thought I saw him, so I am just being cautious."

"It mightn't even have been him."

"I am sure you are right. I am just being an overprotective mom. Thanks."

Chapter 38

It seemed like I blinked, and the next thing I knew it was the middle of August and we were packing for our shopping trip down to Bangor. For my daughter, the trip was all about buying new clothes, purses, and shoes, but for me it was all about the food.

I loved going to Bangor to eat at the different restaurants such as Denny's, IHOP, and Olive Garden.

It was Friday morning at six thirty when the alarm went off to get up and head for Bangor. Normally, it took me calling Abigail two or three times before she got up for school, but today she jumped out of bed the first time I called her. I guess she was excited about going on a shopping trip.

We arrived in Bangor at 1:30 pm but it was too early to check into our hotel, so we went off to the mall to start shopping. We shopped for hours and hours, buying shoes, clothes, and having fun. We were getting tired, so we went to check into the hotel for a rest. It had an indoor swimming pool, so we went down for a swim. The remainder of the evening we decided to just relax and start out first thing in the morning.

We left the hotel right after breakfast to go to my daughter's favorite outlet store, Coach. This whole trip was all about getting a new designer purse and some shoes. Anything else we bought was a bonus. Of course, I had to get a new designer purse, since they had 70% off; now I knew where she got it from.

We also bought a few tops, pants, more shoes, sneakers, winter coats, and boots. My daughter was a natural at this shopping. Tonight, we were going to my favorite restaurant in Bangor, Olive Garden, then back to the hotel to relax. I tell you shopping is a hard job, but someone must do it.

That morning, while we were eating breakfast, I asked my daughter to check her list to see what other stores we had left to shop at. Today was our last day of shopping, and tomorrow morning when we woke up, we were going to pack the car and head home.

When we got back to the hotel that night, we did up our list of what we bought for the border inspectors. You were only allowed to buy $800.00 worth of merchandise to take back over the border. I decided to bring an empty suitcase to take the price tags off some clothes and pretend we brought them with us from home. Everyone that I knew who went shopping across the border did that little trick.

It took us three trips to get everything down to car. I think we went a little bit overboard with the shopping. It was now time to check out and go home. We arrived back at home midafternoon. We finally got everything up to the apartment and just put it on the living room floor.

I didn't feel like cooking, so I ordered a pizza while we unpacked everything. When it arrived, we just relaxed and watched TV for the remainder of the evening. That was when I noticed the picture above the TV was moved over a few inches. I must have moved that a few months ago and forgot. My daughter was still on summer vacation for a few days, so she could sleep in.

I was putting on one of my new outfits for work when I thought my pearl earnings would finish my outfit perfectly. I opened the second drawer of my jewelry box, but I could only find one. I could have sworn both were there. I searched all over my bedroom but couldn't find the other one. It was getting late, and I had to go to work, so I just put on another pair.

When I arrived at work, everyone wanted to know what I bought. I showed them my new outfit, shoes, and purse that I had with me. I told them all about our trip, especially where we had eaten.

It was the end of the day, and I was glad to go home. Sometimes it was hard being a single parent. As soon as I got in the door, Abigail would start to complain about her day and what ticked her off. I wouldn't even have a chance to get my coat or shoes off. I loved my daughter very much, but just occasionally, I would have loved to have five minutes to myself when I got home.

The drama between girls during junior high is unbelievable. I tried to remember back to when I was her age, but my circumstances were different, and I had to grow up very quickly.

People used to tell me the hardest time was when they are little, but I disagree. I believe the toughest time is when they are in junior high.

The next day in the lunchroom, I asked my boss, Jamie, and Grace, who did accounts payable, how they handled the teenaged years with their daughters. I guess I was trying to get some ideas.

"It is a challenging time to get through, but you will make it," Jamie said. "What helped for us was we just concentrated on getting through one day at a time."

"I kept telling myself that granddaughters will be my revenge," Grace said.

We all started to laugh.

"It is almost like a switch goes off in their heads, and my sweet little girl changed into this devil," I said. "She has become sassy, a know-it-all, cranky, believes I know nothing about anything and so dramatic about everything."

"Of course, you don't know anything; you are just her mom in her eyes, and you have never been through it. Hang in there, she will return to a normal young adult in about three more years," replied Jamie.

"You say I have to deal with this for three years!"

"If you ever need to talk or just vent, I am here to listen," Grace said. "I know what you are going through. I went through it twice."

"I don't know if I can make it through once, and you did it twice. You deserve a medal."

"I am so glad I had a boy," said Charlotte. "There isn't as much drama."

The rest of the day went by fast, and I was glad to get out of there for a few days.

As soon as I walked through the apartment door, my daughter came running out of her room. "Can I go to the movies with my friends?"

"Who are you going with?"

"Laura and Robin."

"What movie are you going to see?"

"The new comedy one that just came out."

She only answered the question and didn't give me any more information. I had to ask a million questions.

"What time does the movie start?"

"It's at 6:45 to 8:45 p.m."

"Okay. I will drive you and pick you up when the movie is over."

I was glad that she wanted to go out, since that would give me a couple of hours to myself. All I wanted to do was watch TV and not have to think about anything. I guess I wanted to escape my life for a few hours.

I just got back from taking the kids to the movie theater, and now the next couple of hours were mine to relax. I could never completely relax because I was always thinking about Fred and why he wanted to hurt me.

*

A few weeks before Halloween, my daughter informed me that she was too old for me to take her trick-or-treating. She was going to go with her friends. Now, most parents would be glad to stay at home where it was warm and where the treats were, but for me it was another worry. I knew I couldn't follow her without her noticing me, so I asked Bill what I should do.

"You have to let her go and have fun with her friends, or she will get suspicious. You know she is getting older and smarter every day."

"I know, but how can I protect her from Fred?"

"I will follow her."

"Oh, yeah, that won't look suspicious if you are following a couple of teens. The neighbors will definitely call the police on you."

"Not if I am with a couple of children."

"Whose?"

"My friend's son and daughter."

"What do you mean?"

Bill said, "He is a nurse and has to work the night shift. He tried to get it off but couldn't, so I told him I would take the kids out trick-or-treating then take them over to his mom's house for the night. I could ask Abigail if she wouldn't mind if I tagged along with her and her friends. What do you think?"

"That might work, do you mind?"

"No, I promised you I will do my best to protect your daughter, and I meant it."

On Halloween night I was sitting on the couch watching TV, waiting for my daughter to finish getting ready, when Bill arrived with his friend's children. The boy was dressed up as Spider-Man and the girl was a princess. Then Abigail walked into the living room all dressed up as a witch. The three of them looked amazing, so I had to take their picture.

"Do we have to wait for the kids at each house? They will slow us down," Abigail asked.

I thought she had a point. "No, but before you go to the next street, let Bill know where you are going, deal?"

She let out a sigh. "Okay."

"How long are you going out for?"

"Probably an hour or so."

"Okay, have fun, but please be careful."

"I will."

I decided to go downstairs and help hand out candy to the kids that came to the building. I loved seeing the little kids all dressed up on Halloween; they looked so cute.

We didn't get a lot of kids, since our building was between a bank and a church, so if you didn't know it was there, you could miss it. I always said I had the best place to live, money on one side and the good lord on the other.

Most of the kids that came to our building were the grandkids of one of the tenants, which meant I had more treats for myself. I would sacrifice my waistline to help eat the candy; someone had to do it.

Bill, the two kids, and my daughter walked through the door all looking cold and tired. We went upstairs, and I put on the hot chocolate to warm everyone up.

Normally, Abigail would be after me to check her candy right away so she could eat some, but not this year.

"Abigail, a penny for your thoughts?" I asked.

"A man came up to me and told me to give this letter to you. He knew my name, and I asked how he knew me, but he didn't answer. He just stood there staring at me."

She handed me an envelope, and when I turned it over, the only thing on it was my name. I quickly turned it over, hoping that she didn't see my face. Bill could tell by my panicked expression that something was wrong.

I had bought some candy for me to have as a treat, so I gave some to Bill's friend's daughter and son while we talked to Abigail.

"Is that why you came back to walk with me?" asked Bill.
"Yes. He scared me."
"What did he look like?" I asked.
"He was dressed up like a clown."
"What did you tell your friends?"

"I told them that I wasn't feeling good and for them to continue without me."

"You did the right thing," I answered.

"He knew my name. Who is he and what does he want?"

At that moment, I didn't know what to say. I was scared to tell her the truth, but deep down I knew I had to.

I took a deep breath, let it out, and said, "I am not sure who he is, but he goes by the name of Fred and claims to be my father. All I know is that he wants to hurt me for something that my mom did before she died."

"That is insane. What did Nanny do to make anyone want to hurt her? Everyone loved Suzanne."

"Suzanne wasn't my biological mother. She helped me out when I needed it."

"I don't understand. Where are your parents?"

"They died was I was a young girl. I went to live with my aunt and her family, but some of them started to get hurt. I received a letter when I was sixteen years old from a stranger who told me if I didn't leave my aunt's house, someone would die. I couldn't take that chance, so I left. I had no job, money, and nowhere to stay, so I went to a shelter, and that was where I meet Suzanne. She helped me find a job and get an apartment."

"Why did she help you?"

"She had a daughter that died, and I reminded Suzanne of her. I guess we both needed each other."

"I thought that Suzanne was your mom."

"That is what I wanted you to believe. I loved her as if she was my mom, and she loved you very much."

"I know that. Do you know what your mom did to make this man want to hurt you?"

"I have no idea. I tried over the years to find out why. All I knew was that I had to protect you as much as possible, but with you getting older and wanting more freedom, it was hard."

"That is why you always wanted me to call you as soon as I got home."

"Yes."

"I didn't realize. I thought you were an overprotective mom."

"I know, but I believe the man that talked to you today is the same person that wants to hurt me. Here is a picture of him. If you see him call my cell, Bill, or 911 right away."

"I am scared. What if he comes after me?"

"I am going to do everything in my power to protect you. I take a self-defense class every Tuesday and Thursday night, which shows me how I can protect myself if someone tries to attack me."

"Can I take them too?"

"I was hoping you would want to. We will sign you up this Tuesday night."

After Bill left to take the children home, I gave her a big hug. I could tell tonight shook her up, and she needed it. After a few minutes, she went into the bathroom to remove her makeup while I went through her candy.

She ate some of her treats while we watched TV, since it was Friday night, and we didn't have to wake up early the next day.

Bill came back with a pizza, but Abigail was full of her candy. I had some pizza, and after about hour later she went to bed.

After I was sure she was asleep, I opened the envelope:

My dearest daughter Rebecca,

After all the losses you have been through with family members, I am surprised you let my granddaughter go trick-or-treating without adult supervision. You never know when some crazy person in a costume, let's say a clown, approaches and hurts her.

Could you live with yourself knowing you didn't protect her from harm?

Your father, Fred

    Right away, my hands started to shake, and I couldn't talk. Bill took the paper from my hands and read the note.
"How can I protect her?"
"You can't be with her twenty-four hours a day, 365 days a year. Rebecca, look at me, you are doing everything you can to protect her. Joleen is going to take her back and forth to school. When you go out with the girls, I can come over and stay with Abigail until you get home, if you like."
"Now that we know Fred is here in Toronto, I am going to continue to look for him."
"He talked to her tonight and could have killed her! I couldn't live with myself if she dies too."
"But he didn't hurt her; he just wanted to scare you."
"Well, if that was his mission, he accomplished it. I am scared. I should report this to the police."
    The following morning, I called the police to report the incident. An officer came over to the apartment to talk to Abigail about the clown who talked to her. Since she couldn't identify the person in the costume, there was nothing the police could do.

Chapter 39

It was the end of February when Charlotte decided it was time for a lady's night. At first, they wanted to go on Tuesday night, but I told them I had other plans. I didn't want them to know that Abigail and I took self-defense classes on Tuesday, since they would ask a lot of questions.

It was agreed that we would go out on next Monday night for dinner at Swiss Chalet and then go to the early movie. Bill came over to the house while I was out with the girls so Abigail wouldn't be by herself.

After supper, we drove to the theater, and the lot was full, so I had to park at the end of the lot. Thank goodness, this winter had been a mild one with lots of rain instead of snow.

On our way out of the theater, we couldn't stop talking about how funny the movie was as we headed straight for the bathroom. When I came out, Charlotte was waiting for me while Margaret and Patty were outside having a smoke.

We went outside and walked to our cars while we talked with the other ladies about our favorite parts of the movie. We were at the car when a guy bumped into me. It all happened very quickly; the next thing I knew I could feel a sharp pain in my stomach and fell to the ground.

Charlotte screamed, "Rebecca!"

I touched my stomach when my hand felt the knife and yelled, "I was stabbed."

People rushed over to see what was going on, and the guy disappeared into the crowd.

I could hear Patty on the phone with 911. "My friend has been stabbed in the parking lot of the theatre, please hurry."

"Is the knife still in the wound," asked the 911 operator.

"Yes, it is."

"Put pressure on the wound but don't remove the knife to slow down the bleeding until the ambulance arrives."

Margaret put her hand on my stomach and pushed on the wound, trying not to move the knife. "I am sorry if this hurts, Rebecca."

Charlotte kept asking me questions about the movie. She wanted to keep me awake.

I heard Charlotte asking them, "What hospital are you taking her to?"

The ambulance attendant replied, "Toronto General Hospital."

Charlotte told me she would call Bill right away to let him know what happened.

I was in a lot of pain, and all I could do was nod.

When I arrived at the hospital, the doctor did an ultrasound of my abdomen to see what organs the knife hit. It penetrated my abdominal cavity and hit the liver. The doctor informed me that I would need emergency surgery right away to repair my wounds.

The next thing I could recall was waking up in the recovery room. The doctor came to see me and noticed that I was pale.

"You have to keep arms down by your side," he said. "Every time you curl them up, your blood pressure plummets."

"I can't get warm."

"I will get you another blanket and see if that warms you up, but you have to promise me you will keep your arms down by your side."

As soon as he put the other blanket on me, I started to warm up, and the color in my face came back. He was relieved and told the nurses that I could go to a room.

Within a half hour, Abigail and Bill walked into my room.

"Mom, are you okay?"

"Yes, I am just tired and in some pain."

"Rebecca, the girls are here. They want to see you before going home. Are you up for it?"

"Okay, but just for a little bit."

Bill went out to the waiting room to show the girls to the room.

"Did any of you see the guy?"

"It happened so quickly that I didn't notice you were stabbed until you fell to the ground," said Patty.

The other girls said the same thing.

Charlotte said, "Rebecca, let us know if you need anything, and I will let our boss know in the morning what is going on."

"Okay. Thank you for coming."

The girls gave me a hug then went home.

"Did Fred do this to you?" asked Abigail.

"I am not sure, since I didn't get a look at him."

But deep down inside I knew it was him.

"What about cameras outside of the theater? I am sure they would have them, and maybe it could show us who he is," asked Abigail.

"That is a good suggestion, Abigail, and I am sure the police will talk to the theater," said Bill. "It is getting late, and your mom needs her rest. We should go now."

"Who is going to stay with me tonight?" asked Abigail.

"I will sleep on your couch to ensure you are safe," replied Bill.

"Okay. I will be back tomorrow, Mom, and I love you."

"I love you too honey, and I look forward to seeing you tomorrow."

I was glad they left, since I was having a tough time staying awake.

Bill made a deal with Abigail that she could go and visit me in the morning but go to school in the afternoon.

"Mom, how are you feeling?"

"I am feeling better now that you are here. In a few days, I will be as good as new."

"I am glad."

Later in the morning, the doctor came into the room to check on me. "How are you feeling today?"

"Good, a bit sore."

"You will be sore for a few days until the stitches heal. Rest for today, then tomorrow we will get you up walking around."

"Abigail, would you do me a favor and go downstairs to get us a drink of pop and a chocolate bar?" I asked. "I believe we deserve a little treat today."

After Abigail left the room I asked, "Bill, do you have any leads?"

"No, the guy wore gloves, so there were no prints on the knife. We talked to the theater; they do have a camera, but it only shows a few hundred feet in front of the theater. Since the attack happened at the far end of the parking lot, it was out of the camera's view, so we couldn't obtain a picture. I am sorry."

"It was worth a chance."

"I believe it relates to the letters. I just have this feeling."

"If he wants me dead, why doesn't he just shoot me in the head to get it over? Did the ladies get a look at the guy?"

"No, the guy had his head down texting on his phone, he wore black jacket, hat, and pants. They didn't even know you were stabbed until he was gone. It is a game to him. He wants to torture you by having you on guard on the time, not knowing when or where he will strike."

"I am just getting tired of always having to look over my shoulder. I want to live a normal life."

Abigail came back into the room and gave me my pop and chocolate bar.

About thirty-five minutes later, the nurse came into the room. "Rebecca, it's time for you to get up and walk around."

"Abigail, say goodbye to your mom. It's time for you to go to school," said Bill.

She wasn't happy with Bill, but she did go to school.

That night, Bill brought Abigail back to the hospital to visit with me.

The following day, Abigail's school was closed for an in-service, so Bill brought her to the hospital to spend the day with me.

It was around mid-morning when the doctor came back into to check on me. "Have you been up out of bed yet today?"

"I did get up and use the washroom with the help of my daughter."

"How did you feel?"

"I felt a little dizzy."

"That is normal. I will have the nurses get you up and walk around the unit to see how you do. If everything goes well, you can be discharged tomorrow. I will be back to check on you."

"Thank you."

It was early afternoon and Abigail was reading me a story when the nurse came into my room and said, "Abigail, your mom needs to have a sleep to get better, so you can go out to the family room and watch TV. I will come and get you when she wakes up."

At first, I thought it was a clever idea but then realized that Fred could come into the hospital and get her. At least if she was in my room, if Fred tried to get her, she could scream, and I would wake up.

"She can stay her while I sleep. Honey, can you please read your book while I rest?"

"Yes, I will be quiet."

I slept for two hours, and when I woke up Bill was just entering the room.

"You are done work early?" Abigail asked.

"Yes, I took a few hours of vacation time and came over to see how you two we are doing."

"I am doing good, and Mom just woke up from her a nap."

"Good, who wants supper?"

"I am hungry, how about you, Mom?"

"I could eat something. What do you have in mind?"

"How about Subway?" replied Bill.

"That is perfect. Abigail, can you go with Bill to have a break from the hospital?"

"Sure."

When Bill and Abigail were out getting supper, they stopped at the store and picked up a deck of cards. After we ate, we played a few games of crazy eights.

In a little while, the nurse came into my room to inform Abigail and Bill visiting hours were over and they had to leave for the night.

When I woke the next morning, Bill was sitting there playing a game on his phone. He noticed I was wake and said, "How are you feeling today?"

"I am feeling better but can't wait until I get home to get my comfy clothes on."

"When I dropped Abigail off at school this morning, I promised her I would pick her up early today. That way she can come with me to take you home from the hospital."

"I would like that very much."

Later that afternoon, the doctor signed the papers to discharge me. I couldn't wait until I got home.

On the way up to the apartment, I checked the mail. There was only one envelope with my name on it. Right away, Bill and I knew it was from Fred.

"Who is the envelope for?" asked Abigail.

"It is for me," I replied.

I tried to disguise my voice so she couldn't tell that I was scared, but it didn't work.

"Is that another letter from Fred?"

I wouldn't answer right away.

"Don't lie to me. I am almost fourteen years old, and I can tell when you are hiding something from me," said Abigail.

"Fair enough, from now on I will be honest with you. Yes, it is a letter, and I believe it is from Fred," I replied.

When we went into the apartment, I opened the envelope and read the letter out loud.

My dearest daughter Rebecca,

It seems that you have made a full recovery from the stabbing. You never know when dreadful things are going to happen to you, so please be careful.

Your father, Fred

"Mom, he is threatening to hurt you."
"I know."
"Bill, you are the police, arrest him."
"It isn't that easy. I can't find him, and I can't arrest him without proof that he did something against the law."
"But Mom was stabbed a few days ago, and in the letter, he threatens her."
"He did threaten your mom, but there is no evidence that he hurt her. The knife had no prints on it, and the camera couldn't get a picture of the attacker," replied Bill.
"What about your friends, Mom, did they get a look at him?"
"No, the person was wearing a hoodie and had sunglasses on. It was dark, and it happened so fast," I said.
"That sucks," said Abigail.
"You took the words right out of my mouth," I said.

Chapter 40

I had been working at Sara's Furniture for several years now and was ready for more responsibilities, so I decided to talk to Jamie to see if there were any opportunities for me. At that moment, I realized that I wasn't going to progress any further with this organization, so I decided to look for a new job with more responsibilities.

That night I looked on the job site and found a listing for a property accountant at Matheson Realty, the sister company to Sara's Furniture. Right away, I applied for the job. It would be the perfect job to expand my accounting knowledge.

Two days later Jack, the vice president of Matheson Realty, came over to our office to talk to Jamie. I was in the lunchroom when he walked in and asked me, "What is your last name?"

"Rossi, why?"

"Did you apply to the property accountant position with Matheson Realty?"

I was glad that no one else was in the lunchroom. I nodded.

"Can I talk to you outside?"

"Yes."

"Good."

I didn't want anyone to know, especially Jamie, that I applied for the job at Matheson Realty, just in case I didn't get it. I was a single parent and had to protect the job I had.

"Why do you want to change jobs?"

"I am not using my education enough and feel like I am losing what I learned. I want to expand my accounting knowledge."

"Okay, I understand."

"I have the knowledge, but I don't have the experience, and that is what I want to get."

"If you don't get the job, will you look for another position?"

"I trust you that this conversation will stay between us. To answer your question, yes, I would look for a different position where I can grow my accounting knowledge. However, if you have a stronger candidate and you feel they will be a better fit than me, that is fine with me. I just want you to consider me for the position."

"Fair enough, I will be in touch."

"Thank you."

My lunch hour was up, and I went back to work. I must say that I was a little excited that afternoon since I was being considered for the position.

A few days later, Doug, one of the owners, was coming up the steps when I was on my way home for the day. He stopped me and asked, "You aren't happy here?"

"Yes, Doug I am happy, but I spent a lot of money on my education, and I want to use it."

"Are you sure everyone is being nice to you?"

"Yes, everyone is great, I am just looking for more responsibility."

"Does Jamie know that you applied for the job?"

"No, I didn't tell him in case I don't get the job. I am a single parent, and I need to have a job."

"Okay, goodnight."

"Thank you."

I knew that he was going to see Jamie and he would tell him that I applied. I was incredibly nervous going to work the next day, since I wasn't sure how Jamie would take the news.

When I got to work, I had to walk by Jamie's office to get to my desk, and he didn't look happy. About hour later, he asked me to come into his office. Right away, I got a nervous feeling in my stomach, since I knew that Doug told him I applied for the position.

I walked into Jamie's office, and he looked up from the papers on his desk. "Please close the door and have a seat."

I felt like I was entering the principal's office and I was in trouble.

"I just want to let you know that I didn't appreciate finding out from my boss that you applied for a new job within the company. Why did you apply?"

"I want to use more of my education by expanding my knowledge and start working on financial statements, reconciling banks, etc. Occasionally, I would look at the job sites for an accountant position. Last week there was one at Matheson Realty, so I decided to apply."

"Okay, I understand. Jack called today and wants to set up a meeting with you next week to discuss the job opportunity, would you like that?"

"Yes, I would."

"I will let you know when the meeting will be."

"Thank you." And I got up and walked out of his office.

A few minutes later, Patty came over to my desk and asked if everything was okay, since I was in with Jamie for a long time. I nodded and on break told her that I applied for the position at Matheson Realty. She was happy for me, but I told her not to tell anyone.

It was lunchtime and we were eating when Jamie came in and said to me, "The meeting will be at ten next Tuesday morning, does that work for you?"

"Yes, it does, thank you."

After Jamie left, Patty looked at me and smiled. After we ate, I went outside with her while she had a smoke to tell her the meeting was with Jack regarding the job.

*

I arrived at Matheson Realty ten minutes before my meeting with Jack. Even though I knew him, I was nervous. A few minutes later, he came up to the reception area and showed me to his office.

On the way down the hallway, we passed by the office of Stacy, another accountant, so I waved to her. Before Matheson Realty moved to the other side of Toronto, they were in the same building as Sara's Furniture. Sometimes I would have to go downstairs to take paperwork to Jack and would pass by her office. Sometimes she would call me in to chat so she could have a break.

It was funny, two years ago she told me there was an accountant position at Matheson Realty, and I should apply for it. I didn't send in my resume at the time since I was new with the company. During my training, Jamie promised me he would give me more responsibilities, and I believed him.

Jack went through the history of the real estate side, which I found interesting. He described the duties of the job, the timelines, and what he expected from me as an employee.

Afterward, he asked if I had any questions, and I said no. I thanked him for meeting with me and considering me for the position. He told me since it was the middle of December, he wouldn't be making his decision until the New Year.

A few days later, I was in Jamie's office on a different matter when he said, "How did your meeting go with Jack?"

"I believe it went well. He explained to me the job, the responsibilities, and asked me a few questions. He told me that he won't be making his decision until the New Year."

Jamie's expression changed to a sad one.

"If I get this job, some of it is because of you, who gave me the experience I needed. I would like to thank you for that, and I will miss working with you."

"I know this move will be the right one for you, but we are going to miss you around here."

"Well, I am not sure if I have the job or not, so let's not get ahead of ourselves."

"From what I am hearing, you impressed him a lot."

This was the part that I hate, waiting to hear if I had the job or not.

*

It was Christmas Eve, and Abigail, Bill and I did our traditional drive around the neighborhood looking at Christmas lights.

I felt bad for him since he spent so much of his time with us, it was hard for him to meet someone. I tried to encourage him to go out on dates and someday fall in love, but he never would.

Abigail still asked to open one gift on Christmas Eve. That was my favorite part of the holidays; the traditions that never end. This year she chose to open one of the gifts from Bill, a journal and pen. She loved to work on short stories and poems, and one day she may become an author.

Ever since she stopped believing in Santa Claus, Christmas wasn't the same.

She was writing in her journal when she looked at me. "Why are you looking and smiling at me?"

I was smiling from ear to ear. "Because I love you to the moon and back."

That put a smile on her face. "Bill and Mom, do you want to watch the movie Home Alone with me?"

We both said yes at the same time.

After the movie was over, Abigail gave us a hug and went to bed. Like past years, we would wait about an hour to ensure that she was asleep before bringing out the gifts. When she was younger, if her toys required assembly, that is when we put them together. About four years ago, we started a new tradition to have a glass or two of wine while we waited for her to go to sleep.

We put all the presents under the tree and stuffed her stocking. Then I would bring out Bill's stocking all stuffed, and he would do the same for me. When Abigail stopped believing in Santa Claus, each of us would take her out to the mall so she could pick out what we put in each other's stocking. We would say the stockings were given to us by Abigail.

When she believed in Santa Claus, the rule was to wake me up before going to the living room; that way I could get a picture of her when she first saw all the presents under the tree.

To me, nothing was more exciting than to see the excitement in a child's face when they see all the presents that Santa Claus left for them. It was worth standing in all the line-ups, dealing with the cranky people, and traffic to prepare for that moment. Christmas is really a holiday for children.

Don't get me wrong, I loved the holidays with Bill and Abigail, but since she stopped believing in Santa Claus, Christmas had lost some of the magic for me.

*

I couldn't believe that the holidays were over; they went by so fast. Tomorrow was the first day back to school and work. A new year had begun, and I was thinking that if I got that job at Matheson Realty, I would get a raise.

It was a week later, and I was working at my desk when the phone rang. "Hello, Rebecca speaking."

"Hi, Rebecca it is Jack. If you are still interested in the job, it is yours."

"Yes, I am. I accept."

"Jamie has to hire someone for your position, and Doug wants you to train the person before you start work over here. It will take about four to six weeks. How does that sound?"

"That sounds great and thank you."

After I got off the phone with Jack, I went into Jamie's office to let him know that I accepted the position at Matheson Realty. He wasn't surprised, and he seemed happy for me.

"Okay. The ad for the job will be in tomorrow's paper, and you can tell the others whenever you would like to," Jamie said. "I am happy for you; it will assist with your career growth, but on the other hand I am sad that you are leaving. I have enjoyed working with you and will miss your laughter."

I smiled. "We will still stay in touch and go out every few months to catch up on each other's lives."

After I left his office, I went by Charlotte's office. Patty was in there with her, so I knocked on the door. Charlotte told me to come in, and I told them my news. It was funny how fast news travels around the office; by the end of the day, everyone in the warehouse and office knew about it.

*

A few weeks later, I woke up in the morning all scared and sweaty. I had a nightmare but couldn't remember all of it. All I knew was that the staff at Sara's Furniture were in danger, but I didn't know why.

Over the following two weeks, I couldn't shake this feeling, so I knew I had to do something about it. But what?

I decided that I would hide a gun in the office, but how do I get a gun. That is when I knew I needed Bill's help.

He thought it would be great, so he attained one for me. I didn't ask how he got the gun. I was glad.

I had to tell Jamie in case he found it. How much should I tell him?

It was the following Wednesday, and I knew that he would be working late, so I decided to stay after everyone left.

I walked into Jamie's office. "Can I talk to you?"

"Yes, what's up?"

I took a deep breath. "I need a favor from you, but no one except you and me can know. I want to tape something under your desk so that if I need it all I have to do grab it."

The reaction I received from Jamie was just what I expected, a puzzled look. "What do you want to put under the desk and why?"

"I can't go into details about why without having you more involved, and that will put you at risk."

"Put me more at risk! Am I or the staff in danger?"

"Honestly, I am not sure, but I hope not. There is a guy who is threatening me, and in the past, he has hurt some people that I cared for. I don't want to put anyone here, including you, in jeopardy. That is why I can't go into detail. The less you know, the better for you."

"You didn't answer what."

"A gun. I know it sounds crazy, but I am asking you to trust me."

"This isn't a joke? You are serious?"

"I am totally serious. The gun will be loaded, but the safety will be on, and you aren't to touch it."

"Does this have something to do with what happened in the parking lot of the movie theatre?"

I just looked at him and said, "Yes, it does. This is just a precaution in case one day I need it."

"I shouldn't do this, but the look on your face tells me that I should help you. I am going to trust you on this one. Meet me here on Sunday afternoon at one and we will do it."

"Thank you very much."

Chapter 41

I had only worked in the east end of Toronto, which was fifteen minutes away from my house, but now I had to travel to the other side of the city. I knew the traffic would be heavier, so I set my alarm an hour earlier to give me enough time.

I was nervous about starting a new job, even though I knew Jack, Vice President of Finance, Stacy, another Accountant, Chris, General Manager, and of course Doug, one of the owners. However, I had to get to know all the other people. I would be preparing financial statements, bank reconciliation, budgets, that I never had since I left school, but I knew I could do it.

I was the first one to arrive, and the door was locked, so I just sat in my car and waited until someone arrived. A few minutes later, Jack arrived and opened the door. He showed me all around the office and where everything was. Once everyone arrived, he took me around to introduce me to the other office staff. Lily did accounts payable, Hailey did accounts receivable, Stella was another accountant, Cody was our auditor, Lucy was Chris's assistant, Ethan was operations manager, and Eva was the receptionist.

In the morning, Jack just allowed me to get used to the accounting software, since it was different than what I was using at Sara's Furniture. Stacy sat with me to give me an introduction to the software. After lunch, Jack went over my monthly duties in more detail and the deadlines I had to meet each month. At first, I was overwhelmed and started to have doubts, but I knew once I learned the software it would get easier.

Stacy came into my office and told me that she was just around the corner if I had any questions or needed assistance.

*

A month had already passed, and I was still working on my last monthly duties. Jack assured me that for the first few months he expected me to be late on the deadlines. That made me feel better, and my personal goal was within three months to meet the deadlines.

A week later, Lily, Stella, and I were in the lunchroom when Stacy asked, "tell us about your family. Do you have any siblings or children?"

Even though Sara's Furniture and Matheson Realty were owned by the same family, they were independent. The only time everyone from both companies socialized was at the Christmas party. However, everyone would just sit with the people they worked with, so these ladies wouldn't know about my home life.

"I am a widow with one daughter who is in grade 9. I have no siblings, and my parents died when I was a young child. My aunt who raised me has passed away."

"How long were you married?" replied Stella.

"We were married for five years. He died in a vehicle accident. Now it is just my daughter and I."

"You too must be very close," said Stella.

"Yes, I believe we are," I replied.

"I hope the afternoon goes by just as quick as lunchtime did," said Lily.

We all started to laugh as we went back to our offices.

To me, this afternoon felt like it was taking forever to get through. Finally, it was time to go home, and I was so happy for the weekend.

On my way home, I stopped to pick up a pizza for supper, since I didn't feel like cooking. My hands were full, so I didn't stop to check the mailbox. I would go down later to check it.

When I went into the apartment, Abigail was on the couch watching TV. "Umm, I smell pizza. I am starving; let's eat."

I shut the door and locked the deadbolts then let out a sign of relief.

"Are you okay, Mom?"

"Yes. This week was just one of those weeks that felt like it would never end."

"I am going to eat supper in my room while I watch TV."

I loved my daughter, but sometimes it was nice just to have a little bit of time to myself. I was glad just to put on a sitcom, eat my pizza, and relax for the night.

"That sounds good."

I went into my bedroom, put on my comfy clothes, and ate supper while watching TV.

After I finished, I went downstairs to check the mail. On my way back up to my unit, I was going through the mail when I saw an envelope with just my name on it.

When I came back into my unit, Abigail was in her room, but I had to check to ensure she was okay.

I opened her door. "Honey, do you want any more pizza?"

"No, I'm full."

I put away the rest of the pizza and went over to the couch to open the letter. When I touched the envelope, I could feel something inside beside paper. I was nervous; this was unusual.

I opened the envelope, and a pearl earring fell out. I picked it up, looked at it, and thought I had a pair just like this one. I rushed into my bedroom opened the draw on my jewelry box to see if my pair was still there. There was only one. I looked in every compartment of the jewelry box, and the other one wasn't there. I only wore them on special occasions.

My Aunt Debbie gave them to me for my fourteenth birthday, when I got my ears pierced. They had been in the family for generations, passed down from my great-grandmother to my grandmother to my mom to me. My heart started to beat fast.

I read the letter:

My dearest daughter Rebecca,

I just want to return to you the earing that I took when I was in your house. It was in the second drawer of your jewelry box that sits on top of your dresser. I must say that you have good taste. I like the way you decorated your home.

I love the picture of a lake at sunset in the summer surrounded by the shore that is on your wall above the TV. That is something we both have in common; we like the water. I did notice it wasn't centered on the wall, so I moved it for you.

I see that Abigail and you like to play the games on the PlayStation 4. Let's see what we have here: Knack, Crash, Scrabble, Just Dance, Rocket League and Baseball, just to name a few. I try to keep them for you.

I can see that you took the smaller bedroom for yourself. It is all neat and tidy, just like the rest of the house. I am going to go out on a limb, but I believe you like purple. You have purple curtains, bedspread, and rug.

Now, you are wondering how I was able to get into your apartment. Your door that goes out to the balcony — the lock is old it was easy to pick. You really should have your super replace that.

I took some pictures as proof that I was there. Remember that I can get into your apartment anytime I want to, day or night, and while you are awake or sleeping.

Your father, Fred

I was so freaked out that I couldn't stop shaking while I was looking at the pictures. Tears started to stream down my face. I grabbed my phone dial Bill's number, but it went to voice mail. In a panic voice I said, "Bill, come over to my house now!"

I must have said it loud since, Abigail came out of her room and said, "Mom, is everything okay?"

"No!"

My phone rang, I looked at the number, and it was Bill. "What is wrong?"

"Fred was in my apartment!"

"I am about ten minutes away from you," said Bill. "Keep me on the phone and make sure your doors are locked."

"They are, I am scared!"

"I know you are. I am almost there," replied Bill.

"Mom, what are you talking about that Fred was in our house?" asked Abigail.

I handed Abigail the letter while I paced the floor anxiously waiting for Bill to arrive.

"Mom, he could have come in while we were sleeping and hurt us! We are not safe here!"

"I know! I am just as freaked out as you are!"

There was a knock on our apartment door. I quickly looked at Abigail and whispered, "Go into the bathroom until I come for you."

I walked over to the door and looked through the peephole to see it was Bill. I unlocked the two deadbolts and the door lock.

He rushed into the apartment, and I said, "Quickly, shut and lock the door."

I gave him the letter and pictures to look at while I went down to the bathroom to get Abigail.

"Mom, I am scared, and I don't want to live here anymore!"

"I am too! Go pack some clothes. We are going to a hotel until I can figure out what to do."

"I am calling one of the detectives, we need help," said Bill.

"I can't believe that he was in my house walking around freely as if he belonged here! He was in Abigail's and my bedrooms! The one place that I felt the safest was in my own apartment, and now he has taken that away from me. I feel so violated," I said.

Within thirty minutes, Detective Johnston was at our apartment. I told him everything, from my parents' death right up to receiving the letter today. Abigail told him about the clown that talked to her on Halloween. I gave him all the letters to read. We even showed him the picture we had of Fred and my mom plus the sketch that was done.

"Rebecca, why did you wait so long before asking for help?"

"When I was younger, my aunt and uncle did call the police regarding a letter, but nothing was done. Then I called the police after the clown talked to Abigail four years ago," I said. "They told me since Abigail couldn't identify the man in the clown costume and he didn't touch her, there was nothing they could do."

"We didn't have any fingerprints or DNA from the letters or from the accidents to prove it was Fred Smith. All we had was a picture of Fred Smith with Rebecca's mom that was taken a long time ago. That only proved they knew each other," replied Bill.

"I see. There is no date on this letter, so we don't know when he was here," said Detective Johnston. "It could have been a month ago or yesterday, but he is definitely escalating. He's proven that you aren't safe here."

"I know. I am taking my daughter to a hotel so I can figure what to do," I said.

"Did you ever notice anything that was moved, but you didn't move it or anything that didn't look right?" asked Detective Johnston.

"Yes. The picture above the TV was moved a few inches, but I didn't do it. Fred did it when he was here!" I replied.

"You never noticed before that the earing from your jewelry box was missing," said Detective Johnston.

"A few weeks ago, when I wanted to wear them, I could only find one, but I was running late, so I didn't have time to look. I just thought I missed placed one of them and forgot about it when I got home from work."

"I want both of you to go to a safe house for the next couple of days," replied Detective Johnston. "There will be an undercover police officer with you at the house."

"I will drive them to the safe house," said Bill.

"No," said Detective Johnston, "he knows your car and can follow you there."

"But Fred was a police officer; can't he get the address to the safe house and come for us?" I asked.

"No, he can't access the police system anymore," replied Bill.

"Bill, do you know why he left the police force?" asked Detective Johnston.

"All I could find out is that he filed a wrongful dismissal suit against the department and received $100,000 in compensation," replied Bill.

"We have a few safe houses throughout the Greater Toronto Area, and he wouldn't know which one you are in," replied Detective Johnston.

"Okay, I am going to pack a few things to take with us," I said.

"Did any of you go on the balcony or touch the doorknob?" asked Detective Johnston.

"Not in the past few months. How about you Abigail?" I said.

"I never go out on the balcony," replied Abigail.

"I am going to have the crime scene team dust your apartment and balcony for fingerprints or DNA. One more thing — don't take your cell phones with you," said Detective Johnston.

"Why can't I take my cell?" asked Abigail.

"If he has the right equipment, he can track you by your cell phone, and I don't want to take that chance," replied Detective Johnston.

She wasn't happy leaving her phone but understood the risk.

"This is Mason and Greg, who are the undercover police officers that will be taking turns being at the house with you. For the next few days, I want both of you to call in sick to work and school," said Detective Johnston.

"How can I call school without my cell phone?" asked Abigail.

"Greg and I have a cell phone that can't be traced, and you can use it," answered Mason.

We arrived at the safe house and went inside right away. Mason and Greg searched the entire house inside and out to ensure no one was there.

At this point, it was late, and we were getting tired. Abigail and I went to sleep in the bedroom with the queen bed. Neither one of us wanted to be alone.

The following morning, I woke up first, so I went downstairs to let Abigail sleep in. When I walked into the kitchen, Mason was reading the paper and drinking a cup of coffee. "Did you have a good sleep?"

"Yes, thank you. Now what do we do?"

"We just watch TV, eat breakfast if you are hungry, and Detective Johnston will be here later to talk to you."

"Have you done this before?"

"Yes, we both have, Greg and me. You are safe here, so try to relax."

I was in the living room watching TV when Abigail came downstairs. I looked over and said, "Hi, sleepyhead. Do you want any breakfast?"

"What is there to eat?"

"There is cereal and bread for toast."

"Will you sit with me in the kitchen while I eat?"

"Of course, I will, honey. Let's go."

Mason sat in the living room to give us some space. A couple of hours later, Greg showed up for his shift, and Mason was able to go home.

It was lunchtime when Detective Johnston arrived at the safe house. We all, Abigail, Greg, Detective Johnston, and I, sat around the table.

"We were able to get a fingerprint off the earing, which matches Fred Smith," said Detective Johnston.

"Good, you can arrest him with theft plus breaking and entering," I asked.

"Yes, I am going to get a warrant for his arrest," replied Detective Johnston.

"Great," said Abigail. "Soon this can all be over with."

"I would recommend that you find a new place to live, at least until we capture Fred. You should choose a more secure building with a doorman," said Detective Johnson "We can give the doorman a picture of Fred, so if he comes around the doorman can call 911."

"I have the perfect solution," said Greg. "There is a secure building downtown that is just one block from a police station, and I know the super."

"Do you know the number so I can call?" I asked.

I used Greg's cell to make the call. It turned out that they have one unit vacant on the fifth floor. I made an appointment for the next day so I could see the unit.

Greg drove me to the building. It was a two-bedroom apartment. When I filled out the paperwork I put my middle name, Julie, as my first name and Uncle Jeff's family name, MacDonald, as my last name.

Greg explained to the super my situation, and I was able to pay my rent in cash each month. All the utilities, except for cable, was included in the rent. I also used Julie MacDonald to set up my cable, so Abigail could watch TV.

I didn't want anything in my name; that way it would be harder for Fred to find me.

We were able to move into the new apartment the following week, so we stayed at the safe house until then.

I had Greg sell my car so I could buy a new car. That way Fred wouldn't know what type of vehicle I drove.

It was time to move out of the safe house and into our new apartment. I rented a moving company to move our furniture. I didn't want to go over to the old apartment, since I didn't feel safe there.

On the way to the new building, Abigail and I stopped at Walmart to pick up a couple packages of baby monitors to put them in every room of the apartment. That way if Fred broke in, I could hear him.

A few days later, I took off the afternoon so Bill could take me to the shooting range for more practice. We decided that I would take half a day off every few months so I could practice shooting.

On the way home, Bill gave me a cell phone that couldn't be traced, so Abigail could get a hold of me anytime.

Chapter 42

We had been living in our new apartment for about four months, and I was still afraid that Fred might find us. I guessed I would be that way until the police captured Fred.

It was a Saturday morning, and I was sitting in the kitchen reading a magazine while eating my breakfast.

Abigail came into the kitchen, put some cereal and milk in a bowl, sat at the kitchen table and said, "Mom, do you want to go to High Park this afternoon for a walk?"

"Sure."

"Do you think Bill would want to go with us?"

"I am not sure if he is off today. I will call and ask him."

My daughter was just like any other sixteen-year-old; she only wanted to be with her mom on her time, so when she asked to spend time with me, I always made it a priority.

"Bill will be over in about thirty minutes to go with us."

That made Abigail happy. Whenever we went outside, she wanted Bill with us. I guess she felt safer that way.

It was a beautiful sunny day, perfect for a walk in the park. It took about an hour to get there, so we left right after breakfast. The Park was busy; it seemed like everyone had the same idea. We didn't talk about anything much; it was about spending quality time with my daughter.

We walked around the park for about three hours and started to get hungry. We decided to head back to the car and stop on our way home for lunch.

We just arrived back at the parking lot when out of the corner of my eye I saw Fred going into the park.

I turned to Abigail and said, "Stay with Bill. I will be right back." Then I started to run into the park after Fred.

"Mom, where are you going!" Abigail yelled.

I didn't want her to know, so I just pretended that I couldn't hear her.

When I entered the park and went around the first bend, I saw Fred staring at me. When he raised his right hand, I saw a gun pointing at me. We were about thirty feet apart.

At the same time a couple came around the corner and saw Fred with the gun. They both screamed, "There is a man with a gun! Call 911!"

That was when I heard a bang. I fell to the ground with a sharp pain in my leg. The people must have startled Fred, which I believe saved my life. I placed my hand on my leg.

I could see Fred running off into the woods.

The couple rushed over to me and saw blood running between my fingers. The lady put pressure on my wound while the man called 911 on his phone.

A couple of minutes later Bill and Abigail were running toward me.

Abigail started to scream, "Mom! Mom! You are bleeding!"

Bill looked at my leg and realized I was shot. "What happened?"

"It was Fred. I saw him entering the park when we were in the parking lot, so I ran after him. He pointed a gun at me, and when he saw her and him come around the corner, he shot me."

"I think we frightened the man and that is why he had bad aim," the lady said.

Bill started to go after Fred, but Abigail said, "Please stay with my mom and me! What if he comes back and hurts us?"

The police officers arrived at the scene and asked, "Did anyone see where the shooter went?"

"He went into the woods," I replied.

Two officers took off into the woods, while the other one started to take statements from witnesses. Before long more police officers came to help with searching the park for Fred.

The ambulance arrived shortly afterward and rushed me to the hospital. When the doctors examined my leg, they didn't see an exit wound. The doctors asked me if I was hurt anywhere else, and I shook my head. The doctor told the police the bullet was still in my leg.

When I opened my eyes after the surgery, I saw Abigail holding my hand with tears running down her face. I squeezed her hand.

"Mom. Why did you go after Fred?"

"I wanted to capture him and to have this over with. All I want is for you to have a normal life." I looked at her and smiled.

The nurse came in right away to check on me.

Abigail started to cry. "I am going to be just fine, honey, don't you worry."

"These are happy tears. I am going to call Bill to let him know that you will be okay. He stayed at the park to help with the search."

The doctor came into the room. "You are awake. How are you feeling?"

"My leg hurts a bit, but I am okay."

"I will have the nurse give you something for the pain. You are lucky, the bullet just missed the femoral artery in your leg."

Bill arrived and visited with me for a couple hours, then he went home. Abigail didn't want to leave me, so the nurses arranged to have a cot brought into my room for her.

The next morning, Bill walked into my room. "Hi, Rebecca, how are you feeling?"

I put a finger over my lips and said, "Shhh, Abigail is still sleeping. Good only tired. I am used to sleeping on my stomach, but it hurt my leg too much, so I didn't get a lot of sleep."

"Why did you tell me that you saw Fred? I would have gone with you."

"I know, but I wanted you to stay with Abigail to keep her safe."

Abigail opened her eyes and said, "I am sorry, Mom, but I fell asleep. I couldn't stay awake."

"That's okay, honey, you were tired. I dozed off and on all night."

The nurse came in to see how my night was, and I told her that I didn't have a good sleep. My leg was hurting, and I couldn't get comfortable.

"If you like, I can give you a sleeping pill so you can get some rest."

"Okay, thank you."

Bill said, "Abigail, let's go out for breakfast while your mom has a sleep."

"Sure. Mom, do you want me to bring anything back for you?"

"I would like it if you could go home and bring me back some clothes?"

"Sure thing."

I had to stay in the hospital for a week, so Bill stayed at the apartment with Abigail. Every day, they came to visit me, and sometimes they would bring me treats.

Chapter 43

I couldn't believe that my daughter started high school this fall — where did the time go? I remembered her first day of school, how excited she was to go, but I was nervous.

It was a Thursday night in November, and we were eating supper when Abigail asked, "Mom, can I go with my friends to the mall on Saturday so we can shop for Christmas gifts? We will get the bus there and back."

"Okay but be careful and if you see Fred or anyone acting suspicious, please call me right away."

It was Saturday afternoon, and I just finished putting the groceries in the trunk of the car when my phone rang. I opened it but didn't recognize the number.

"Hello."

"Mom, is that you?"

"Yes."

"Can you come and pick us up?"

"Of course, are you okay?"

"Yeah, how long will you be?"

"I will be there in about ten minutes."

I could tell by the tone of her voice that something was wrong.

"Did you ladies have an enjoyable time shopping?" I asked when I arrived.

"Yeah, there were a lot of good deals," answered Abigail's friends.

"That is great."

I looked over at Abigail, but it seemed like she was a million miles away.

"Honey, are you okay?"

In a faint voice she whispered, "Can we talk when we get home?"

I knew she didn't want her friends to hear, so I just nodded. As I was dropping off her friends, I couldn't help but wonder what happened.

As soon as we went inside the apartment, Abigail said, "We were at the food court having a snack when I had to go to the bathroom. After I came back, my friends told me a man dropped this enveloped off for you. I asked them to look around to see if they could point him out to me."

"Could they?" I asked.

"No, he disappeared into the crowd. That was when I got that scared feeling in my stomach, so I called you."

"So, no man actually talked to you?"

"No."

"Okay. Do you think if I showed Fred's picture to your friends, they could tell me if it was him?"

"I am not sure, but we could ask them."

"Did you open the letter?"

"No. Mom, it gave me the creeps, and I just wanted to come home."

"Honey, you are home now, and I am here to protect you."

"I want you to read the letter to me."

"Okay."

My hands were shaking when I opened the letter:

My dearest daughter Rebecca,

It seems that you have healed nicely from your bullet wound back in the summer. You are incredibly lucky that the couple came around the corner it caused the shooter to have bad aim.

I went to your apartment to drop off this letter when I ran into one of your neighbors who told me that you moved out. I had no choice but to wait until you left work yesterday to follow you to your new home. Also, I was surprised to find out that you bought a new car.

Since your new building has a doorman, I couldn't leave the envelope there without him seeing me, so I left. I knew with Christmas coming, if I just hung out at the food court, one day I would see my granddaughter.

I went to the table to give her the letter, but she was in the bathroom. I tried to wait a few minutes, but I had to go, so I gave it to her friends. They seem like nice young ladies.

I believe you are trying to hide from me. You can run, but I will always find you. I thought by now you would realize that.

Soon we will meet in person.

Your father, Fred

I wanted to call Bill right away, but I knew he was working, so instead I called Detective Johnston.

"Hi, this is Rebecca Rossi and I have received another letter from Fred."

"Where are you?"

"I am at my apartment."

"Make sure your door is locked, and I will be there shortly."

"Okay."

About thirty minutes later, the doorman called to inform me that Detective Johnston was on his way up. When he knocked on my door, I looked out the peephole to ensure it was him before I unlocked the two deadbolts. I knew we lived in a secure building, but I still didn't feel safe unless I had two deadbolts.

"Please come in."

I handed him the letter.

"Did he talk to Abigail?"

"No. Let me have Abigail come out to the living room to tell you what happened."

I went down the hallway to her bedroom and knocked on the door. "Honey, the detective is in the living room and would like to talk to you."

She opened the door and walked out to the living room. I followed. She sat down on the couch and told the detective what took place.

"Detective Johnston, could you show the picture of Fred to her friends to see if it was him?" I asked.

"No, I don't want to involve my friends. What if he tries to hurt them?" said Abigail.

"Fred isn't interested in hurting your friends, or he would have done it at the mall," replied Detective Johnston. "All he wants is to hurt your mom. At least this way we will know if he gave the letter to your friends."

"I guess that will be okay. What if they ask why?"

"I will tell them it is a family member that your mom has been trying to find," replied Detective Johnston. "If it makes you feel better, for the following few days I will have more police patrol the neighborhood they live in."

"Yes, that will make me feel better," answered Abigail.

"I will call their parents tomorrow to set up a meeting at their house. I will let you know the outcome," said Detective Johnston.

"Thank you for coming over, and I will wait to hear from you," I answered.

The following day, I told Bill what happened. He was going to talk to his boss to have a police car drive by my building a few times a day, so if Fred was watching he would see the police presence.

A few days later, Bill stopped in for a visit while Abigail and I were watching TV when my phone rang.

It was Detective Johnston letting me know that it was Fred who gave the envelope to Abigail's friends. He has rented an apartment under the name of Jeffery Woodley, who is deceased. He must have stolen his identity.

Chapter 44

The bosses were away at meetings all day, and no one felt like working. I guess the old saying when the cat is away, the mice will play was true. We were just sitting in the lunchroom eating homemade cupcakes that Lily brought in as a treat when Eva came in and told me that she had a phone call for me.

"Okay, put it through to my office. Hi, Rebecca speaking."

"Hello, Rebecca, this is Fred, and I am with your coworkers over at the accounting department. If you want to save their lives, you will be here within thirty minutes. If you are late, I will kill someone for every five minutes until you get here. I suggest you leave now. Goodbye, see you soon."

Suddenly, I couldn't hear anything. It was like everything just stood still for a minute, and I was frozen. All I could do was stare into space, and at that moment Stacy and Lily walked by my office. They could see that my face was white as a ghost. They could tell that something was wrong.

"Rebecca, are you okay? What is wrong? Talk to me," Stacy asked, shaking my arm to try to get me to say something.

"No. I have to go over to the warehouse," I replied.

I called Bill right away to tell him about the phone call. Within ten minutes, he was in my office. Before we left the office, he held me as tight as he could, as if he was afraid this was going to be the last time, he saw me alive.

"What is going on?" asked Lily.

"I don't have time to explain everything right now. There is a crazy man at the warehouse holding the accounting department hostage. He wants me, and if I am more than thirty minutes, he is going to hurt someone."

Lily just stood there in disbelief.

"Detective Johnston is vacating the remainder of the building as we speak, and I am going to drive you over," said Bill.

I took a deep breath. "Okay, let's go."

It seemed like it was taking forever to get there. My heart was pounding so hard, the blood was just shooting through my veins, and I couldn't help but wonder if I was going to die today.

I couldn't stop my mind from working in overdrive. I kept thinking, why take any hostages, and why them? I haven't worked over there for the past few years.

"Rebecca, the police aren't going to let you go into the office."

"I know, that is why I want you to drop me off on the other side of the building. I am going to break a window to get into the warehouse. I will text Detective Johnston to tell him I am in the building."

We finally arrived, and I jumped out of the car before Bill had time to put it in park.

"Please be careful. You have three minutes left," Bill said.

I nodded then as fast as I could I ran toward the window, picked up a rock, and broke the glass. When I went inside, I wasn't used to how quiet it was. You could hear a pin drop. Normally, eight to ten men would be putting together furniture for tomorrow's deliveries.

I texted Detective Johnston that I was in the building. He sent me back a text telling me that I shouldn't have gone in. He was right, but I couldn't take the chance that Fred would kill them before the police raided the office.

I went up the four flights of steps and barged into the accounting offices. When I went around the corner, I saw him pointing a gun at Patty's head.

"I am here on time. Let her go."

Fred looked at his watch then pushed Patty to the floor and told her to go and sit with the others.

"Patty, are you okay?"

She nodded since she was too scared to talk.

I looked into Fred's eyes and knew that he was a killer. He had this cold, angry, and empty look in his eyes. I never saw that look in anyone's eyes before. I thought it was strange that he was wearing a police uniform. It must have been the one he wore when he was working on the force.

He told one of the guys to frisk me to ensure I didn't have a gun.

Fred pushed me into a chair and told Jamie, my boss at Sara's Furniture, to handcuff my hands together.

I yelled at Fred, "Let them go! This has nothing to do with them. No one else has to get hurt."

"No one will get hurt if they just sit there and don't try to help you. But if they try to stop me, I will have no choice but to kill them."

I could hear a few of the lady's gasp and start to cry.

"If you hurt any one of them, I promise I will kill you."

"You won't be able to kill me since you will already be dead. Please forgive my daughter for her rudeness and not introducing me. I am her father."

"You aren't my father! You killed him and my mom when I was a little girl."

"Rebecca, dear, I am your biological father."

"No, you're not! I don't believe you!"

"Brent wasn't your real father, I am. I met your mom at the park, and we started talking. After several months, we started a physical relationship. You must realize that your mom was a sexy, and I knew she missed being touched by a man, so I took care of her. Our affair lasted for four months, until she felt guilty and ended the relationship with me. I didn't want the relationship to end. A few months later, I saw her at the grocery store and realized that she was pregnant. I knew right away the baby, you, were mine. It was a feeling, call it father's intuition."

I couldn't stop staring at his face, wondering if I really did resemble this crazy man. Could he really be my father, and if so, did that mean I got some of the crazy genes?

I didn't know my mom that well, since I was only young when she died. Could he be right? Did she have an affair with this man?

"I told your mother how I felt and demanded that she got a paternity test done to see who your biological father was. She didn't want to get the test done; she kept on insisting that Brent was your father. I knew you were mine. I told her if she didn't get the test done, I was going to tell Brent about our affair, so she had no choice but to get it done. I know she was hoping that Brent was your father, but it turned out that I was right all along. I am your biological father. Your mother told me that you were going to be raised believing that Brent was your dad and not me."

"I don't believe you. Do you have a copy of the test results?"

"No, your mom didn't give me a copy."

"So, all I have is your word. My mom wanted the relationship with you to end. Why couldn't you just leave us alone?"

"Because I am your father, not Brent!" Fred yelled and slammed his fist on the wall. "Rebecca, you are part of me, I helped create you, and I needed you in my life. All I wanted was to see you from time to time and watch you grow up, but your mom took you away from me. She and Brent moved you to another province where I couldn't see you."

"If I am your daughter, why do you want to kill me? Normally, parents don't want to hurt their children."

"I made a promise to your mom that if she took you away from me, she would be sorry, and you won't see your fortieth birthday. I was right, she was sorry when I killed her, and your fortieth birthday is coming next month. I intend to keep my promise to your mom."

"You killed my parents!"

"I had to keep my promise to her, didn't I?"

"Just because she wouldn't divorce my father, she didn't deserve to die!"

"I am your, father not him!"

"Why do I have to pay for a mistake my mom made over forty years ago?"

"Sometimes life isn't fair, and children have to pay for their parent's mistakes."

"You are crazy, and that is why my mom didn't want you around me!" Jamie jumped up and ran toward Fred. He pointed the gun in Jamie's face. "If you take one more step toward Rebecca, I will blow your head off."

Jamie just stood there having a staring contest with Fred.

I screamed, "Jamie sit back down, he will do it!"

Jamie turned around and went back to sit on the floor. I took a deep breath. "You have me now. Let everyone else go. No one else has to get hurt. They didn't do anything to you."

"I know, but I want them here to watch me kill you."

Everyone just stared at me with tears running down their scared faces.

"No! Rebecca doesn't deserve this. She is a wonderful person," said Grace.

"Let them go. No one needs to witness my death."

"No, everyone stays! Now it is time to play a game. In this gun, I have one bullet, and I am going to put the gun to your forehead and pull the trigger. Either you are going to die or live for a few more minutes, but eventually, I will get to the bullet. Then you can say hi to your mom for me."

Fred walked over to me and put the gun against my forehead. I remember feeling a sensation of cold. I wasn't sure if it was the gun or me just realizing that I was going to die that day.

"Quiet!" Fred yelled. "The next person that talks or moves, I will kill them with this gun."

He pulled out a different gun and fired a shot into the ceiling. Dust came down in the air. You could hear a pin drop. Jamie knew then that this guy was serious, and I needed his help.

He pulled the trigger. Everything went black, and I was numb. I opened my eyes and had to think if I was alive or dead. A few people started to cry again, then the room went incredibly quiet.

Jamie's face started to turn red from choking on the dust in the air, so he stood up. He bumped into my chair, which caused me to fall to the floor.

Fred quickly pointed the other gun at Jamie and was ready to shoot when Jamie yelled, "It was an accident! I didn't mean to do it! My eyes were all watery from choking. I couldn't see the chair. I will pick her up."

After Fred stared into Jamie's eyes, which felt like an entirety, he lowered the gun and pushed him over to where the others were.

Again, Fred put the gun to my forehead, and I closed my eyes. I heard the trigger being pulled. I was frozen, just like the last time, until I realized I was alive.

At first, I didn't know why Jamie knocked into me until I realized I was closer to his office door. I knew that I didn't have much time left, especially since I didn't know if the next time, he pulled the trigger would be the bullet. I quickly worked on the knots while Fred was going on about how much he loved my mom and how happy he would have made her. Thankfully, he didn't check the knots as I was starting to loosen them.

Again, he put the gun to my forehead and pulled the trigger. I closed my eyes and prayed that I could make it out of this situation. The only thing going through my mind was my daughter and how much Bill had helped me over the years.

I knew that Bill would be developing a plan to save me, but I didn't know if it would be in time, so I had to make a move. All I needed was one more distraction to give me enough time to get into Jamie's office.

I looked over at Jamie, and by the look on his face he knew what I was thinking about. To tell you the truth, it was a little eerie. Then Jason suddenly put his hand over his heart and started to scream in pain.

Jamie said, "Jason, what is the matter?"

"I have a pain in my chest. I think I am having a heart attack."

Fred's attention was on Jamie and Jason, so I knew this would be my only opportunity. I jumped out of the chair and grabbed the gun from under the desk. I yelled, "Everyone take cover!"

I shot Fred in the shoulder. He fired back at me but missed. I ducked behind Jamie's desk.

I could hear people running to the door and down the steps. The hostages must have known this was their only chance to escape. When Fred realized what they were doing, he shot Grace in the leg, which made her drop to the floor. He ran over to her, pulled her up by her hair, and pointed the gun at her head.

"Rebecca, if you don't come out in ten seconds, I am going to put a bullet in her head."

Grace whimpered, "Rebecca, please help me! I have been shot in my leg. I don't want to die!"

I knew I had to surrender to save her life.

"Okay! I am coming out. Just don't hurt her anymore."

I stood up and walked out from behind the desk.

"Throw your gun on the floor," yelled Fred.

Then he pointed his gun at me, at the same time as he pulled the trigger Grace fell to the floor. Instead of the bullet going into my chest it entered my stomach, and I fell to the ground. He let go of Grace, who was crying and screaming, "No! No!"

He walked over to me, pointed the gun at my chest, and pulled the trigger. At that point, I realized that today I would die. I closed my eyes.

I heard three more shots, but I didn't know who was shooting. Was it the police or Fred? If it was the police, was Fred alive or dead?

I couldn't see what was going on. I could only hear screaming from the hostages.

Bill rushed over to me and took my hand. "Look at me! Don't give up! Fight! Your daughter needs you."

That day the last thing I remember Bill was yelling, "I need paramedics quickly."

As I was being rushed to the hospital from the warehouse, I was drifting in and out of consciousness. I knew I was hurt badly, since the last thing I heard was a paramedic saying, "We need to have blood on hand at the hospital. She lost a lot," on the radio.

Chapter 45

Suddenly, I felt a warm hand squeezing mine. When I opened my eyes, I was looking around, trying to focus on something to see if I was alive or in Heaven when I saw Abigail and Bill.

Abigail saw that my eyes were open. "Mom you are alive! I love you so much!"

She pressed the nurse's button while she was wiping tears from her eyes. The nurse rushed into my room and smiled at me when she saw me awake.

"Please, don't try to speak," said the nurse. "We have a breathing tube down your throat. We will remove it then you can talk."

The nurse requested that Abigail and Bill leave the room while she took out my breathing tube and assessed my condition. She informed me that I had been in a coma for the past month, and I lost a lot of blood. They didn't believe that I was going to survive. I couldn't believe I had been asleep for a month.

The nurse went to tell Abigail and Bill it was okay for them to come back into my room.

Abigail came right over and gave me a hug. "How are you feeling, Mom?"

"I have had better days, but I am glad to be alive, Abigail, can you go downstairs and get me a pop?"

"Mom you just came out of a coma from being shot twice, and the last thing you need is a pop. I want to know exactly what is going on, especially if Fred is still out there. He probably will try to hurt you again."

"Okay. Bill did the police get Fred?" I asked.

"No, with all the confusion he got away. He was wearing a policeman's uniform, the one he had from when he was on the police force. No one would have stopped him," Bill said.

I looked over at Abigail and could see her face go white. I squeezed her hand. "I will do anything to protect you. I thought I hit him in the shoulder. Did the hospitals have anyone that went in with a gunshot to the shoulder?"

"No, either he had a friend that fixed his shoulder, or he wore a bulletproof vest."

"What if he went to a different hospital?"

"I called all the hospitals within a few hours of here and sent them a picture of Fred, but no luck. Detective Johnston put out an all-points bulletin on Fred to all the police departments in the province of Ontario. Every police officer and Mountie is hunting for Fred."

"I relived my whole life while I was in the coma. I can't believe that I survived. I thought I was going to die," I said.

"That would explain why your heart rate and blood pressure increased. We thought we were going to lose you," replied Abigail.

"How is Grace?" I asked.

"She is doing great, her leg healed, and she has no permanent damage," replied Bill.

I was thinking that this wasn't over when the alarm on the machine started to sound. The nurse ran into my room. "Rebecca, your blood pressure is too high. You must calm down. I am going to give you some medicine to help bring it down."

The nurse looked over at Abigail. "For your mom to get better, she needs her rest. You can come back tomorrow morning."

"I almost lost her. I am not leaving here until I know she is going to be okay."

"Okay, but you have to let her get some rest, or you will have to leave. The chair you are sitting in reclines, so you can sleep too."

"I can't protect Abigail if I am sleeping," I said.

"There is a police officer outside of your room to protect Abigail and you."

The last thing I heard was Abigail saying, "Mom, you need your rest. Please go to sleep, and I will read my book."

A few hours later, I woke up and saw Abigail all curled up in the chair, sleeping. I looked at the position of her head and thought she was going to have a stiff neck when she woke up.

I remembered sleeping in those chairs when Matteo was in the hospital after he was shot at our wedding reception. There were a few times when I woke up my neck and back were extremely sore.

I must have fallen back to sleep, because when I woke up again Abigail just walked back into the room with a tea and bagel from the coffee shop downstairs.

"Hi, Mom, how are you?"

Before I could answer, the nurse came into the room and asked me the same question.

"My legs and back are sore, plus I am tired."

"Your back and leg muscles are weak from not being used in over a month. This is common with people who have been in a coma. Today we are going to get you up and walk around for a few minutes."

Shortly after the nurse left, another hospital worker walked in with my breakfast. Normally, hospital food isn't the greatest, but this was good, a bowl of oatmeal, glass of orange juice, and red Jell-O, which I guess would be hard to mess up.

About an hour later, the nurse came back into my room. "How was your breakfast?"

"It was good."

"You must have been hungry; it is all gone. It's time for your walk. I want you to stand up wait a couple of minutes then start to walk. If you feel dizzy, let me know right away."

"Okay."

I took a breath, stood up, and my legs started to shake, so I sat down for a minute then stood up again. The second time I started to walk, the pains in my legs started to go away. I went about quarter of the way down the hallway but started to get dizzy, so the nurse decided that was enough for now and helped me back to my room.

As soon as I sat down, Bill and Detective Johnston walked into my room.

"Hi, Rebecca, how are you feeling?" asked Detective Johnston.

"Okay. I am weak, but every day I am getting stronger," I replied.

"I am glad to hear. I need to take your statement. Is this a suitable time." asked Detective Johnston?

"Yes."

"I am going to tape the statement then have it typed up for you to read and sign."

"Abigail, why don't you and I go home so you can have a shower plus get your mom some clothes to make her feel more comfortable."

Abigail didn't want to leave, but she realized she needed to get cleaned up.

After they left, I asked, "It is my understanding that Fred got away. Do you have any leads?"

"No."

I put my hands to my face and started to cry when Detective Johnston said, "I am not going to stop until we find and arrest him. You have my word on that. Are you sure you are well enough for this?"

"Yes, maybe there is something in my statement that could help you find him."

The detective turned on the tape recorder. "Tell me what happened from when you entered the warehouse to now."

It took about two hours to give my statement. Sometimes we had to stop for a few minutes as I was getting upset.

"If you remember anything else, call me. Is there anything I can get you before I go?"

"How am I going to protect Abigail and my coworkers from this lunatic if he decides to go back?"

"Calm down! Bill changed his work hours and has been driving Abigail back and forth to school. Over the past several weeks, there has been some gang violence in the area, so the police put an undercover cop in the school. I told him what was going on, and he has been looking out for your daughter. We have an undercover police officer at the warehouse in case Fred returns. When you go back to work, we are going to have a police officer there in case he shows up. You remember Mason and Greg from the safe house?"

"Yes."

"Well, Mason is going to be at the warehouse, while Greg will be at your office."

"Okay, that makes me feel better, thank you."

"You are welcome. I see that you are getting tired, so I will leave you to have some rest."

"Okay."

I must have been tired, since the next thing I knew I woke up two hours later.

A few minutes later, Bill and Abigail arrived back at the hospital.

"Abigail, while Fred is still out there somewhere, I don't want you to leave the house without Bill or me. Also, I am going to have an alarm installed at the apartment, and it has to be on at all times."

Bill and Abigail agreed to this.

A few days later, Detective Johnston came into my room with my typed statement for me to review. After I finished reading it, I signed.

Over the following few weeks, I was healing from my injuries and getting stronger every day. Abigail and Bill would go to school or work then come to the hospital to visit me. Sometimes they would bring me a treat like pizza since I was getting tired of hospital food.

It was a Wednesday afternoon when the nurse took me for another walk. This time I could go all around the unit without any issues. When we arrived back to my room, the doctor came in to examine me.

"How are you feeling?"

"I feel good but would like to be in my own bed. When can I go home?"

"Your vitals look good. The nurses told me that you have been up walking around without any issues. If you are feeling good tomorrow, then you can go home. I will come in around lunch to check on you before I sign your discharge papers."

A big smile spread across my face. "Great."

I was discharged from the hospital the next afternoon, but I couldn't return to work until the following week. The doctor wanted me to have a few days off to rest and deal with what happened. It was great to get home to sleep in my own bed.

Bill decided to take the rest of the week off to be with me until the alarm was installed just in case Fred came after me.

After Bill returned from dropping Abigail off at school, I asked him, "What do you think about me carrying a gun for protection?"

"I think that would be great."

"It has been a few months since I shot a gun, so could you take me back to the shooting range?"

"We will go tomorrow afternoon."

"But wait, where is my gun?"

"Your gun is at the police station in the evidence room."

"Then we will go, and I will buy one."

"Why don't you get some rest, and I will purchase the gun for you."

I went to bed, and when I woke up it was after lunch. I called Jamie to let him know that I would be coming in for a visit on Monday morning to see how everyone was doing.

*

It was Monday morning. Bill went with me to the warehouse for support. When I walked through the door, the guys that worked in the warehouse came over to see how I was doing.

"We thought he was a police officer, but if we knew he was going to hurt you, we wouldn't have let him up," one of the warehouse workers said.

"That wouldn't have stopped him. It only would have put you in danger," I replied.

We went upstairs. At first, that day came all rushing back to me, and I was overwhelmed. Bill took me into the kitchen to sit down for a few minutes before saying hi to everyone.

I stood up, went out of the kitchen and to the center of the cubicles and said, "Hi, everyone."

Patty got up from her desk, walked over to me, and gave me a hug. Everyone came out of their cubicles to say hi.

Then I saw Grace coming over. I felt bad that she was hurt but was glad it was only her leg. "How is your leg?"

"It is doing well. I am all healed."

"I would like to say I'm deeply sorry to each one of you. I had no idea that he was going to come here. The last thing I wanted to do is put any of you in danger."

"Is he really your dad?" asked Charlotte.

"Who knows? He claims to be, but I am not sure."

"What do you mean?"

"He has no proof that he is my biological father, so honestly, I really don't know."

"Why did he want to hurt you?" asked Grace.

"He blames my mom for taking me away from him, but I am not sure why."

"Was he responsible for you getting stabbed outside the movie theater?" asked Charlotte.

"I believe so."

"What if he comes back here looking for you and hurts one of us?" asked Grace.

Mason stood up. "I won't let that happen."

Grace shouted out. "Who are you, and how are you going to stop him!"

"I am an undercover cop here to protect all of you until we capture Fred. This is just a precaution in case he comes back," replied Mason.

"Will he come back?" asked Jamie.

"Honestly, I can't answer that question. I really don't know what he is going to do, but I don't believe he will come back," answered Mason. "He will know that we will be watching this place very closely."

"If he does show up, Mason will call for backup, and the police will be here within minutes," replied Bill.

"What if a man comes in with a police officer's uniform? How will we know if it is a real police officer or Fred?" asked Jamie.

"I know what Fred looks like, so if he comes back dressed as a police officer I will arrest him," replied Mason.

I could see that some people were still worried. I tried to reassure them they were safe, but honestly, I couldn't guarantee that.

I looked at Bill and said, "We better go now. I told Jack I would be at Matheson Realty by 1:00 p.m."

When we arrived at the office, I went into the boardroom, where Jack had gathered everyone.

I walked into the room, and everyone went silent. "Hi, everyone."

"Hi, how are you?" asked Lily.

"I am good, thank you. I know you all have heard of what happened at the warehouse. I will give you the quick version, then if you have any questions, I will answer them. There is a man who claims to be my biological father who wants to hurt me. I am not sure why."

"If he is your father, why does he want to hurt you? Don't fathers want to protect their children?" asked Hailey.

"That is the million-dollar question that I have been trying to figure out. With a parent like that, who needs enemies?"

"Will he come here and shot one of us, like he did at the warehouse?" asked Stacy.

A man walked into the boardroom. "We can't guarantee that he will or will not come here. However, if he does, I will be here to protect you."

"Who are you?" asked Lily.

"My name is Greg. I am an undercover cop that will be here every day until we arrest Fred."

For the next hour, I answered questions. I tried to reassure them that if Fred did show up, we had help there to protect them. I knew some of them are worried, and truthfully, so was I.

I arranged with my boss to have every second Friday afternoon off so Bill could take me to the shooting range for practice before picking up Abigail from school.

*

I had been back to work for two weeks, and nothing out of the ordinary had happened. It was a typical day, I thought, but little did I know that night I would get the shock of a lifetime.

When I arrived home and checked the mail, there was a letter with my full address on it and a return address in Pickton, Ontario. At that time, I knew it wasn't from Fred, but I thought to myself, I don't know anyone that lives in Pickton. I looked it up on the computer to find out it was a small town three hours away from Toronto.

I opened the letter:

Hi Rebecca,

I know this is going to come as a complete shock to you. Ryan and I are alive. Please don't be angry with Bill. It was my decision to take Ryan away. I did what I thought was in the best interest of our son.

If possible, Ryan and I would like to see you tomorrow morning at ten at the food court in the Eaton Center Mall. We will wait until eleven, and if you don't show up, I will understand.

You must have a lot of questions, and I will answer them. I hope you can forgive me and meet us.

Love always, your husband, Matteo

It can't be possible that my husband and son were alive!

Chapter 46

I couldn't believe what I was reading. They couldn't be alive; I saw the car, and it was totaled — or could they be? This could be a trick to set me up so Fred could kill me. I thought this could be a way to capture him.

After the shock wore off, I called Bill to come over to read the letter. I didn't know what to do. He asked if we had supper yet. I told him no, so he was going to stop and pick up a pizza for supper.

A few minutes later, Abigail came out of her bedroom and said, "What's for supper?"

"Bill is on his way over with a pizza. He should be here in about half an hour or so."

"Okay. Do I have to sit with you guys while I eat?"

I didn't want to sound too eager to say no, so I waited a few moments. I was glad since I wanted to talk to Bill about the letter.

"No, are you okay?"

"Yeah, I just don't feel good. I am on my period and having a lot of pain. I just want to lie down in my bed."

"Okay. How about you go and lie down? When Bill comes, I will bring you in a slice of pizza and a glass of pop."

"Thanks, Mom, I love you."

"I love you too."

For the next thirty minutes, I tried to watch TV but couldn't stop thinking about the letter. I went around the apartment to ensure all the doors and windows where locked. Then I called down to the doorman to inform him that Bill was on his way over.

When my phone rang, it was the doorman telling me that Bill was on his way up. A few minutes later, I heard a knock on my door.

As always, I would look through the peephole to ensure it was Bill before unlocking my dead bolts.

"I hope you are hungry?"

"A little bit. Just put it on the table. I will get us some plates and pop."

"Where is Abigail?"

"She is in her room, not feeling good tonight. I am going to take her a slice of pizza and a drink while you read the letter."

I returned to the table, poured a glass of pop, and started to eat a slice of pizza while Bill finished reading the letter.

"I believe this letter is from Fred. What do you think about us setting up a sting operation to arrest Fred? We can have a few undercover cops sitting at different tables while Detective Johnston is waiting in line to order some food."

Bill took a deep breath and said, "Rebecca, this letter is from Matteo. They are both alive."

"What! What are you talking about?"

"They didn't die in the car accident that day."

"No, no. It can't be true. I saw the car. There was no way they could have survived the accident."

"I know this doesn't make sense, but it is true."

"How do you know this for sure?"

"I helped him fake the car accident."

"You did what!"

"I know you are furious at me."

"Of course, I am! Wouldn't you be?"

"Yes, but Matteo made me promise not to tell you. He didn't want you to worry about their safety."

"You knew all of these years that Matteo and Ryan were alive but didn't tell me!"

"Yes."

"You watched me for two years drink myself numb praying for them to be alive. I was on a path to self-destruction, and you just watched me! You call yourself a friend, but a devoted friend would never intentionally hurt me, and that is exactly what you did."

It was so quiet the next few minutes, you could hear a pin drop.

"I am so sorry, Rebecca. I didn't mean to hurt you, but you must understand it was the only way to protect them. I made a vow to Matteo I wouldn't say anything to you."

"Then what did you expect to happen? I mourned for them all these years while you knew they were alive and safe. You sat there and lied to me. I don't want to hear it."

"Are you going to meet them tomorrow morning?"

"Of course, I am. Now I want you to leave. Get out!"

It was about twenty minutes later when Abigail come out of her room. "I thought Bill was here.

"He was tired, so he went home."

"Are you okay, Mom?"

"Yes, I just had a rough day at the office."

"I am going to bed, goodnight. I love you."

"Goodnight, honey, I love you too."

I tried to get some sleep, but I just couldn't turn my brain off. I kept thinking what do they look like? What am I going to say to them?

The following morning, Bill showed up to take Abigail to school while I called in sick to work. I was just like a teenage girl and couldn't decide on an outfit to wear.

I didn't want to take my car in case Fred was watching me, so I decided to take the bus. I went out the back door of the parking garage then three blocks to the bus stop. In order, to get to the mall from this bus stop, I had to take two buses.

When I arrived at the mall, I went straight to the food court, and over in the corner with Bill was two men. As I was walking over to them, tears started to run down my face, "Rebecca, it's me, Matteo."

"No, it can't be."

"It's true, we are alive."

"But–but the police showed me pictures of the car. There was no way you could have survived. I was told there were two people that died in the car accident, a man and child."

"I know this is hard for you to believe, but it is really me."

Matteo recited his wedding vows to me to prove it was really him.

I started to cry. "It's actually you! You remember our wedding vows after all of these years!"

"That is what kept me going."

We stood up and held each other for what seemed like a long time but was only a few minutes. Then he took his hands, placed them on my face, and gave me a soft, beautiful kiss.

"I missed that! I forgot how good of a kisser you were."

When I looked at Ryan, I couldn't hold back my tears. I walked toward him with open arms. It was hard to hug him, since he was six feet tall, but I did. I didn't want to let him go. I was scared if I did, I wouldn't see him again.

He had brown eyes, light brown hair, and was very fit. He was the perfect likeness to his father. I wanted time to stand still so I could enjoy my husband and son.

Through the tears, I managed to get out, "Hi, Ryan. Did you know who I am?"

"Yes., my mom. I am happy now that I have been reunited with you. I have dreamed about this day for so long."

The tears started to stream down my face again.

"Remember, we asked someone to take a picture of the three of us at the zoo a few weeks before the crash?" said Matteo. "Well, I framed it and put it on the wall in Ryan's bedroom so he would know who his mother is. Ryan would look at this picture every day and wished he could see you in person. I would tell him maybe someday."

I sat there while Ryan filled me in on his life. He told me what his favorite subject in schools was, what grade he liked the best, and that he just graduated from university. I just sat there staring, amazed at what a wonderful job Matteo did raising our son.

Ryan turned to Matteo. "Why did you lie to me about Mom?"

"I had to keep you safe. There was a man trying to hurt your mom and threatened yours and my safety," replied Matteo. "I was just doing what I thought was best to keep you safe."

"Is the man still trying to hurt you?" asked Ryan.

"Yes," I replied.

Over the next hour, I told Matteo and Ryan everything about Fred and what was happening.

"Can I see you again?" asked Ryan.

At first, I want to say yes but then realized that I was being selfish.

"No. It isn't safe for you two to be around me."

"I just reconnected with you," answered Ryan. "I want you in my life."

"Rebecca, Ryan and I aren't going anywhere. We are a family," said Matteo. "We are going to get through this together, helping each other like families do."

"But I couldn't live with myself if something happened to either one of you. I already lost you once; I can't do it again."

"See, Dad, I told you Mom was still alive."

I took out a piece of paper and pen from my purse, wrote down my cell number, and gave it to Ryan.

"You can call me anytime, day or night."

"Ryan, how about you and I go to get something to eat while your parents talk," said Bill.

"How do you know my dad?" asked Ryan.

"My late wife and your dad's mom were best friends. I knew your dad ever since he was born," said Bill.

"That's cool," said Ryan.

"Bill, please watch him," I said.

"I will," replied Bill.

"I am not a kid. I can protect myself," said Ryan.

I smiled, looked at him, and said, "Yes, you can, and I love you."

"I love you too," replied Ryan.

They walked away, and I turned to Matteo. "How did you survive the car crash?"

"Remember that you didn't want to marry me since you were afraid the man was going to kill me, and I told you that I just wanted to be married to you? Two weeks prior to our fifth anniversary, I received a letter at work telling me that he was going to kill Ryan. I knew he meant it and that Ryan was in danger. The only way I could keep him safe was to stage our deaths, change our names, and move to a new area so no one would know who we were."

"Why couldn't we have died together as a family and started over with new identities?"

"Bill felt that the man would have scrutinize the bodies more closely. I know it was selfish on my part, but I felt that was my only option. Besides, Bill could only get one adult cadaver."

"How did you do it?"

"I did it on our anniversary because it was the only time that you aren't going to be in the car. Bill chose the spot, since there were a lot of car accidents on that stretch of road. He was there in another car, waiting for us. I gave Ryan to him, backed up our car, and drove right into the median. I jumped out of the car just before it crashed. Bill took two cadavers from the science department to put them in the car. I was assured the accident was bad enough that the police couldn't identify the bodies."

"Didn't the science department miss the cadavers?"

"Bill staged it as a break-in. The police never found out who was responsible for it."

"How did you leave Toronto?"

"Bill took us to the bus station and gave us new identities, money, and a bus ticket to Pickton, a small town three hours away. In the following few days, I read in the paper that there were two bodies found in the car, but they could only be identified by using dental records. Bill gave the police a fake set of dental records that matched the cadavers. The police assumed it was Ryan and I that died."

"I can't believe that Bill knew Ryan and you were alive for the past eighteen years and never told me. I was so angry with him last night."

"It wasn't his fault. I made him swear to me that he wouldn't tell you. The last thing I wanted to do was hurt you, but that was the only way I knew how to keep Ryan safe. For the past eighteen years, I raised Ryan on my own but told him all about you and what a wonderful person you were. I kept in touch with Bill over the years, and he kept me informed of how you were doing. I asked him to try to keep you safe, and he told me he will do his best."

"Did Ryan ask where I was?"

"Yes, on several occasions. I told him that you died, but he wouldn't believe me."

"Why did you come? He is still trying to kill me and almost succeeded a few months ago. If he finds out that Ryan and you are alive, you won't be safe."

"I realized that, but Ryan hired a private investigator to find you. He kept telling me that deep down he knew that you were alive. When he told me that he knew where you worked and he was going to confront you, I knew there was no stopping him. The one trait that he received from you is his determination, so I told him I would take him. I called Bill to set up a meeting. He suggested meeting in a mall since Fred knew where you worked."

"I have a sixteen-year-old daughter that doesn't know anything about Ryan and you. I thought both of you were dead and never dreamed that I would see you again. When you and Ryan died, I took it extremely hard and started drinking. After a while, I was drunk more than sober. I met this guy at work who liked to drink too, so we would party together. After a while, one night we were drinking, one thing led to another, and the next thing I knew we were in bed together. I just wanted to feel alive."

"You don't owe me any explanation. You thought I was dead and had every right to start a relationship with anyone you wanted to."

"I was drinking so much that it almost cost me my job. My boss gave me a second chance, and when I sobered up a month later, I started to feel sick. That's when I realized that I was pregnant. This was my second chance at being a mom, and I couldn't pass that up."

Bill and Ryan returned to the table and overheard me asking Matteo, "How long are you in the city for?"

"I am going to live here from now on. I want to be near you, Mom. I am only going back to Pickton to pack up my things. I will be back in two days," said Ryan.

"I guess we are moving here," said Matteo.

"Matteo and Ryan, what about your home, work, and friends you have in Pickton? You are going to miss them," I said.

"I just finished university, so I am looking for a job in my field. There will be more employment opportunities for me here in the Greater Toronto Area," answered Ryan. "As far as my friends go, they can come and visit me here. Sometimes I can go back to visit them."

"What about you, Matteo?"

"I now work in the IT industry, which allows me to work from home. All I must do is go into the office once a month for meetings. I can commute from here," replied Matteo.

"I guess there is no sense in trying to talk you out of it for your safety, Ryan and Matteo," I said.

They exchanged a look, then Ryan said, "Our mind is made up. We are moving to the city near you."

"Matteo, just promise me you will find an apartment building that is secure," I asked.

"Mom, Bill told me that you live in a secure building," said Ryan. "Are there any apartments available?"

"You can't move into my building. Fred followed me home one day, and if he sees you and your dad going in or out of the building, you won't be safe," I said. "Please promise me you will live in a different part of Toronto?"

They both agreed.

"Ryan, you have a half-sister," I said.

"I have always wanted a sibling. How old is she?"

"Abigail is her name, and she is sixteen."

"Does she know about my dad and me?"

"No. How could she? I just found out last night that you two were alive."

"Oh, yeah, that's true. Can I meet her?"

"How about when you and your dad come back from Pickton, we will set up a meeting."

"I can't wait to meet her."

"Matteo, are you married or in a relationship?" I asked.

I wanted the answer to be yes since all I ever wanted was for Matteo to be happy. However, on the other hand I also wanted the answer to be no so I would have a chance to be with him. I had always and would always love him.

"No. I tried to date, but it never felt right."

I was so happy to hear those words. I tried not to smile, but I couldn't help it.

"I still can't believe it that Ryan and you are alive! I feel like I am dreaming, and when I wake up it won't be true."

Before I left Matteo and Ryan, I gave them each a hug and squeezed as tight as I could. Deep down, I didn't want to let go but knew I had to.

Chapter 47

After Bill and I left the food court, he offered to drop me off at home. On the way over to my apartment Bill said, "Can you forgive me for lying to you all these years?"

"Yes. Matteo went to you for protection, even though it meant lying to me. I realize now that you were only doing what was best for them."

"Thank you. I must do some errands before I pick up Abigail after school. When are you going to tell her about Matteo and Ryan?"

"I was thinking about tomorrow afternoon. Maybe you can be there in case she has any questions that I can't answer?"

"Yes, I will try to answer any questions she has."

"How does one o'clock sound to you?"

"Good. I will see you then."

I was glad to have some alone time, since this morning was emotional, plus I didn't sleep well last night. All I wanted to do was take a nap.

When Abigail came home from school, I was sitting on the couch watching TV.

"Mom, you are home. Is everything okay?"

"Yeah, I wasn't feeling good this morning at work, so I left early."

"That sucks. How are you feeling now?"

"I am feeling better. I slept this afternoon. I think I was just overtired and needed some rest."

For the rest of the night, we just sat on the couch and watched TV. We had the leftover pizza and garlic fingers from the night before for supper. Abigail and I were both just worn out.

I had just finished the housework when Abigail came out of her bedroom. She was a typical teenager who loved to sleep in.

"Can we have bacon, eggs, and home fries for breakfast?"

"Sure. Bill is coming over this afternoon to discuss something with you."

"Did you receive another letter from Fred?"

"No, it isn't about Fred."

"Then what is it about?"

"I will tell you when Bill arrives."

Abigail could tell by my tone that I wasn't going to say anything until later, so she offered to help me with breakfast. I just finished the dishes when the doorman called to tell me that Bill was on his way up.

Abigail was already sitting on the couch, watching TV.

"Thanks for coming over this afternoon," I said. "Abigail, would you please turn off the TV and come over to the table so we can talk."

She quickly came over to the table, eager to find out what was going on.

"I did receive a letter but not from Fred. It was from another man, Matteo."

"Who is Matteo?"

"It was about six or seven years before you were born. I was married to the love of my life, and we had a son. On our fifth anniversary, my husband and son were involved in a car crash and the police told me they died. I just found out yesterday that they are alive."

Abigail's jaw dropped open and she yelled, "What! I have a brother and stepfather!"

"Yes, you do."

"OMG, what are their names?"

"My husband is Matteo, and your brother is Ryan."

"How old is Ryan?"

"Twenty-one."

"This is so bizarre! I don't understand, why did the police tell you they were dead? Why didn't they come back to you?"

"Matteo received a letter from Fred threatening to kill Ryan and him. Matteo knew he had to do something to protect Ryan, so he staged a car crash and moved away to raise Ryan. The police thought it was a real accident. The only other person that knew was Bill."

Abigail looked over at Bill said, "You knew they were alive all these years but never told my mom. What type of friend are you?"

"In order to keep Matteo and Ryan safe, the police had to think they were dead. Otherwise, Fred would have killed them," replied Bill.

"I am so sorry, Mom. That must have been hard on you."

"At the time I was devastated, but now I realize that was the only option Matteo had."

"Okay, but I don't understand. Fred is still out there somewhere, so why did they come out of hiding now?"

"That is a good question honey. Matteo told Ryan that I died, but he never believed him, so Ryan hired a private investigator to find me. It worked. Ryan told his father that he was going to Toronto to find me, so Matteo called Bill."

"I set up a meeting at the food court yesterday so Matteo and Ryan could be reunited with your mom," said Bill.

"Do they live in Toronto?"

"They live in a small town called Pickton, three hours away from here. However, they are moving to Toronto in the next few days," replied Bill.

"If Fred finds out that they are alive, he will try to hurt them," said Abigail.

"I know that is the risk, but Ryan doesn't care. He wants to move to Toronto to be near your mom," said Bill. "All the police departments in Ontario are looking for Fred, and hopefully we will find him soon."

"Are they going to live with us?"

"No. Ryan wanted to, but I told him it was too dangerous because Fred knew where we lived. Matteo and Ryan are going to rent an apartment on the other side of town," I replied.

"Do they know about me?"

"Yes, I told them both."

"Do they want to meet me?"

"Of course, they do. You are my family, just like them."

"I still can't believe it. This is just like something out of the movies."

"But you can't tell anyone about Matteo or Ryan for their safety. Promise me."

"I promise I won't tell anyone. When can I meet them?"

"It probably will not be until the end of next week when they come back into the city."

After Bill left, Abigail asked me a few questions about Matteo and Ryan when we lived together. I tried my best to remember, but it was a long time ago.

It was Sunday night when Ryan called to invite us to dinner at the New Town Family Restaurant on Wednesday night.

*

Abigail and I had just arrived at the restaurant. I wasn't sure if they were there yet, so I looked around, saw them, and walked over to their table. I took a deep breath and said, "Abigail, this is Matteo and Ryan, and this is my daughter."

Abigail hugged each of them. "It's nice to meet you."

"I have a sister!"

"Abigail, you look a lot like your mom," said Matteo.

"A lot of people comment on that, and it drives her crazy," I said. "You know she is at the age where being like Mom isn't cool."

"Ryan, you look more like your father, but I can see Mom in you," replied Abigail.

"Yes, I do, but he tells me I get my stubbornness from our mom."

"I am stubborn too, but she blames it on my father. Maybe it comes from her."

"What is this, pick on Mom day?"

Everyone started to laugh.

"Where is your father?" Ryan asked.

"He isn't in the picture," Abigail replied. "Mom told me that you are moving to Toronto. Did you find a place to live?"

"Actually, we just signed the lease this afternoon and we are moving in this weekend. It is in a building on the other side of the city," answered Matteo.

For the next couple of hours, everyone got to know one another. Ryan and Abigail would talk about what traits they received from me, good and bad. It was like the universe was getting back at me for the bad traits I blamed on Abigail's father.

After that, Ryan and Abigail talked about likes and dislikes in school, music, and movies. It gave Matteo and I a chance to get to know each other again.

Mostly I would just watch how Matteo, Ryan, and Abigail were interacting. I thought about how much I had to lose, which made me a little sad.

I looked at my watch and said, "Oh my, the restaurant is closing in about twenty minutes. But before we go, I want to give you a picture of Fred Smith, the man who wants to hurt me. This way you will know what he looks like. If he approaches you, please call Bill or the police."

"One more thing, Ryan — I bought you a pocketknife for your protection. Please have it on you at all times."

"I will, thanks, Mom."

I handed one of the detective's cards to Matteo.

Chapter 48

Ryan and Matteo were calling me every day, sometimes just to say hi. As the days went by, I was falling increasingly in love with Matteo. I had my second chance to be a family with my husband, son, and daughter.

It was Tuesday evening when my phone rang. "Hello."

"Hi, Mom, I have an interview on Thursday morning," said Ryan.

"That is wonderful, dear. Where is your interview?"

"It's at an office building on Bay Street across from the Eaton Centre."

"I only work about fifteen minutes away from there. What is the company's name?"

"CJT Software."

"After my interview, maybe we can have lunch."

"I would like that."

The following evening, I called Ryan to wish him good luck at his interview the following day.

"How are you getting to the interview?"

"Dad is going to drive me, so he will be with us for lunch."

"That sounds good. When you are done the interview, call me, and I will meet you at the food court in the Eaton Centre for lunch."

"I will, and Dad says hi."

"Tell your father hi from me."

*

It was Friday afternoon, and we just finished the monthly accounting meeting when I went back to my desk. I noticed there was an envelope on my desk with my name on it. Right away I knew it was from Fred:

My dearest daughter Rebecca,

I was having lunch with a friend at the food court in the Eaton Centre yesterday when I couldn't believe my eyes. I saw Matteo, Ryan, and you in lineup at the Chinese place. I see your husband and son were hiding for all these years. You must have been in shock when you saw them alive and well, since Matteo wanted you to believe they were dead. It must have been quite a family reunion for Abigail to find out that she has a brother and stepfather.
   You know, playing dead, for all these years could turn into the real thing. I took some pictures of the three of you at lunch yesterday, since it might be the last time you are together, alive.

Your father, Fred

   Right away I showed Greg the letter. We went to talk to Eva to find out who dropped off the envelope, but she told us it was already against the door when she came back from the washroom. Eva was worried that Fred might come into the office, so Greg changed the small meeting room out in the reception area to use as his office. That way he could see everyone that came into the office.
   While Greg was calling Detective Johnston, I went back into my office, picked up the phone, and called Bill. "I received a letter from Fred. He knows that Matteo and Ryan are alive!"
   "I am on my way."
   Fifteen minutes later, Bill and Detective Johnston rushed into my office. I showed them the letter.
   "Fred was there yesterday at the food court watching us eat! He took pictures and sent them in the envelope. I love Matteo and Ryan so much, but I wish they never found me. Fred wants to hurt me, and by killing them it would destroy me. I can't let that happen," I said.

I started to cry. Bill put his arms around me. "We are going to do our best not to let that happened."

"We have to put them in protective custody," said Detective Johnston. "I am moving them to a safe house. Has either one of you talked to Matteo or Ryan today?"

"No, I normally don't talk to them until I get home in the evening," I replied.

"I haven't heard from either today," said Bill.

"Rebecca, call Matteo cell to let him know I am sending a police car over to pick them up immediately," said Detective Johnston.

I called Matteo's cell, but there was no answer. I tried again just in case he didn't hear the phone, but no answer.

"Neither one is picking up their phone," I cried. "We have to go over to their apartment right away!"

I folded my hands, put them up to my lips, and started to pray for their safety.

"Let's take my car," said Detective Johnston. "We can get there faster."

As Detective Johnston, Greg, Bill, and I were running out of the office, I shouted to Eva, "I don't know when I will be back."

We were on the way to Matteo's apartment when Detective Johnston received a phone call. I could only hear bits and pieces of his side because I was in the back seat.

After he hung up the phone, he looked over at Bill, who was sitting in the front seat, and I could by his expression that it wasn't good.

"Is that about Matteo and Ryan?"

"Yes, Matteo has been shot in the chest," Detective Johnston replied. "They are doing CPR on him while waiting for the ambulance. Ryan isn't there."

"Fred must have him!" I replied.

Within a few minutes, we arrived at the apartment. I ran upstairs to Matteo's unit to see the ambulance attendance working on him. I squeezed his hand. "I love you so much Matteo. I need for you to fight and come back to me. I need you so much!"

I overheard Detective Johnston telling Greg to always stay with Matteo and keep us inform of his condition.

After the ambulance attendants left with Matteo, Detective Johnston said, "Rebecca, there is an envelope on the table addressed to you."

I opened the letter:

My dearest daughter Rebecca,

After seeing Matteo and Ryan at the mall with you the other day, I waited to follow them home. This afternoon, after I dropped off the letter at your office, I went to Matteo's apartment to my surprise to find all three of them there. I thought I would have to get Abigail after I had Ryan. I shot Matteo in the chest and told Abigail and Ryan if they didn't go with me, I would do the same to them.

Your father, Fred

Chapter 49

"My worst dreams are coming true. Fred has my children!" I said. I started sobbing.

Bill looked at me and said, "We are going to look everywhere for them."

The police, Detective Johnston, Bill, and I looked everywhere we could think of where Fred might be holding Abigail and Ryan hostage. Abandoned buildings in the area were searched, we showed Fred and the kids' pictures to all the hotels, and put their pictures on the news, hoping someone would have seen them.

Detective Johnston's cell phone rang, and I jumped. I was so scared to find out that they found my children dead. It was Greg let us know that Matteo made it out of surgery.

"Where are my kids? Why can't we find them?"

With each passing hour, I was getting increasingly scared that they wouldn't be alive when we found them.

*

It had been twenty-eight hours since I last talked to Ryan and Abigail.

Then my cell phone rang. I looked to see the number. It was Abigail calling me. "Honey, where are you?"

"Well, hello, Rebecca, that is a wonderful way to answer the phone."

Immediately I tensed up, my hands started to shake, and my heartbeat was so fast, I thought I was going to pass out.

In a shaky voice, I said, "Who is this?"

"Rebecca, it is your father, Fred. I have two special people here with me, and I know you want them to be safe, but that depends on you."

"How do I know you did hurt them? Let me speak to her!"

"Mom, he has Ryan and me!"

"Did he hurt either one of you?"

"No, but I am scared."

"It is going to be okay, trust me. Abigail! Abigail!"

"Now that you know they are alive for the time being."

I closed my eyes, and tears started to run down my face. I was scared, but I wasn't going to show him any fear, so I cleared my throat. "What do you want?"

"I want to exchange your children for you. Let's see it is Saturday evening at seven. I will give you until ten tomorrow morning to find us. I will give you a hint, go to where it all started. If you are late, they will be dead."

Click. Then a dial tone.

I put my hands on my face. Bill walked over to me, and put his arms around me, and whispered, "We are going to get the kids back. What did he say?"

"He just told me to go where it all started." I thought hard about what he meant then realized where they were.

"I got it! He is in Tignish, PEI — that is where it all started. Mom had the affair, conceived me, and I was born there. It has to be there!"

I called Greg to let him know what was going on.

Greg said, "Just please call me as soon as you have any information about the kids so I can let Matteo know."

"Thank you! Please tell him that I love him, and that Bill is with me. That way he knows I didn't go alone."

"I will. Be careful."

We called the airlines. The only available seats were on the morning flight, which wouldn't get us there on time. Detective Johnston pulled some strings and was able to get a plane to fly us to Tignish, PEI.

While we were in the air, I said, "Bill, when we arrive in Tignish, how do we find them?"

"Detective Johnston is talking to the chief of police to let them know what is going on. Maybe they can start looking and have some leads by the time we arrive."

When we arrived at the airport in Summerside, we rented a car and drove to Tignish.

We arrived at the police station in Tignish and went inside, where the chief of police was waiting for us.

"Hi, I'm Stan Wilson."

"Hi, I'm Bill and this is Rebecca."

"I have had my men out looking all night at abandoned places, hotels, and driving all over the town watching for anything suspicious. Are you sure he came here?"

"I am almost positive. He told me to come where it all started, and this is where I was born. If what he is telling me is the truth, that my mom and he had an affair, and I was the outcome of the affair it has to be here."

"We have three possible addresses: 36 Main Street, 89 Autumn Drive, and 23 Millwood Lane," Stan said. "Two more police officers are on their way from Charlottetown, so we can each take an address."

As soon as I heard the address, I recognized it. That must be where Fred had the kids, but I knew Stan wouldn't let me go alone.

"How much longer before they get here?" I asked.

"They will be here in about twenty minutes."

I knew that it would be too late, so I told Stan and Bill I had to go to the bathroom but left the building instead. On my way to the car, I googled how to get to Autumn Drive from the police station on my phone.

When I left the parking lot, I texted Bill that I was on my way to 89 Autumn Drive.

It was so strange; when I turned onto the street right away, I knew which house it was. I had a flashback to when I was four years old. Nancy, Billy, my mom, and I were playing in the snow in the front yard while Dad went to the store to get us a treat. A man came into the yard and started talking to my mom. It must have been Fred.

I parked the car just a few houses up the street.

I walked up the sidewalk to the house and opened the white picket fence gate. I walked up the steps to the porch that had a rocking chair on the left-hand side and opened the door. As I walked in the house, on my left was the living room, in front of me were stairs that led to the second level, and in between them was a hallway that I believed went to the kitchen.

"Fred, I am here before the deadline. Let me see Abigail and Ryan!"

There was no response, so I started to go through the house looking for them when I heard, "Mom! We are upstairs."

It was Abigail's voice, so I ran up the stairs. At the top there was a full bathroom and three bedrooms off the hallway. I looked in the first room, and no one was there, so I continued down the hallway until I found them in the third bedroom.

At first all I could see was Fred having one arm around Abigail's neck while holding a gun to her head with the other hand. When I went all the way into the room, I saw Ryan tied up to a chair. He had tape over his mouth so he couldn't talk. I could see the scared look on his face.

"I am here. Now let Abigail and Ryan go as you promised."

"I lied. Rebecca, I am going to play the same game with Abigail as I did with you at the warehouse. You do remember what that was. Let's play Russian Roulette."

"You promised you would let them go!" I yelled.

"What game is that?" asked Abigail.

Fred explained the game to Abigail, and she started to cry.

He pointed the gun at the side of her head and pulled the trigger. I screamed. I couldn't bear to see my child die in front of me. Then I heard Abigail cry out. I knew the chamber didn't fire the bullet.

I knew something had to be done quickly before it was too late. I didn't know if the next time he pulled the trigger, it would be the bullet. However, if I shot at Fred, he would just use Abigail as a shield. But if I managed to hit him, his reflexes could make his gun go off and kill her.

I kept my eyes on Fred and Abigail while I checked on Ryan, so Fred wouldn't see me loosening the rope a bit. I was hoping Ryan would realize what I did, so he would continue until he got his hands free.

Abigail screamed, "What did my mom do to you that made you so angry?"

"It isn't what she did. It is what her mother didn't do," Fred said.

I realized at that point Abigail was trying to change Fred's focus.

"That isn't fair. My mom had no control over what her mom did."

"It is about time that you realized that life isn't fair."

"What did you want my mom to do?" I asked.

"To leave Brent and move in with me. That way we could have been a real family. But she wouldn't. She told me that she loved Brent and regretted having an affair with me."

I don't know if Fred realized that while he was talking about my mom, he lowered the hand holding the gun. Ryan leaped up, pushed Abigail to the floor, and stabbed Fred in his side with the pocketknife I gave him as a present.

Fred fell to the floor and the gun was knocked out of his hand.

I screamed, "Abigail and Ryan, run!"

I took out my gun, but before I had a chance to fire, Fred grabs his gun, stood up, and at the same time we both pulled the trigger. I hit him in the leg, while he hit me in the stomach. I fell to the floor. I could hear Fred crawling over to me, so the adrenaline running through my body let me turn around toward him and said, "This one is for all the people you killed that I loved."

I believe I shot him straight between the eyes.

The next thing I heard was Bill racing up the stairs while Abigail and Ryan were crying next to me.

Bill rushed over to us while Stan checked Fred.

I looked at Bill said, "I killed him! I killed him!"

"You had no choice. He was going to kill Abigail, Ryan, and you."

I started to cry. I couldn't believe it was finally over. My children were okay, and I had my life back.

I took off my sweatshirt and removed the bulletproof vest that I took from the police station. That vest saved my life. If I wasn't wearing it, the bullet would have killed me.

"I love you both very much."

"We love you too, Mom."

"I need a phone to call Greg to see how Matteo is." Bill handed me his phone.

"Hi, Greg, can I talk to Matteo?"

"Hold on," Greg said. "I will give him the phone."

"Hi, Rebecca, is everyone okay?" asked Matteo.

"Yes, we are all fine and Fred is dead."

All I heard was Matteo feeling relieved.

"It is finally over."

"Yes, Matteo, it is over."

I handed the phone to Ryan so he could talk to his father. When Ryan gave me back the phone, I told Matteo that we had to spend the night in Tignish to give our statements, and we would be heading home first thing in the morning.

It finally hit me what I almost lost today.

After we finished giving our statements, Stan gave us a lift to the hotel. That night we just watched the comedy channel, ordered pizza, and tried to relax. None of us talked. I guess there were no words for what we had been through.

Chapter 50

In the morning, there was a knock on the hotel door. Bill looked through the peephole. "It's Stan."

He opened the door.

"Good morning. I thought you might want some clean clothes to change into. They might not be your style, but at least they are clean."

"Thank you very much for everything, Stan. I will always be grateful to you for saving my family and me," I said.

"You are welcome."

"Let's go and get some breakfast and head home," I said.

Everyone was in total agreement.

We arrived at the hospital just after supper to see Matteo. When we walked into his room, he started to cry. We all did, but this time they were happy tears.

*

A few weeks later, Matteo was being discharged from the hospital. He and Ryan came to stay with Abigail and myself. The following morning, I was the last one to wake up. I went in the kitchen, and everyone was eating their breakfast. Even Bill was there. He had dropped in to see how we were all doing.

"Hi, everyone, I would like all of us to go on a road trip," I said.

"Where?" asked Abigail

"To Nova Scotia."

"Why?" asked Matteo

"I have family there, and I want to take all of you to meet them," I answered.

"But I have school," said Abigail.

"I started my new job on Monday, so I can't go," said Ryan.

"Abigail, I will call the school and let them know you will be out for the week. Ryan, can you please call your work and ask if it would be okay to start the following Monday? You can tell them we have a family situation to deal with," I said.

"Okay, I will call and let you know," replied Ryan. "I thought your family died."

"Fred was responsible for my parents' death, and after they passed, we went to live with our Aunt Debbie and Uncle Jeff. I have a brother who I am hoping is still alive. While I was living with my aunt and uncle, Fred killed my sister, hurting my Aunt Debbie and cousin Monica. That was when I received my first letter from Fred saying that if I didn't leave my aunt's house, more of them would die, so I left. When I arrived here, I stayed at a shelter, and I met Suzanne."

"I am sorry. That must have been hard on you," said Ryan.

"It was, but I had no choice. So, are you with me?"

Matteo, Abigail, and Ryan all at the same time said, "Yes."

I looked over at Bill. "How about you?"

"You want me to go too?"

"Why not? You are part of this family. You help Matteo and Ryan to stay alive. Also, you have helped protect Abigail over the years. If that isn't family, then I don't know what is. Can you get the time off?"

"Yes. Yesterday I asked my boss for two weeks off, and he agreed that it would be a wonderful idea."

"We will leave tomorrow morning early at 6:00 a.m. It will take us two days to drive there."

Even though Abigail moaned when she heard to leave at six, she was ready and in the van on time. She was reading her books, Ryan was listening to his music, and Bill, Matteo, and I took turns driving. We would stop every two to three hours to stretch our legs, use the bathroom, and if hungry have something to eat.

The first day, traffic wasn't that bad, so we managed to get more than halfway there before stopping at the hotel for the night. The next morning, we decided to sleep in and leave by 9:00 a.m.; that way we should arrive by late afternoon.

Due to an accident, we were stuck on the highway for three hours. That put us arriving in Nova Scotia in the evening, so I decided we would get a good night's sleep then go to my aunt's house in the morning.

The next morning, we went downstairs to the continental breakfast in the hotel restaurant. Abigail noticed that I wasn't eating. "Mom, you aren't eating?"

"My stomach has some many butterflies. I am not hungry. I guess I am too nervous to be hungry."

"What are you nervous about?"

"What if they don't remember me? What if they are mad at me for leaving? What if it is too late and they have passed away?"

"Once you explain everything, I am sure they won't be angry at you for leaving. I will be there for you."

Deep down, I knew she was right, and I gave her a huge hug.

"Before we go over to my aunt's house, I just want to say thank you to all of you for coming with me. I am not sure how this meeting is going to go, but I know with your support I will be fine."

I turned onto the street and parked across from her house. I just sat there staring at the front yard, waiting for Aunt Debbie or Uncle Jeff to come outside. For all I knew, they could have sold this house and moved to a different one.

Matteo put his hand on my hand and squeezed it. "You aren't going to know if they still live here until you ring the doorbell."

It was as if he was reading my mind and gave me the push I needed. "You are right. Let's go, everyone, and meet my family."

We walked up the driveway to the steps that led to the front door, and I rang the doorbell. A few seconds later a lady opened the door. "Aunt Debbie, it is me, Rebecca."

She started to cry. "Rebecca! Rebecca, is it really you?"

I couldn't hold back the tears. "Yes, it is. I love you, Aunt Debbie."

We hugged for a few minutes.

She screamed to Uncle Jeff, "Come here right away?"

I heard a loud noise coming up from the basement. Uncle Jeff took one look at me. "Rebecca, you are alive. Come in, come in." He hugged me, and I could hear him tearing up.

"Why did you leave and never contact us before now?" asked Aunt Debbie.

"I will tell you everything, but I just have one question: is my brother, okay?"

"Yes, he lives just a few streets over from here, and he will be so happy to find out that you are alive. Jeff call Billy and tell him to come over right away."

"Good. I would like to introduce my family. This is my husband Matteo, our children, Ryan and Abigail, and a really good friend of mine, Bill."

Within ten minutes, the front door opened, and Billy walked through. He was in complete shock when he saw me. I hugged him so tight as he said, "Rebecca, I am having a tough time breathing."

"I am sorry."

We all went into the living room, and I told them the whole story. They couldn't believe what I went through to protect them.

"About a year after you left, I found two envelopes in a book that belonged to your mom. Both were addressed to you. I will go and get them." Aunt Debbie came back into the living room and handed me the two envelopes. I opened the first one:

Dear Rebecca,

I want to explain to you what happened before you were born. I loved Brent, the man who you thought was your dad, but he was working thirteen-hour days and I was lonely.

I know that is no excuse, but a few houses down the street was a man who at first would say hi to me every morning when I would take you and your siblings for a walk. He was a widow and had no children; at least that was what he told me. He seemed so normal, and I loved the attention that he was giving me. His name was Fred.

After a few months of talking to him, the next thing I knew we were having an affair. Every Tuesday night I would get a babysitter for a few hours to spend time with him before your dad would come home. I loved your dad, but I missed have the emotional connection that Fred gave me.

The affair lasted for about eight months before I ended, but Fred didn't want the relationship to be over. He told me that if I didn't continue the affair with him, he would tell Brent everything. I knew if that happened your, dad would leave me, so I continued in the relationship with Fred for the next six months.

At the point, I found out that I was pregnant but wasn't sure if your dad or Fred was the father. Your dad and I were intimate, but not as often as with Fred. When Fred found out that I was expecting a child, he automatically thought he was the father. I needed to know the truth, so after you were born, I took some of your dad's hair from his brush and had a paternity test done.

Fred was right, you are his daughter. I tried again to stop the affair, but he wouldn't take no for an answer.

When your dad got the job in Nova Scotia, I thought it was the best thing for the family. Fred would have no choice but to accept the fact that the relationship between him and me was over. I would raise you as Brent's daughter.

Fred was so angry with me that he threatened to hurt me, and you if I took you away from him. If you are reading this letter, that means he went through with his threat, and I am dead.
A copy of the paternity test, along with your birth certificate, is in the envelope.

Love Mom

The second envelope had the test results and my birth certificate. I guess Fred was telling the truth about being my biological father. I let Aunt Debbie read the letter. "I wish your mom would have come to me. I would have helped her."

"Rebecca, we were just talking about you last week," Uncle Jeff said. "We received a letter asking us to give you part of a picture when we saw you. I never thought we would see you again, so I just put it in my drawer. I will go and get it."

Uncle Jeff returned to the living room and gave me an envelope.

I opened the envelope and turned the picture around. "That is Fred. He was responsible for my parents' and Nancy's deaths. Also, for everyone getting hurt. I guess he didn't want me to see who else was in the picture," I replied.

I put the picture in my purse and started thinking is it over and who else was in the picture?

Printed in Great Britain
by Amazon